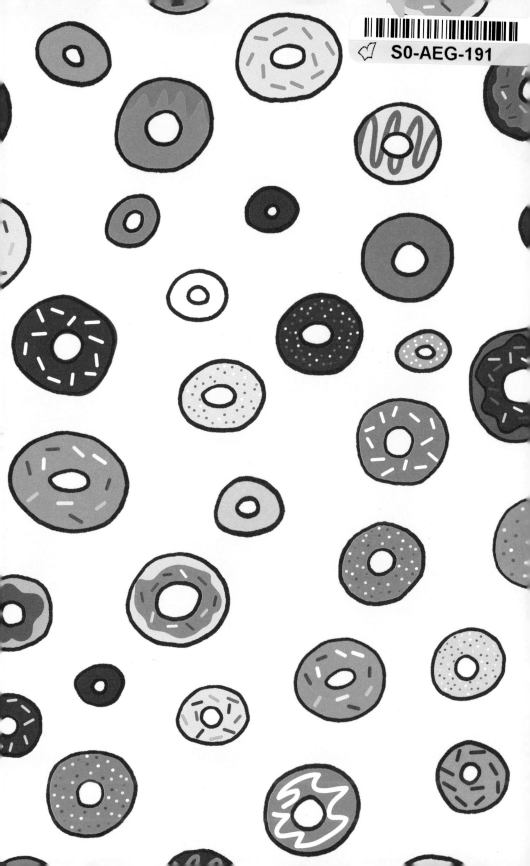
S0-AEG-191

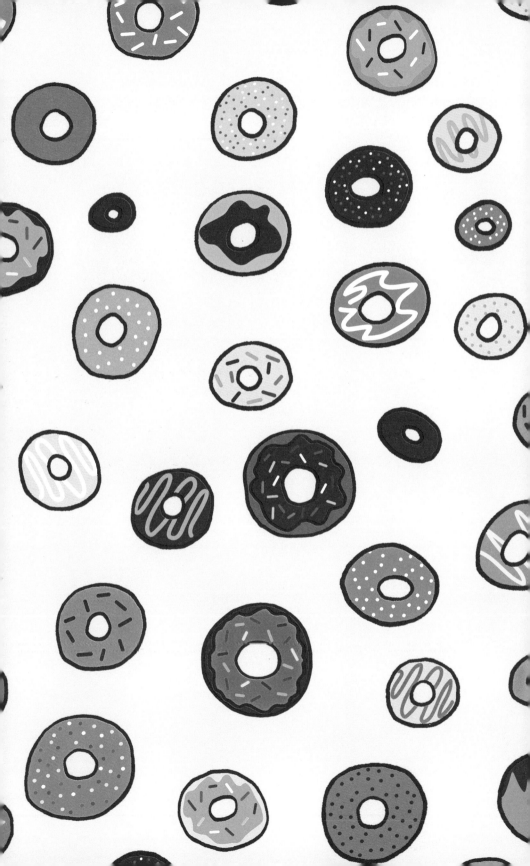

THE NOT-SO-SECRET CLUBHOUSE!

WRITTEN BY STEVE METZGER
ILLUSTRATED BY BRIAN SCHATELL

WITH COLOR BY
BEN SCHORR AND GARY FIELDS

Reycraft Books
145 Huguenot Street
New Rochelle, NY 10801

Reycraftbooks.com

Reycraft Books is a trade imprint and trademark of Newmark Learning, LLC.

Text © 2023 Steve Metzger
Illustrations © 2023 Brian Schatell

All rights reserved. No portion of this book may be reproduced, stored in a retrieval system, or transmitted in any form or by any means, electronic, mechanical, photocopying, recording, or otherwise, without written permission from the publisher. For information regarding permission, please contact info@reycraftbooks.com.

Educators and Librarians: Our books may be purchased in bulk for promotional, educational, or business use. Please contact sales@reycraftbooks.com.

This is a work of fiction. Names, characters, places, dialogue, and incidents described either are the product of the author's imagination or are used fictitiously. Any resemblance to actual persons, living or dead, is entirely coincidental.

Sale of this book without a front cover or jacket may be unauthorized. If this book is coverless, it may have been reported to the publisher as "unsold or destroyed" and may have deprived the author and publisher of payment.

Library of Congress Control Number: 2022920338

Hardcover ISBN: 978-1-4788-8193-3
Paperback ISBN: 978-1-4788-8194-0

Author photo: Courtesy of Rob DeSantos Jr.
Illustrator photo: Courtesy of Jane E. Gerver

Printed in Dongguan, China. 8557/0523/20217

10 9 8 7 6 5 4 3 2 1

First Edition published by Reycraft Books 2023.

Reycraft Books and Newmark Learning, LLC, support diversity and the First Amendment, and celebrate the right to read.

To my comedy heroes: Abbott and Costello, the Marx Brothers, Lucille Ball, Stan Freberg, Charle Chaplin, Carol Burnett, Bob and Ray, Jerry Lewis, Steve Allen, Jackie Gleason, Laurel and Hardy, Allan Sherman, Sid Caesar, and Jack Benny
—S.M.

For Jackie Morris and Lynne Moerder
and Rachel Rankin and Zane
—B.S.

CHAPTER 1 - SWAMPLAND!

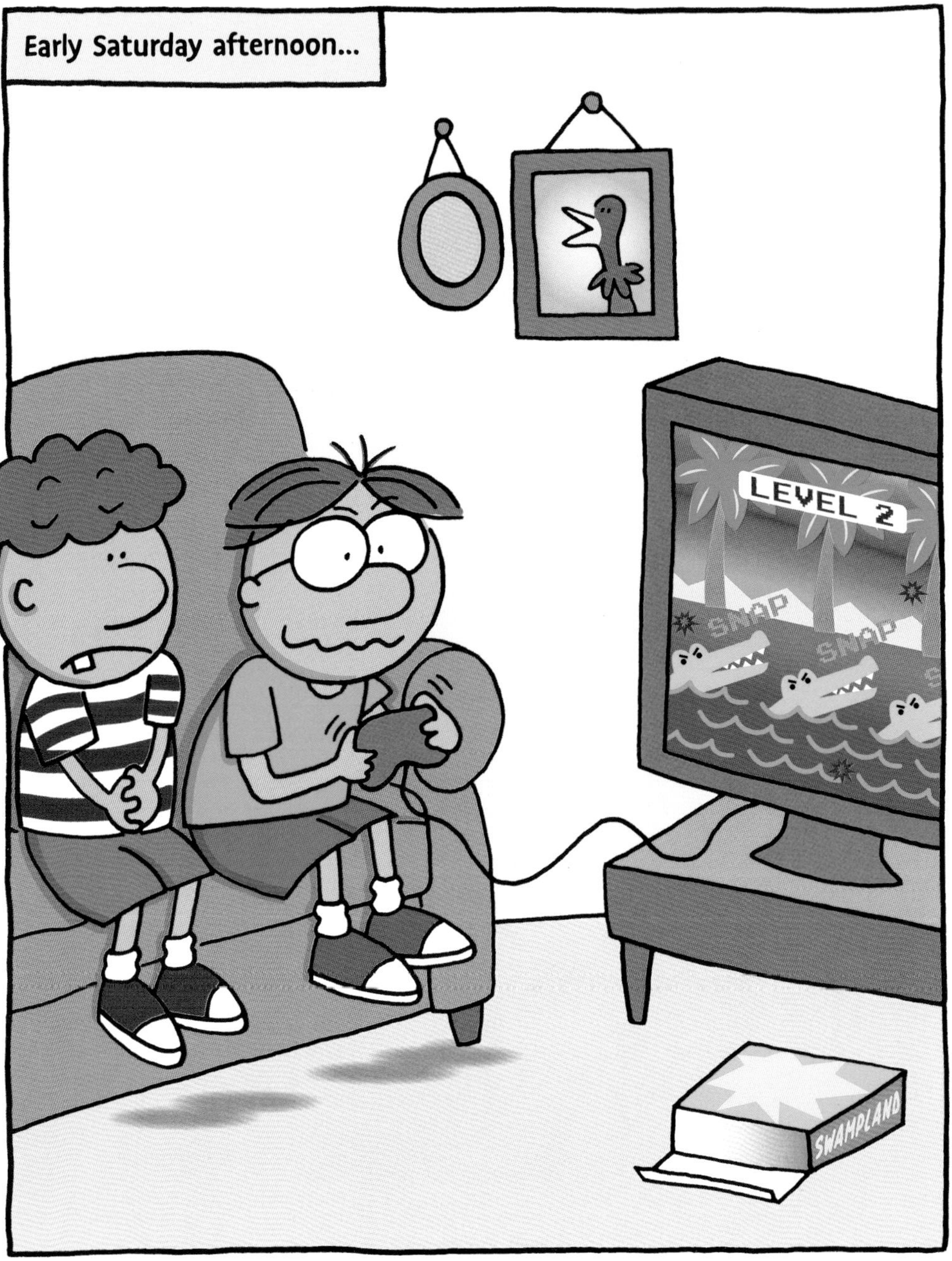

Early Saturday afternoon...
LEVEL 2
SNAP
SNAP
SWAMPLAND

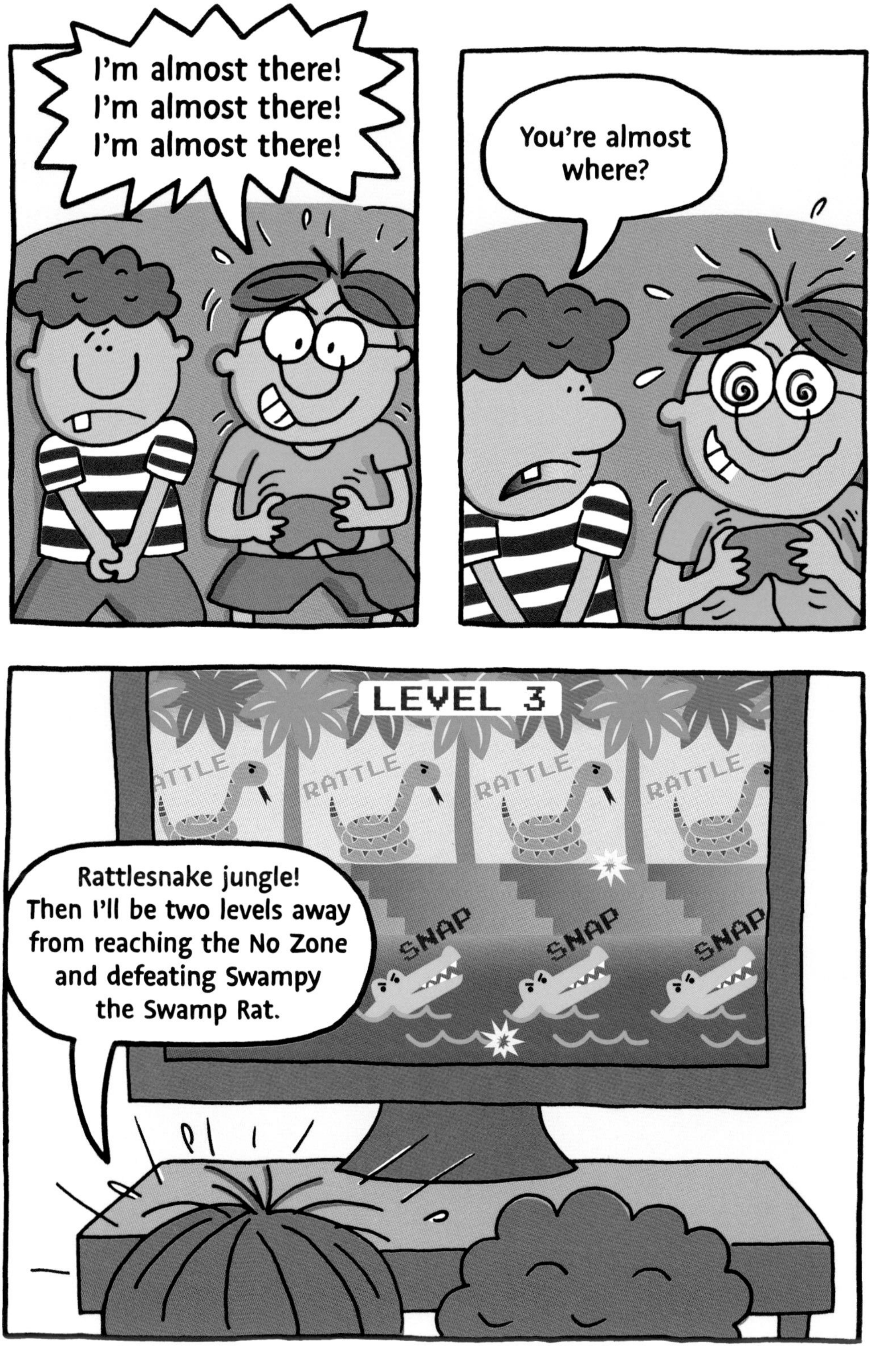
I'm almost there! I'm almost there! I'm almost there!
You're almost where?
LEVEL 3
RATTLE
RATTLE
RATTLE
RATTLE
SNAP
SNAP
SNAP
Rattlesnake jungle! Then I'll be two levels away from reaching the No Zone and defeating Swampy the Swamp Rat.

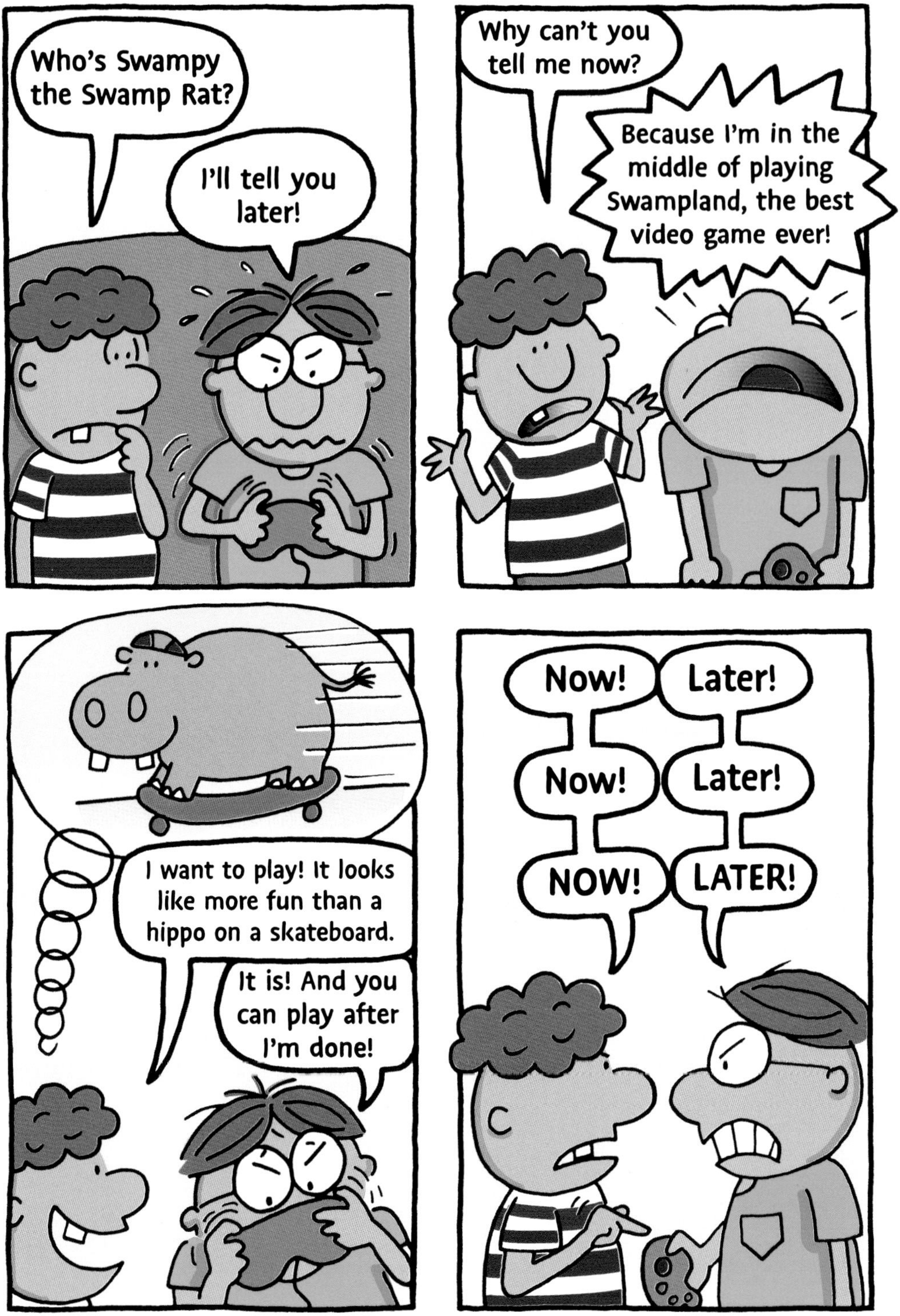
Who's Swampy the Swamp Rat?
I'll tell you later!
Why can't you tell me now?
Because I'm in the middle of playing Swampland, the best video game ever!
I want to play! It looks like more fun than a hippo on a skateboard.
It is! And you can play after I'm done!
Now!
Later!
Now!
Later!
NOW!
LATER!

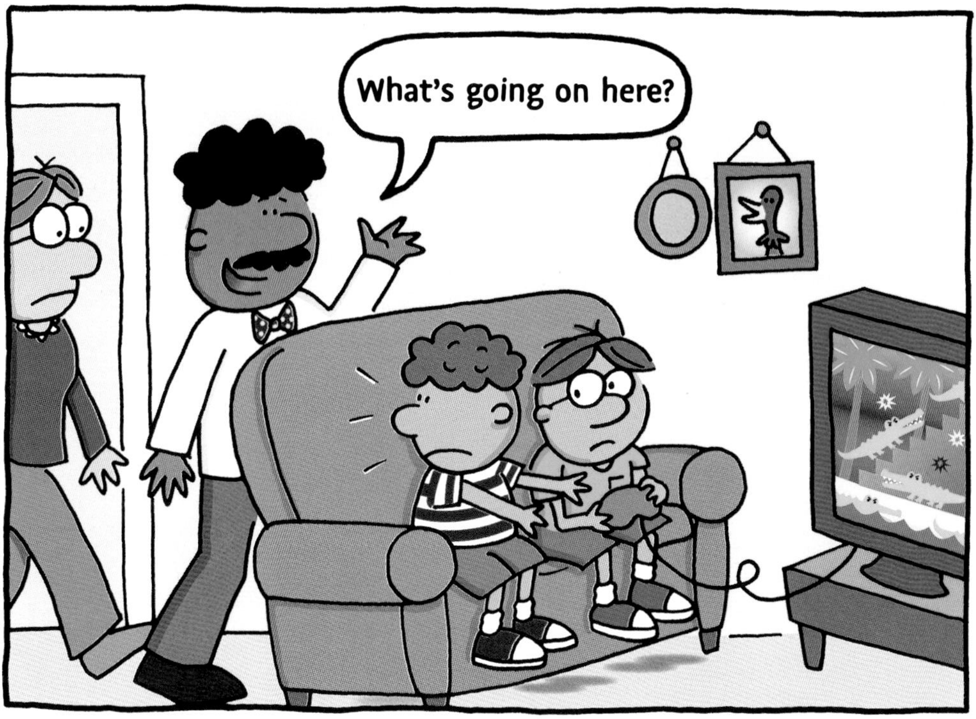
What's going on here?

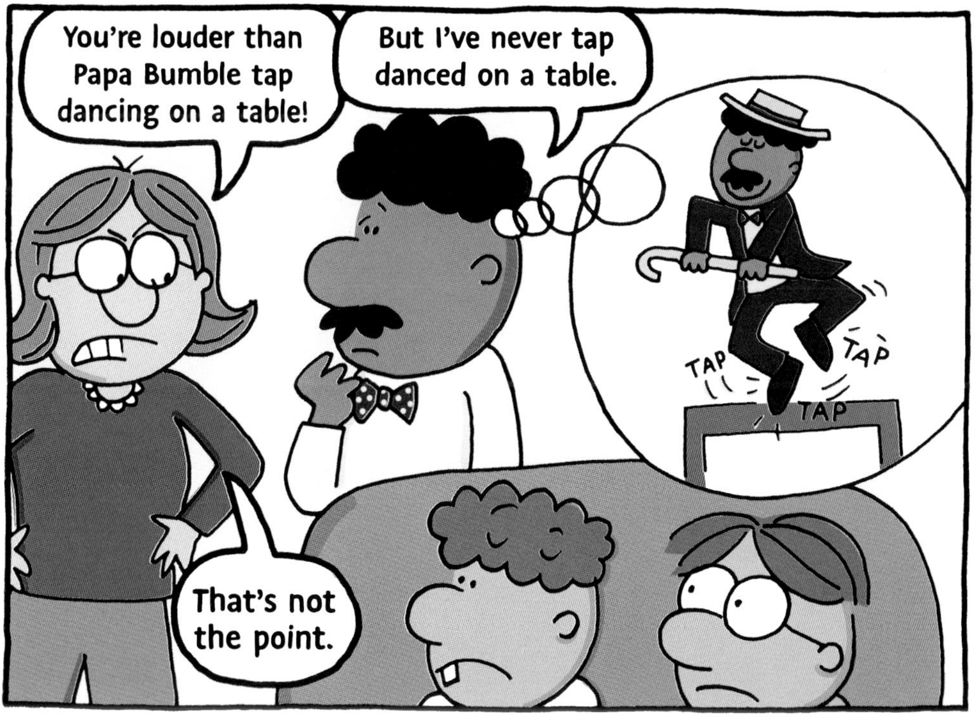
You're louder than Papa Bumble tap dancing on a table!
But I've never tap danced on a table.
TAP
TAP
TAP
That's not the point.

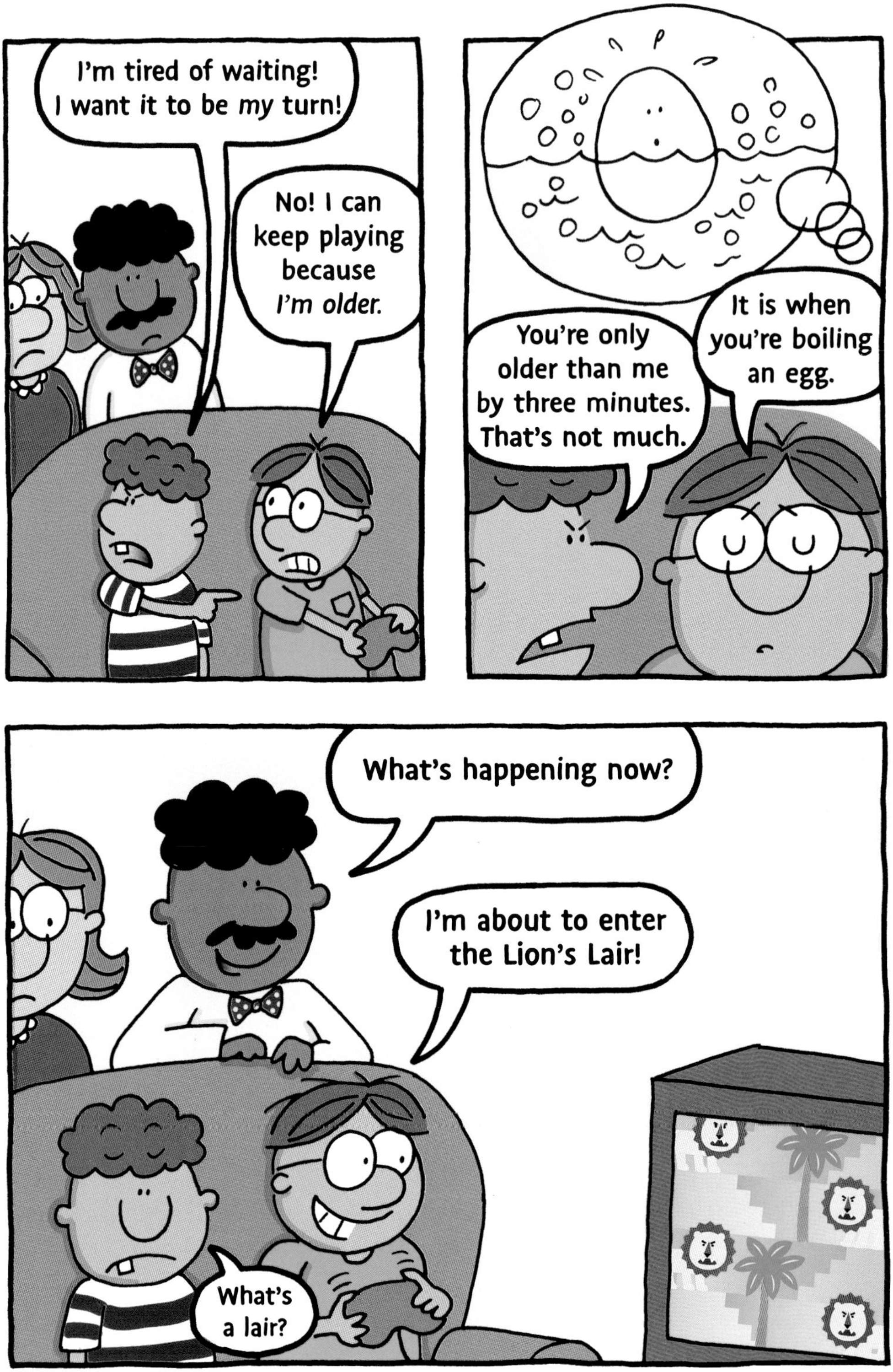
I'm tired of waiting! I want it to be *my* turn!
No! I can keep playing because *I'm older.*
You're only older than me by three minutes. That's not much.
It is when you're boiling an egg.
What's happening now?
I'm about to enter the Lion's Lair!
What's a lair?

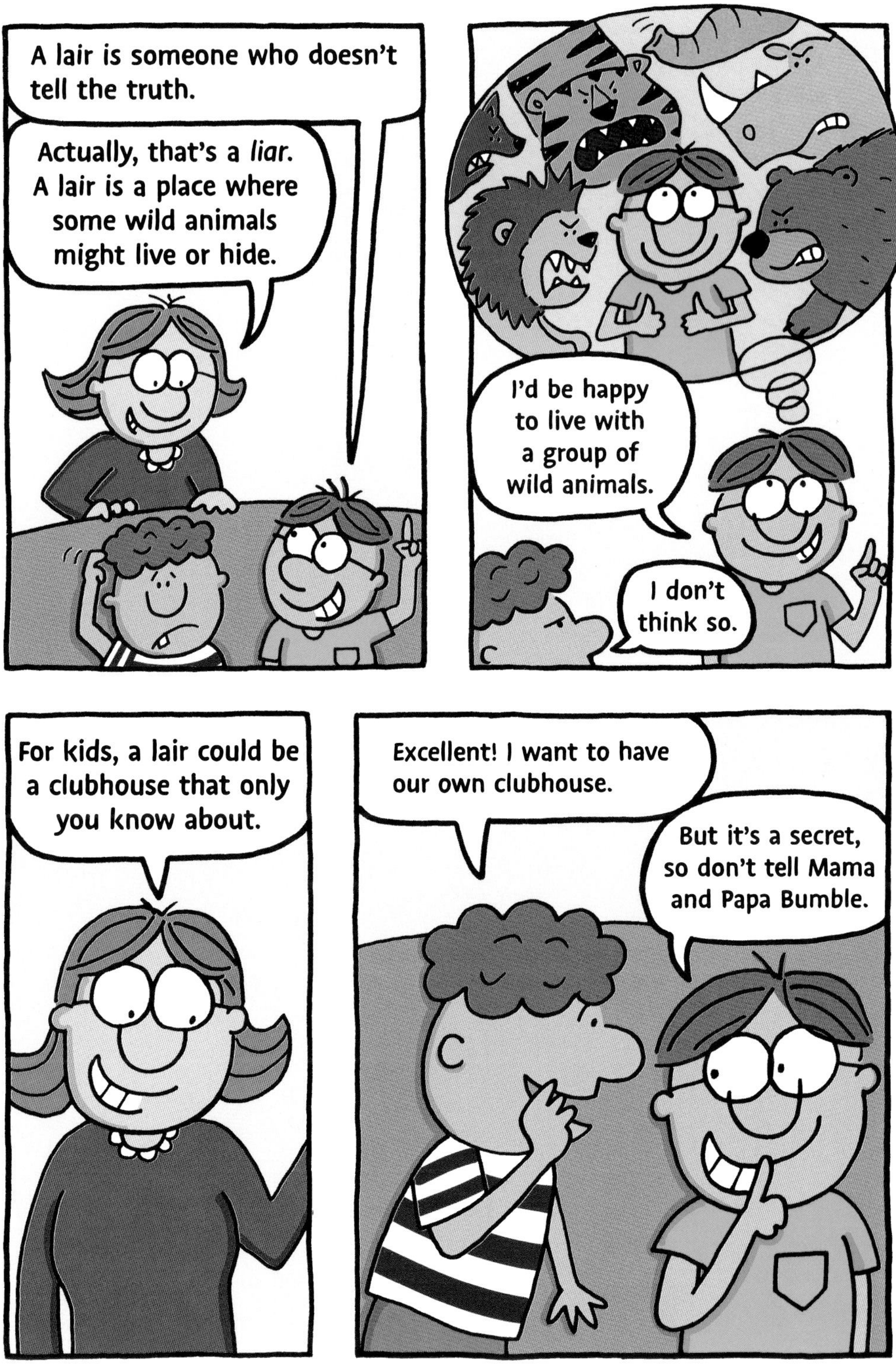

A lair is someone who doesn't tell the truth.
Actually, that's a *liar*. A lair is a place where some wild animals might live or hide.
I'd be happy to live with a group of wild animals.
I don't think so.
For kids, a lair could be a clubhouse that only you know about.
Excellent! I want to have our own clubhouse.
But it's a secret, so don't tell Mama and Papa Bumble.

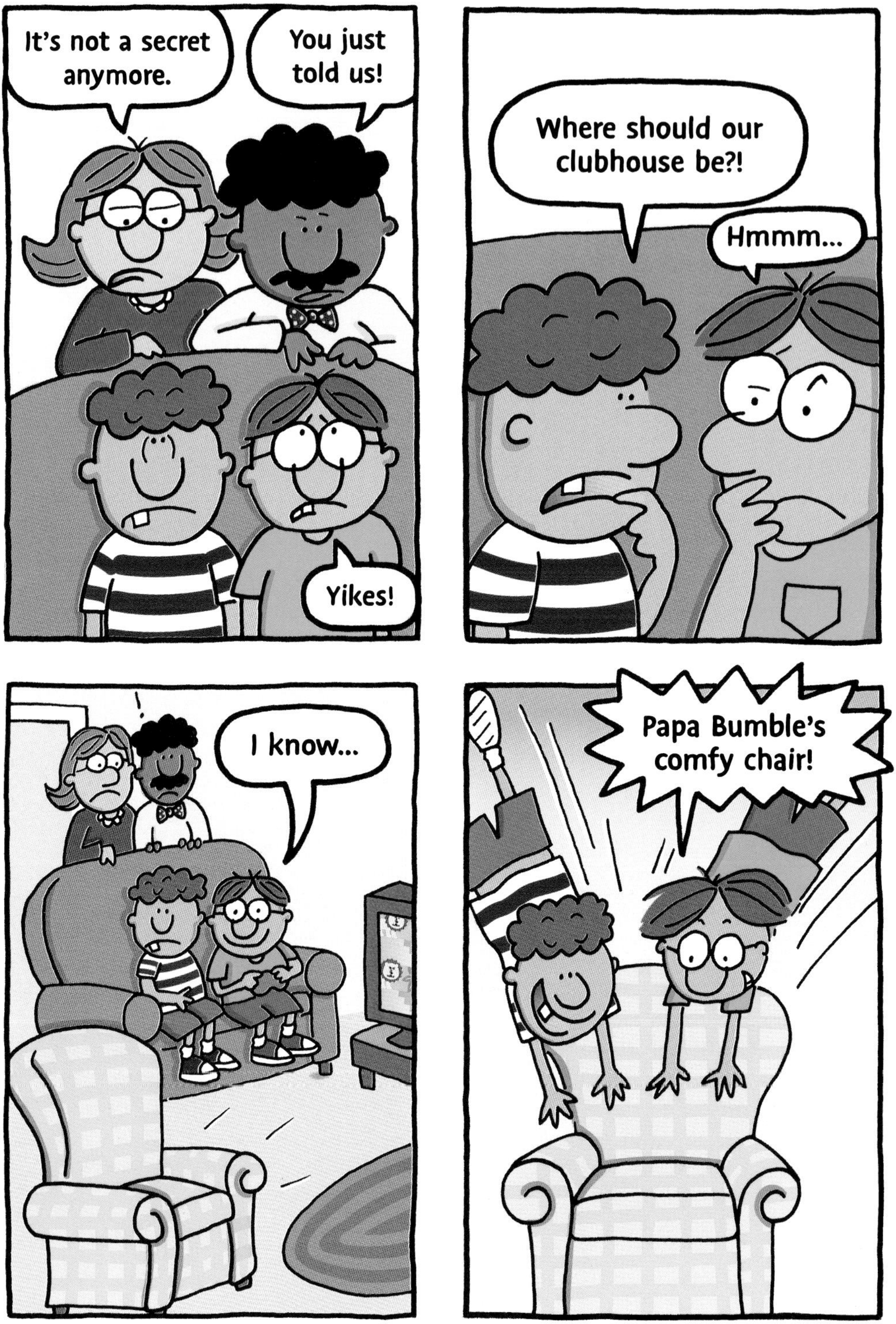
It's not a secret anymore.
You just told us!
Yikes!
Where should our clubhouse be?!
Hmmm...
I know...
Papa Bumble's comfy chair!

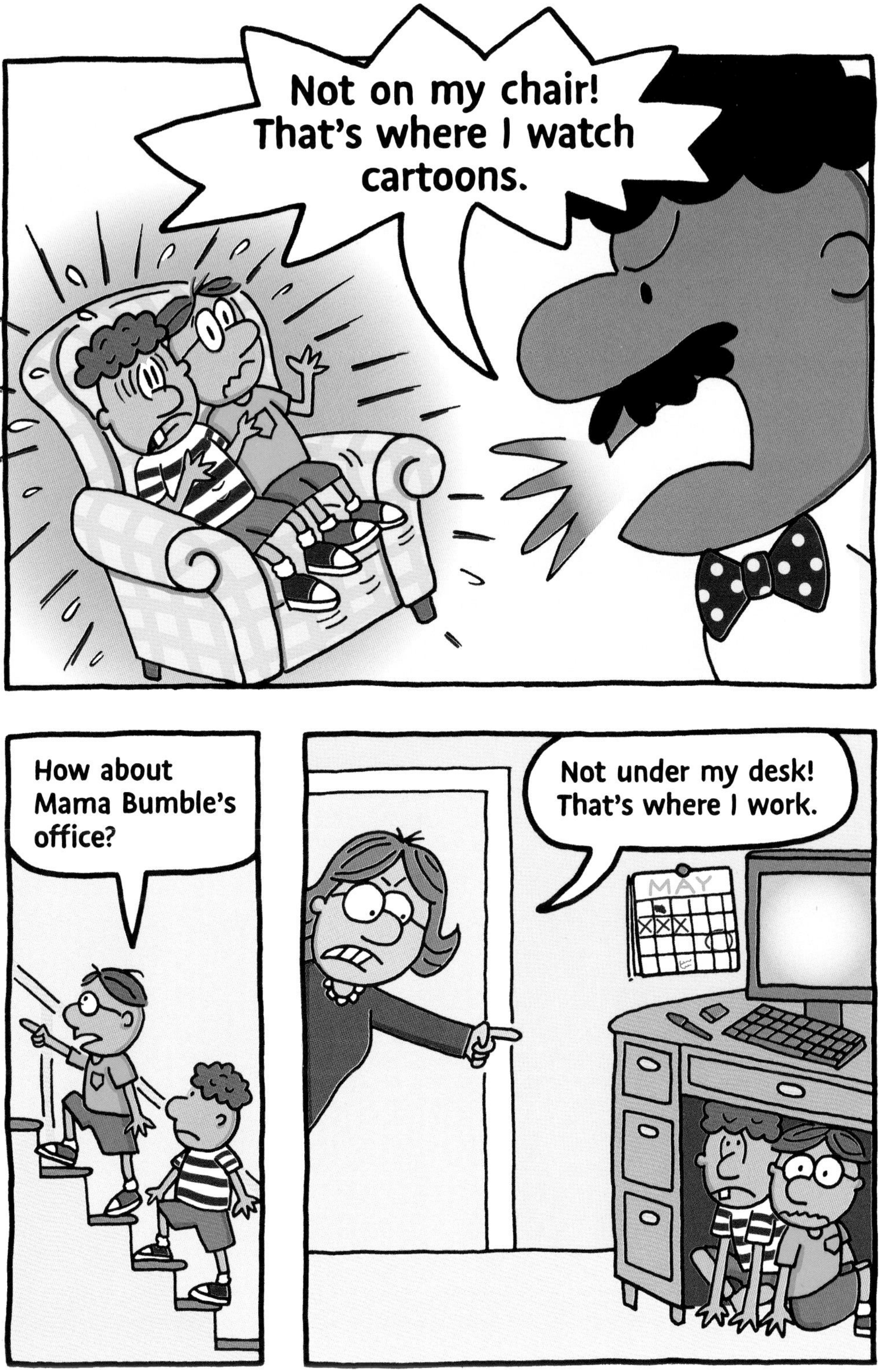
Not on my chair! That's where I watch cartoons.
How about Mama Bumble's office?
Not under my desk! That's where I work.
MAY

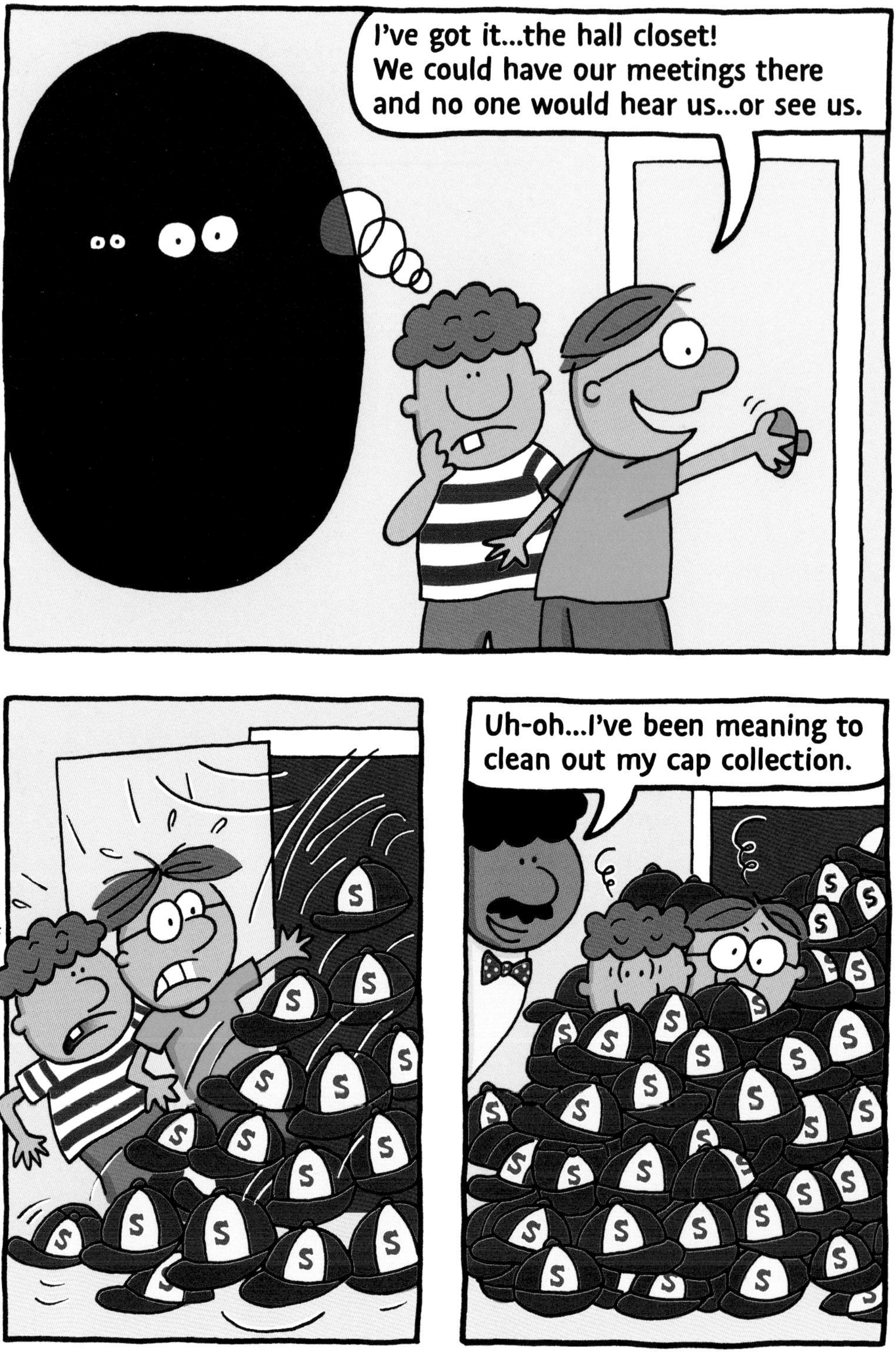
I've got it...the hall closet!
We could have our meetings there
and no one would hear us...or see us.
Uh-oh...I've been meaning to
clean out my cap collection.

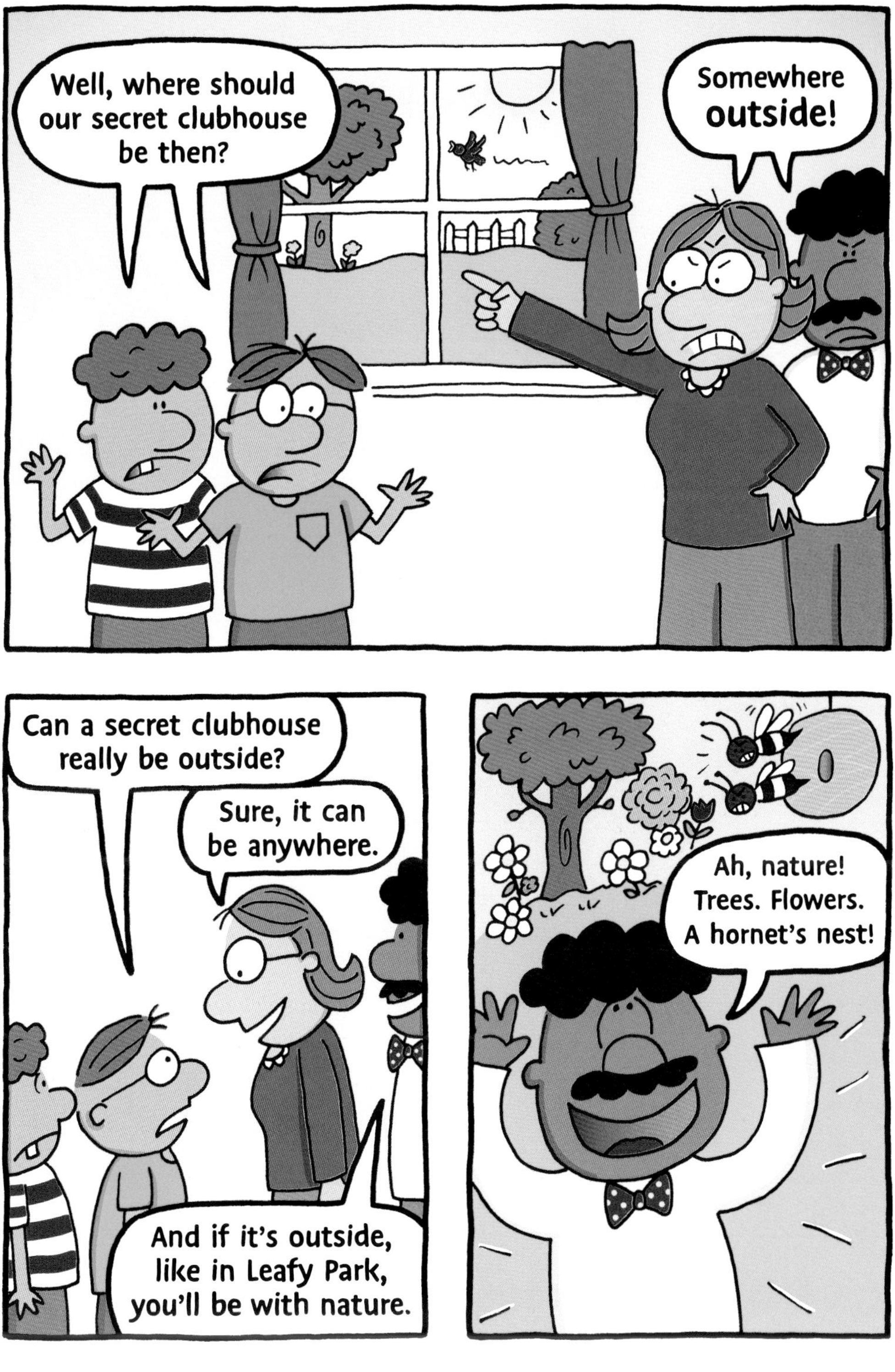
Well, where should our secret clubhouse be then?
Somewhere outside!
Can a secret clubhouse really be outside?
Sure, it can be anywhere.
And if it's outside, like in Leafy Park, you'll be with nature.
Ah, nature! Trees. Flowers. A hornet's nest!

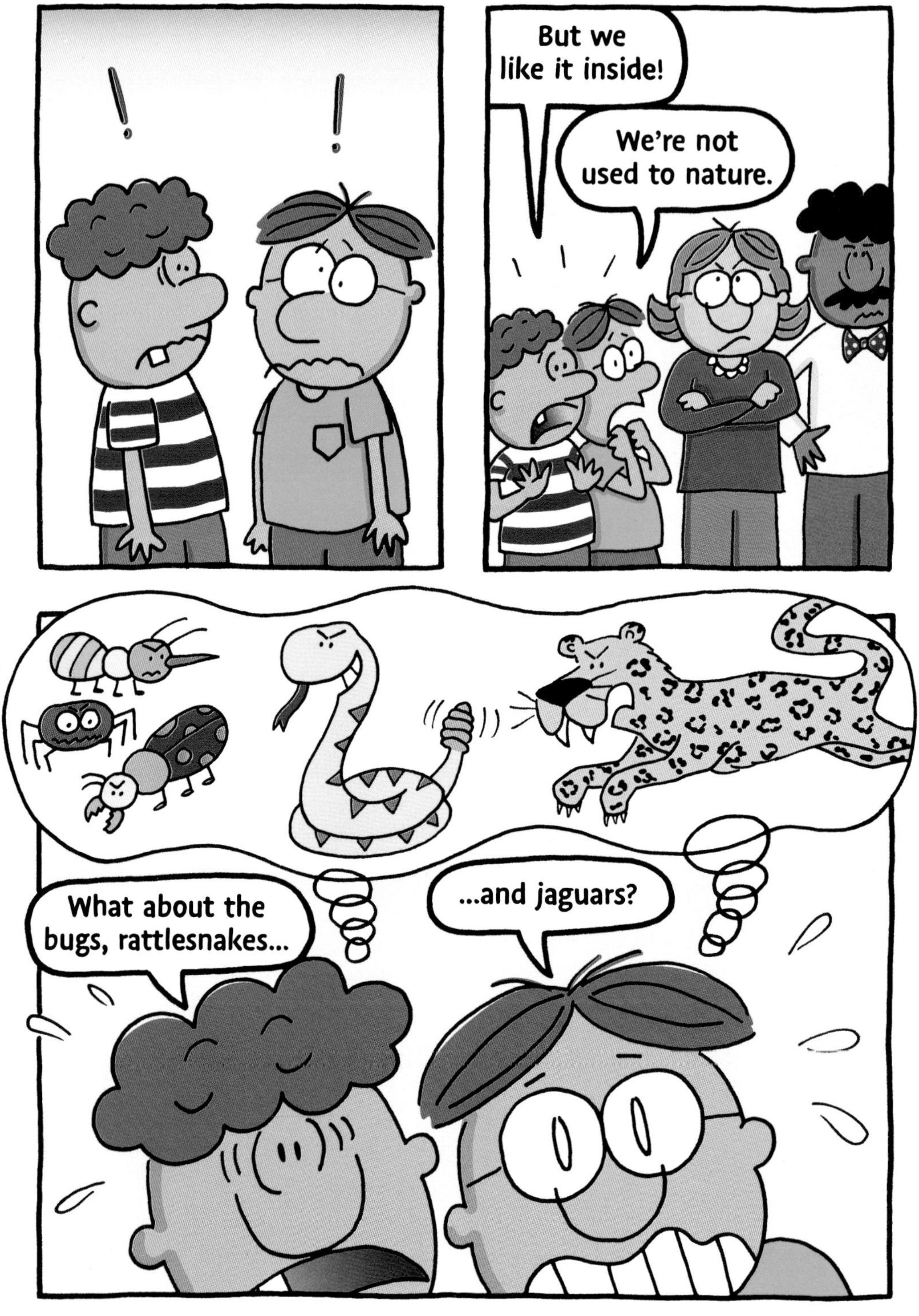
!
!
But we like it inside!
We're not used to nature.
What about the bugs, rattlesnakes...
...and jaguars?

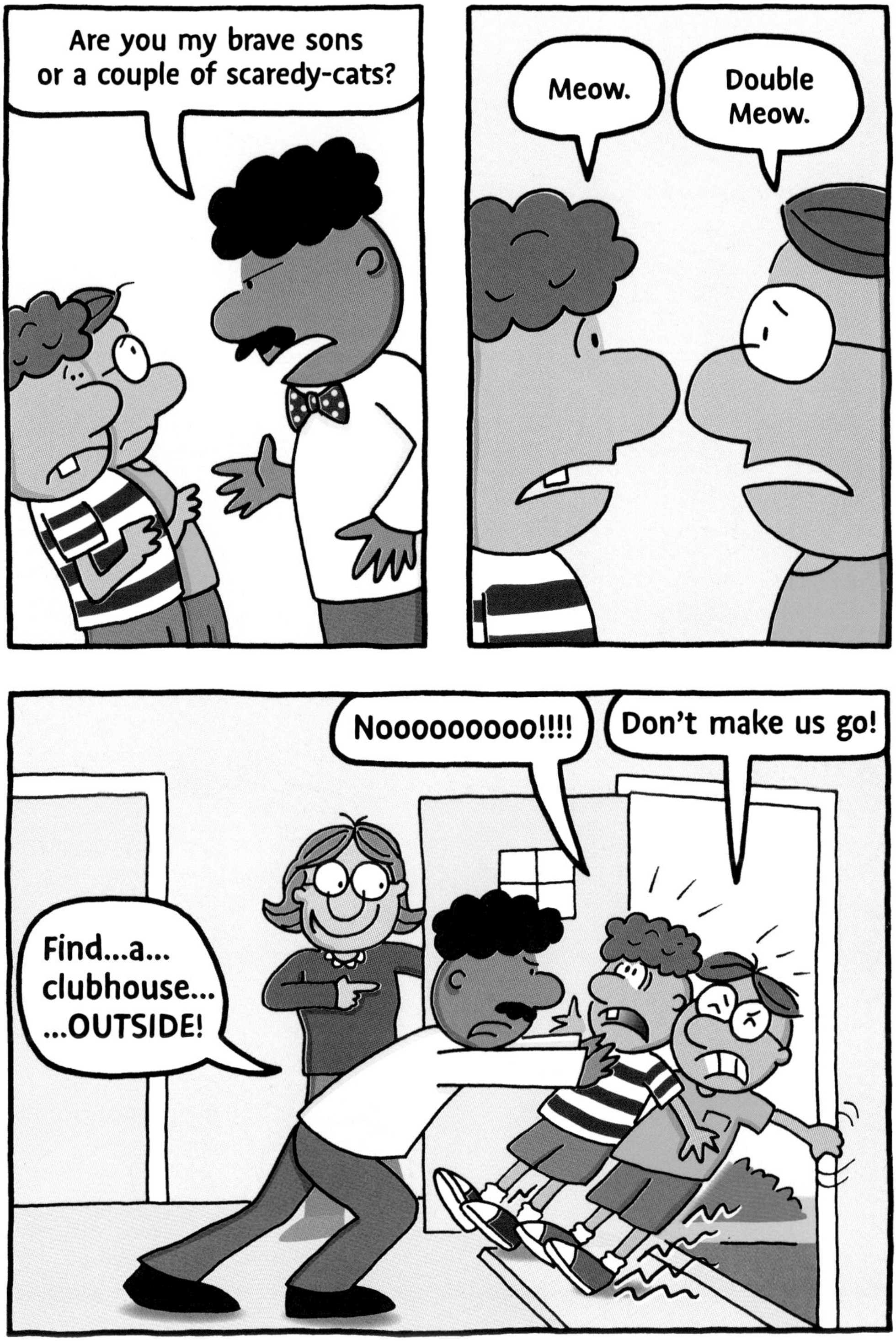
Are you my brave sons
or a couple of scaredy-cats?
Meow.
Double
Meow.
Nooooooooo!!!!
Don't make us go!
Find...a...
clubhouse...
...OUTSIDE!

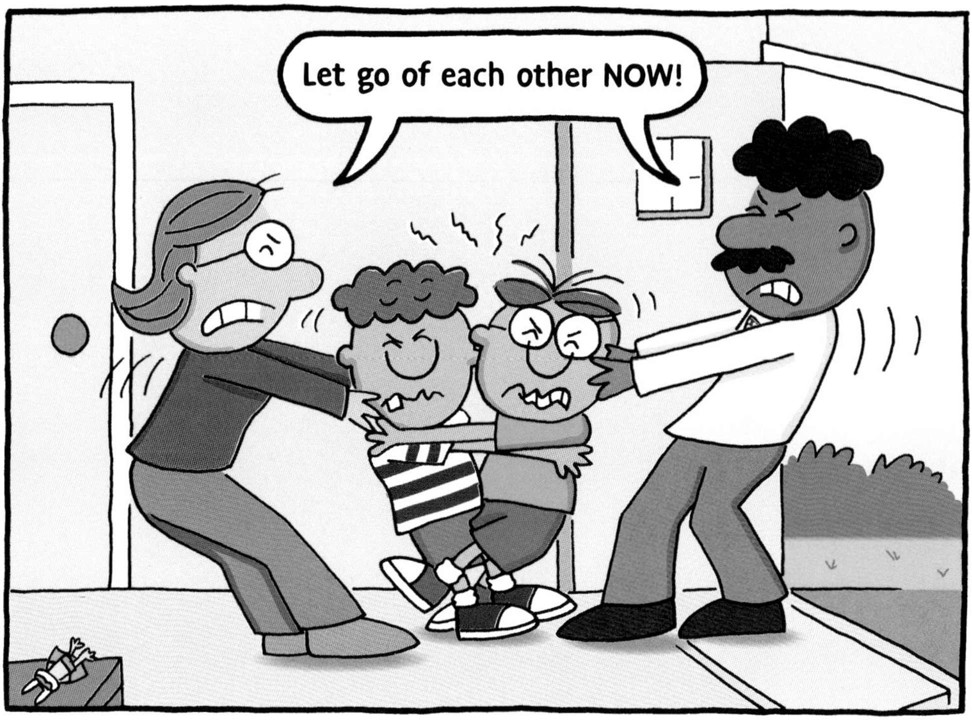
Let go of each other NOW!

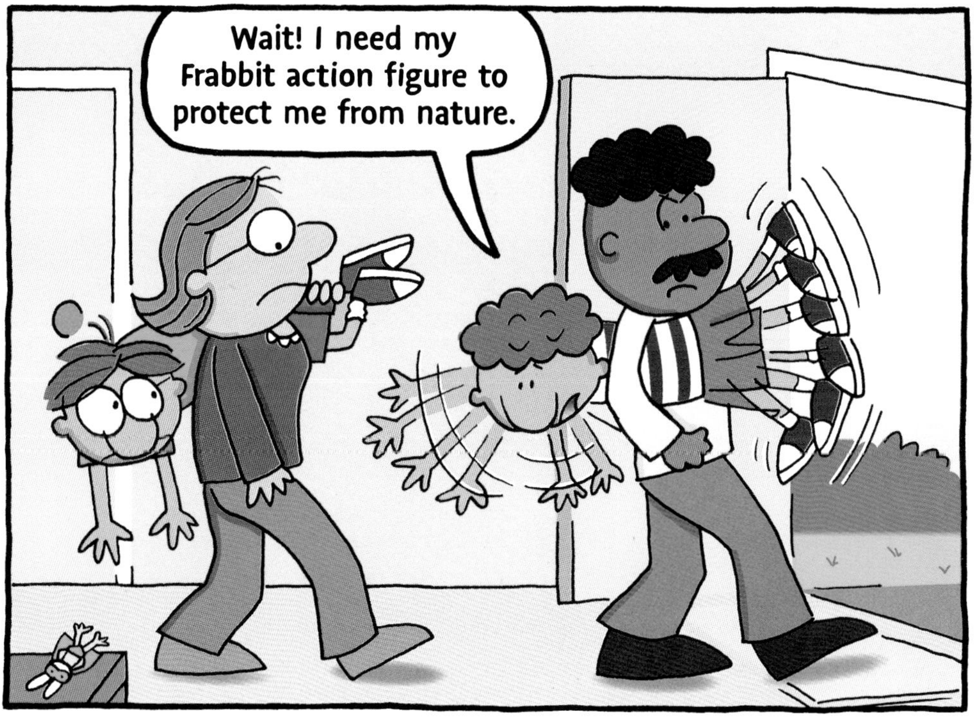
Wait! I need my Frabbit action figure to protect me from nature.

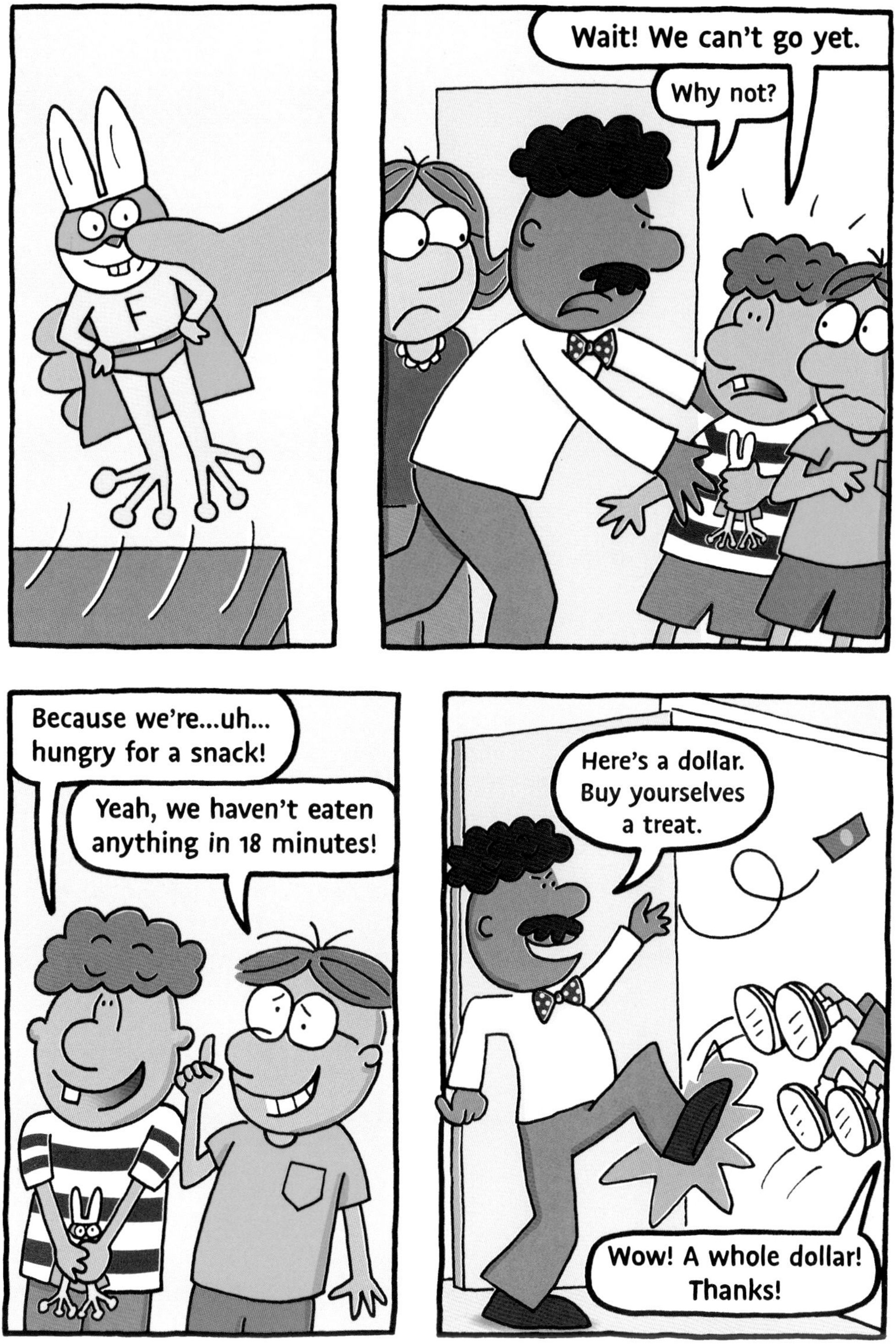
Wait! We can't go yet.
Why not?
Because we're...uh... hungry for a snack!
Yeah, we haven't eaten anything in 18 minutes!
Here's a dollar. Buy yourselves a treat.
Wow! A whole dollar! Thanks!

CHAPTER 2 - GOTTA HAVE A DONUT!

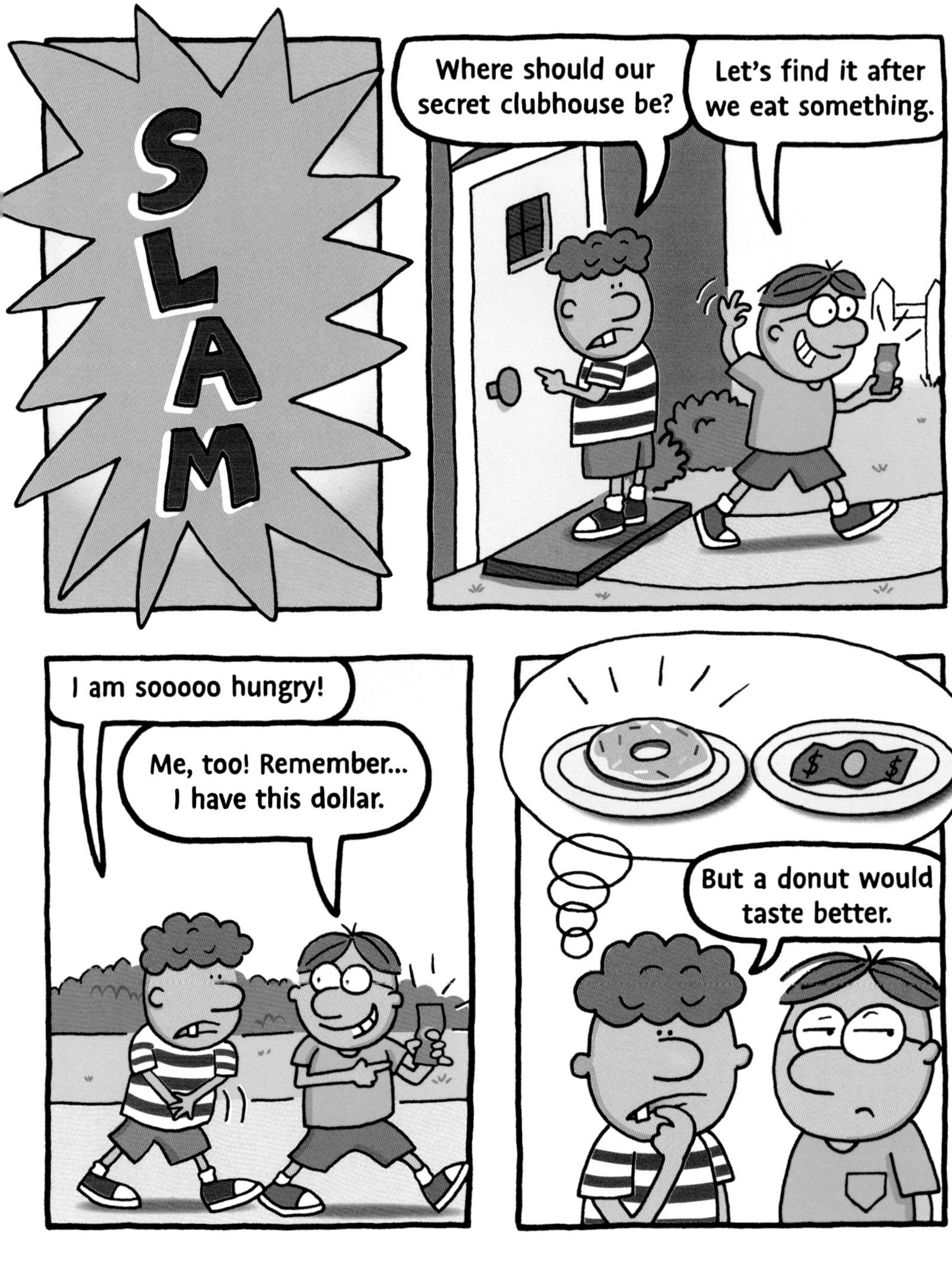
SLAM
Where should our secret clubhouse be?
Let's find it after we eat something.
I am sooooo hungry!
Me, too! Remember... I have this dollar.
But a donut would taste better.

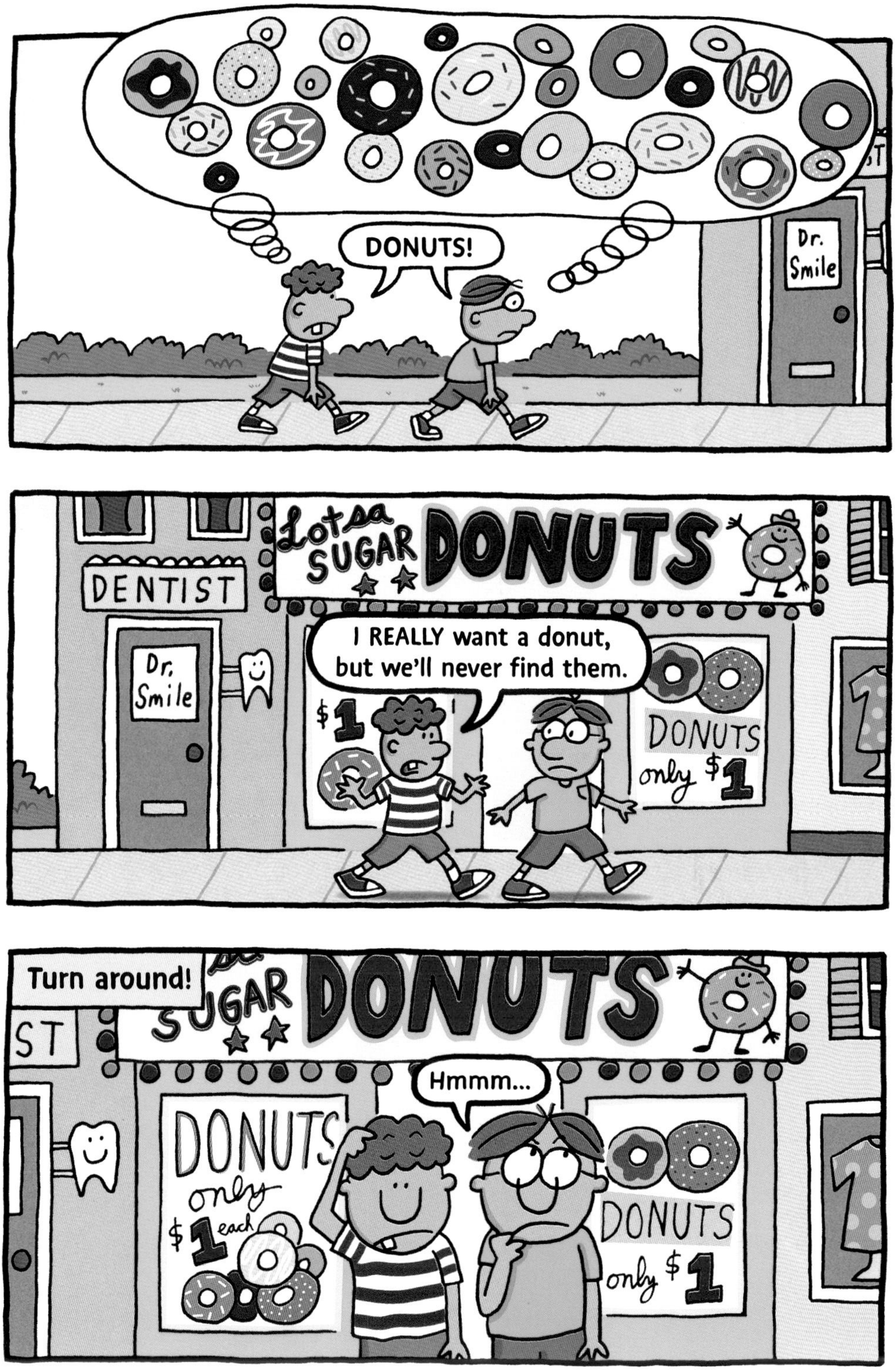
DONUTS!
Dr. Smile
Lotsa SUGAR DONUTS
DENTIST
Dr. Smile
I REALLY want a donut, but we'll never find them.
$1
DONUTS only $1
Turn around!
SUGAR DONUTS
ST
DONUTS only $1 each
Hmmm...
DONUTS only $1

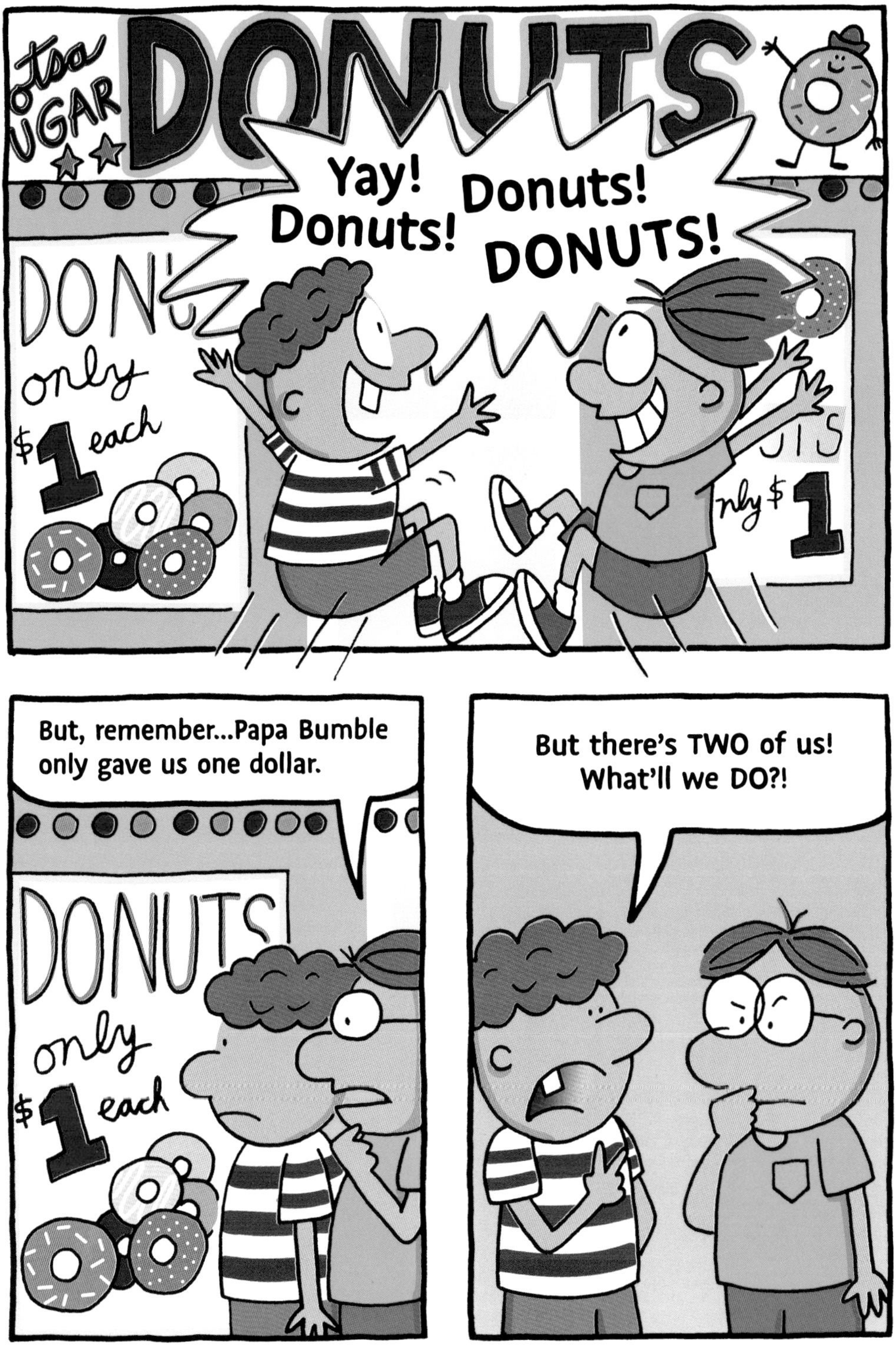
DONUTS
Yay! Donuts! Donuts! DONUTS!
only $1 each
But, remember...Papa Bumble only gave us one dollar.
DONUTS
only $1 each
But there's TWO of us! What'll we DO?!

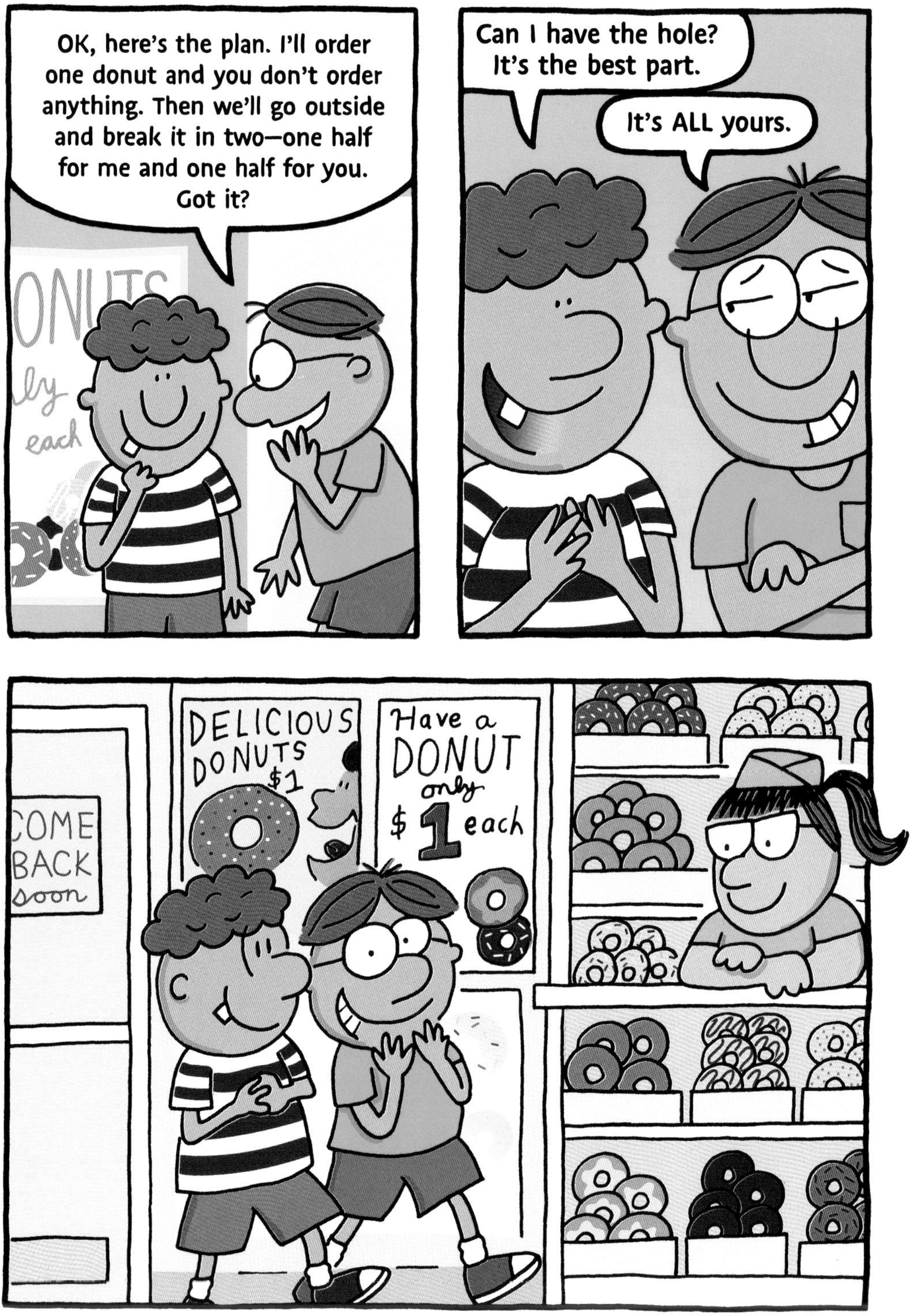
OK, here's the plan. I'll order one donut and you don't order anything. Then we'll go outside and break it in two—one half for me and one half for you. Got it?
Can I have the hole? It's the best part.
It's ALL yours.
DELICIOUS DONUTS $1
Have a DONUT only $1 each
COME BACK soon

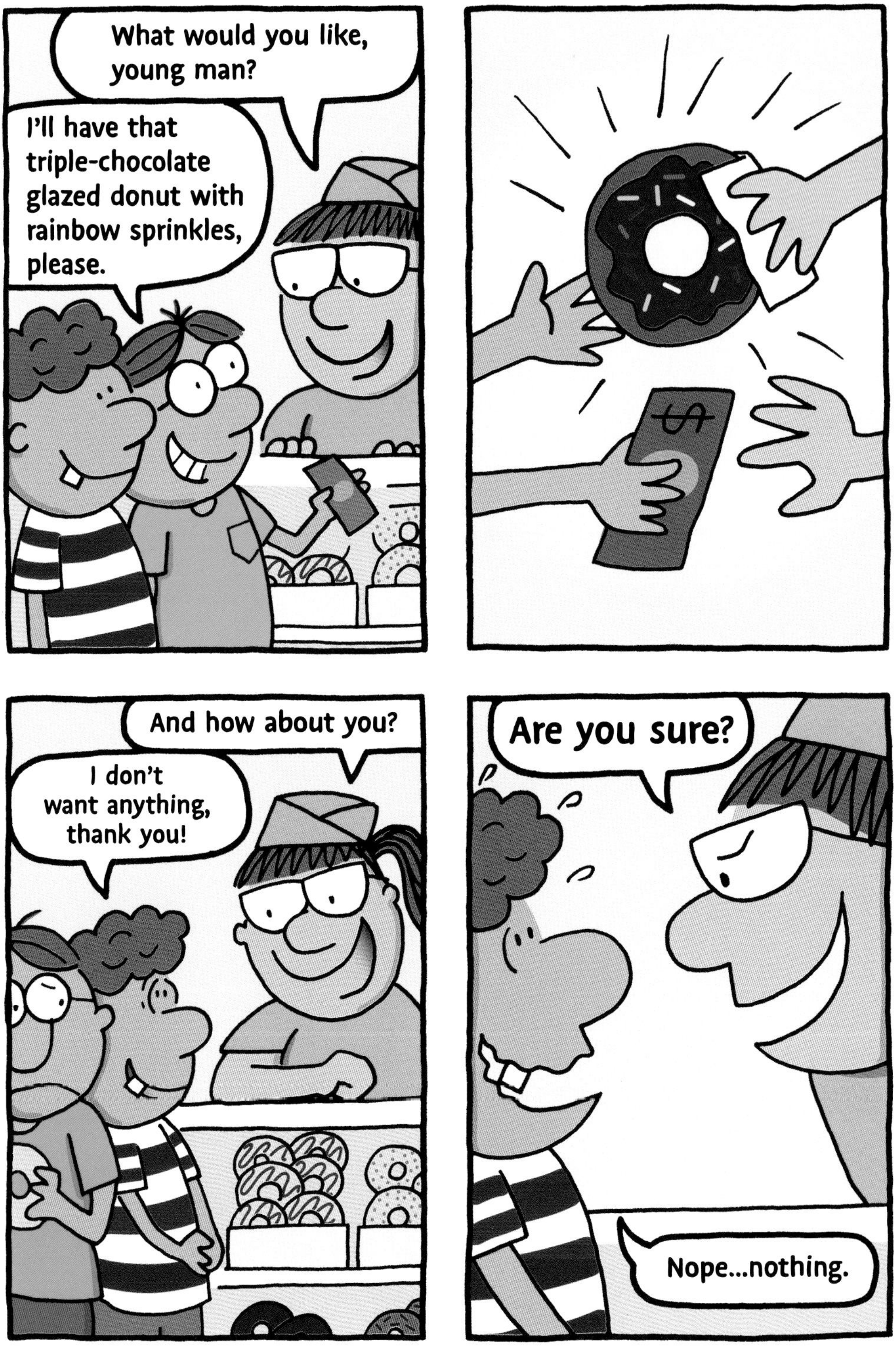
What would you like, young man?
I'll have that triple-chocolate glazed donut with rainbow sprinkles, please.
And how about you?
I don't want anything, thank you!
Are you sure?
Nope...nothing.

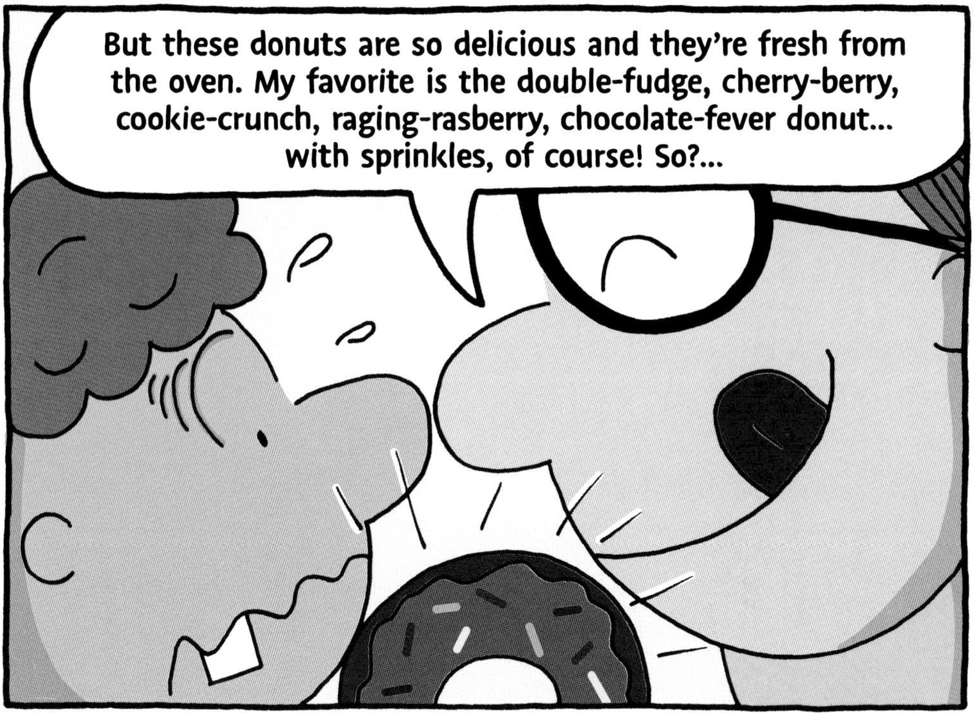
But these donuts are so delicious and they're fresh from the oven. My favorite is the double-fudge, cherry-berry, cookie-crunch, raging-rasberry, chocolate-fever donut... with sprinkles, of course! So?...

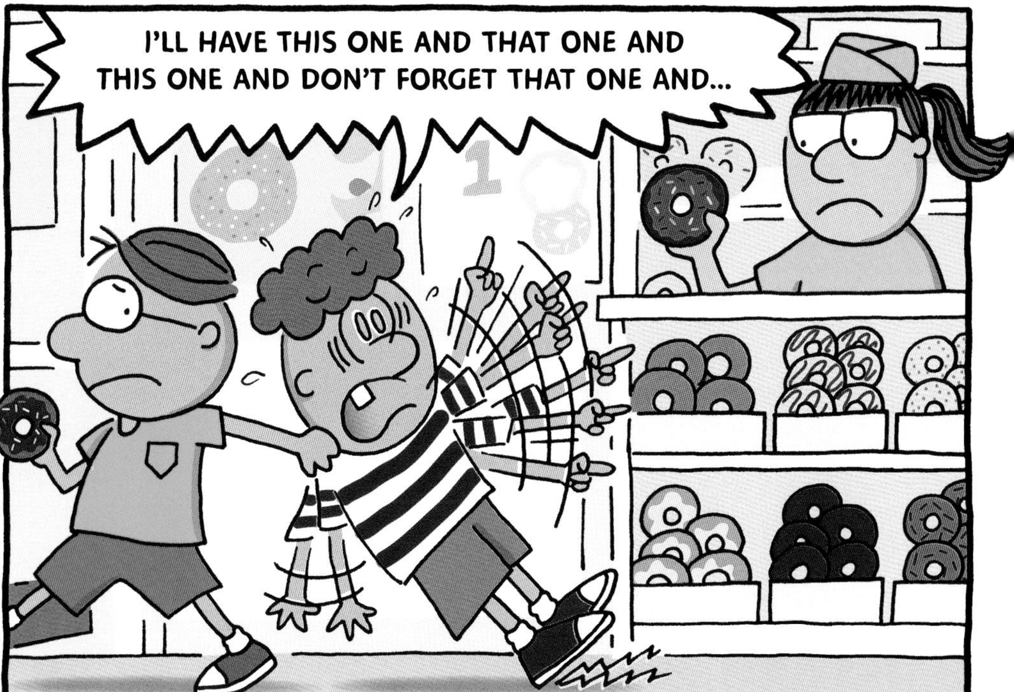
I'LL HAVE THIS ONE AND THAT ONE AND THIS ONE AND DON'T FORGET THAT ONE AND...

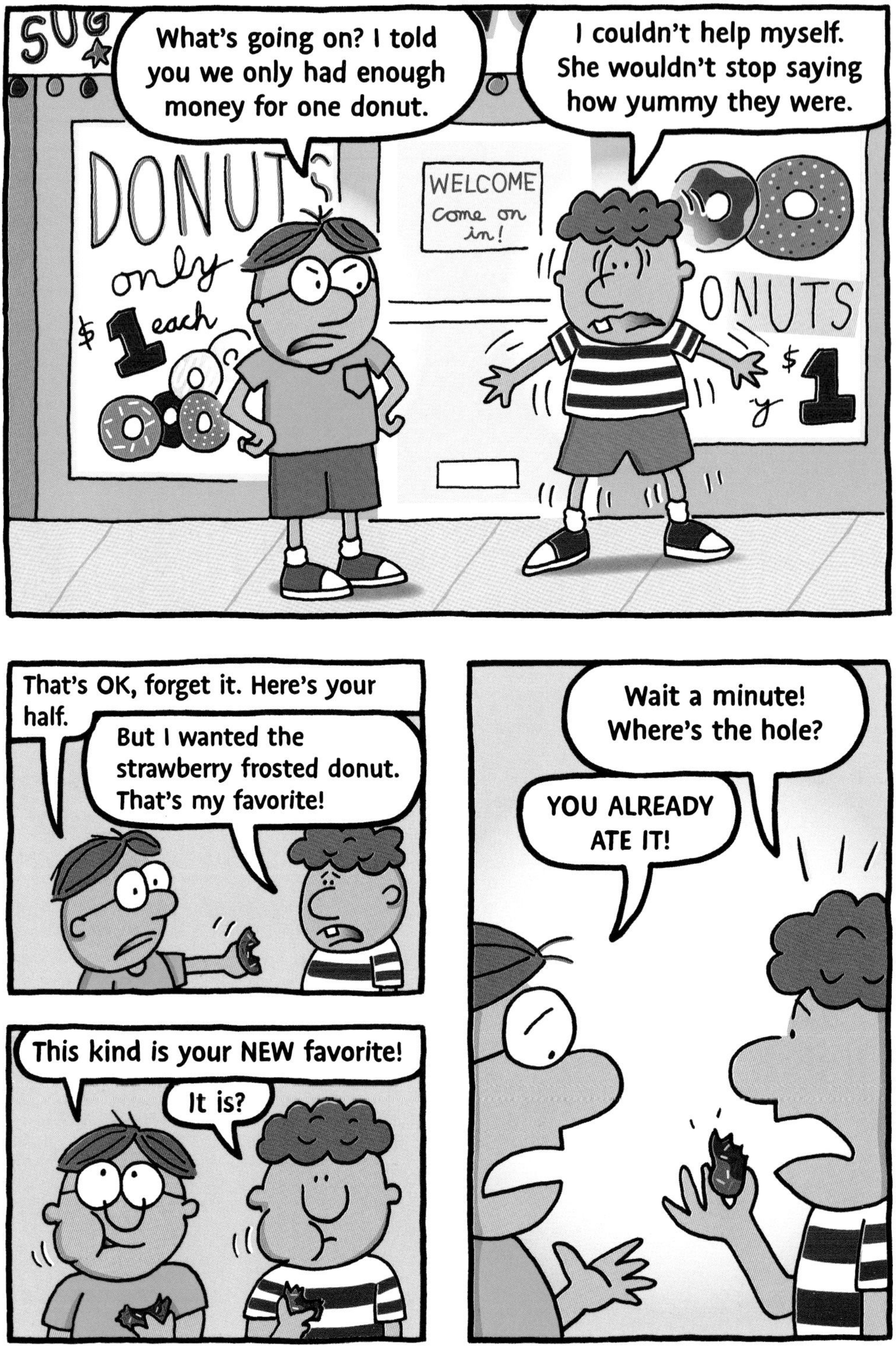
SUG
What's going on? I told you we only had enough money for one donut.
I couldn't help myself. She wouldn't stop saying how yummy they were.
DONUTS
only $1 each
WELCOME
Come on in!
ONUTS
$1
That's OK, forget it. Here's your half.
But I wanted the strawberry frosted donut. That's my favorite!
Wait a minute! Where's the hole?
YOU ALREADY ATE IT!
This kind is your NEW favorite!
It is?

CHAPTER 3 – HELLO, REBECCA WOOD!

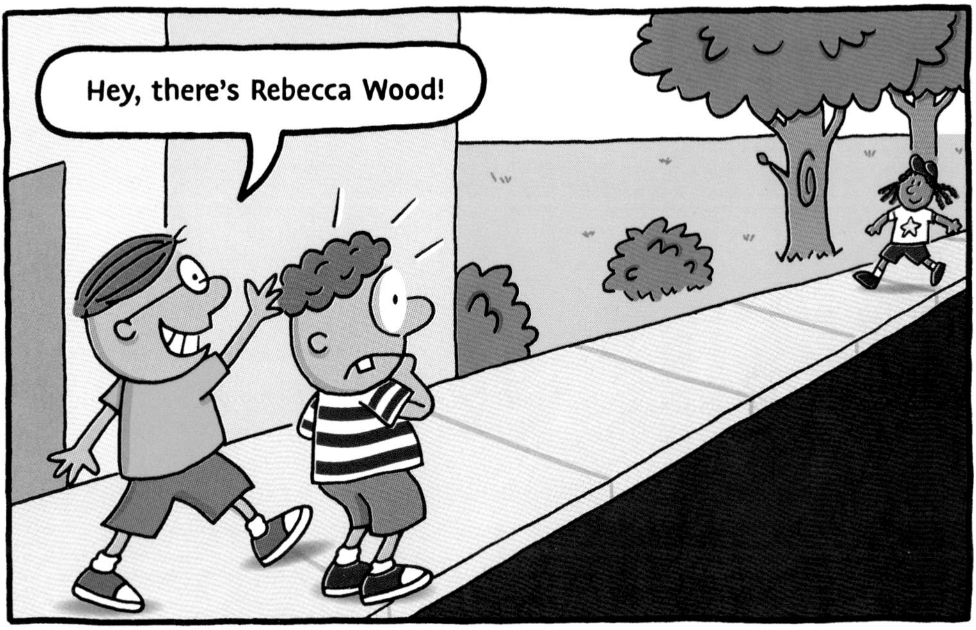
Hey, there's Rebecca Wood!

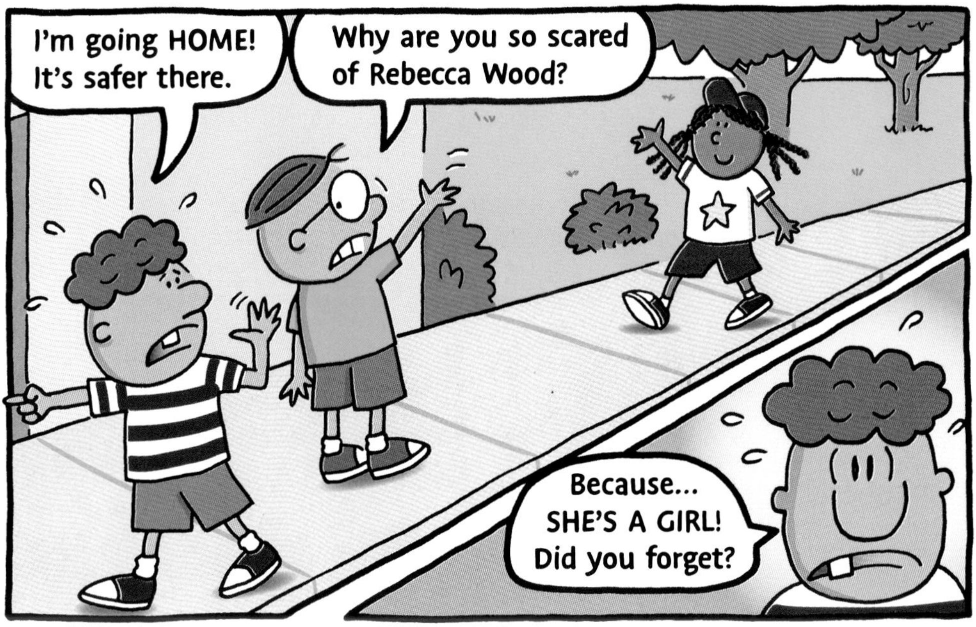
Why are you so scared of Rebecca Wood?
I'm going HOME! It's safer there.
Because... SHE'S A GIRL! Did you forget?

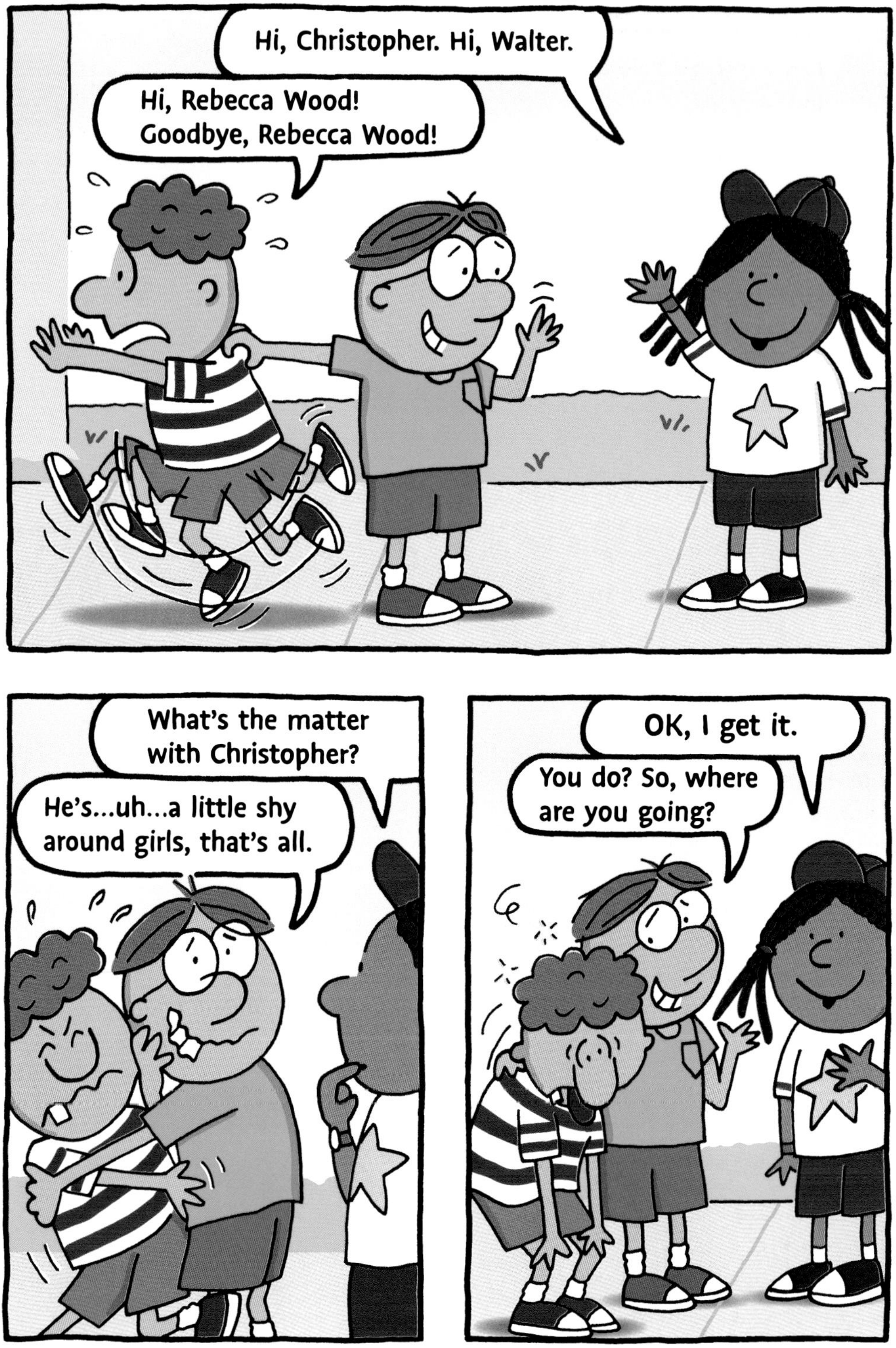
Hi, Christopher. Hi, Walter.
Hi, Rebecca Wood! Goodbye, Rebecca Wood!
What's the matter with Christopher?
He's...uh...a little shy around girls, that's all.
OK, I get it.
You do? So, where are you going?

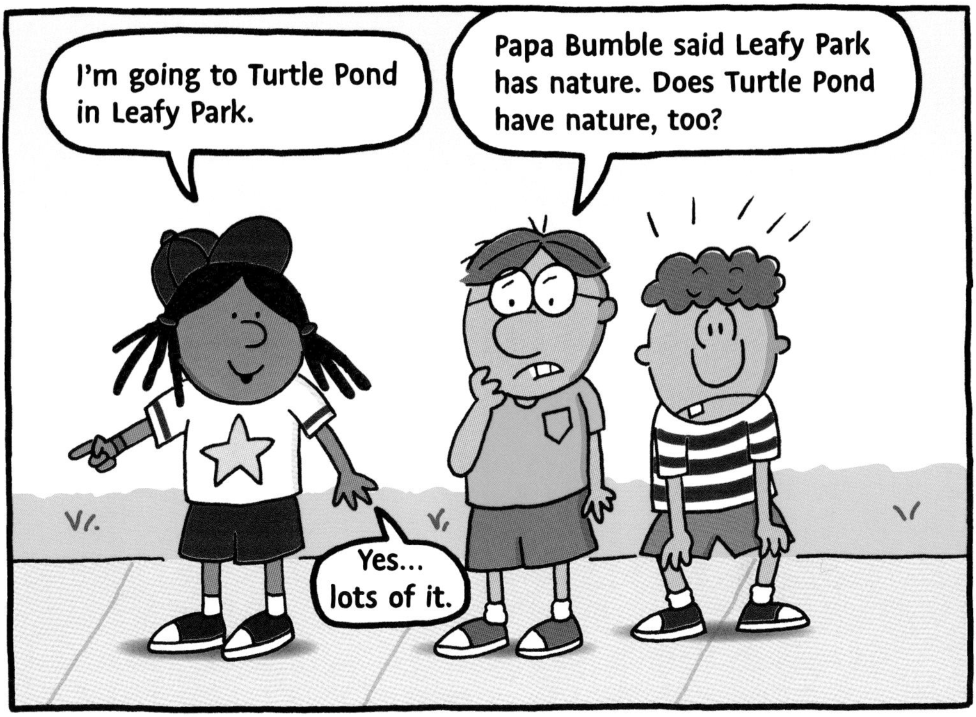
I'm going to Turtle Pond in Leafy Park.
Papa Bumble said Leafy Park has nature. Does Turtle Pond have nature, too?
Yes... lots of it.

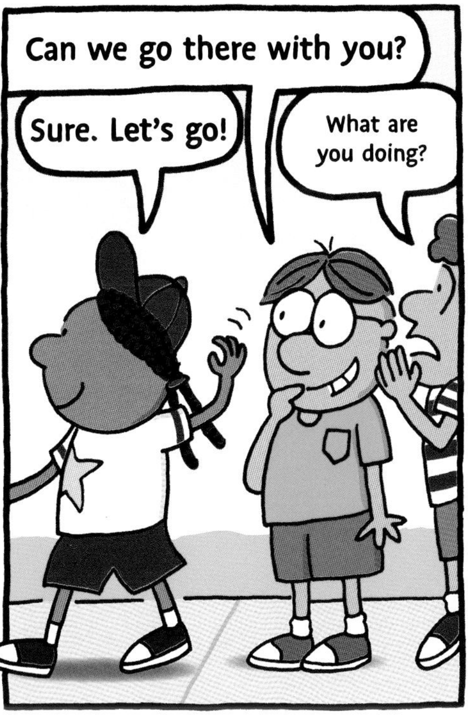
Can we go there with you?
Sure. Let's go!
What are you doing?

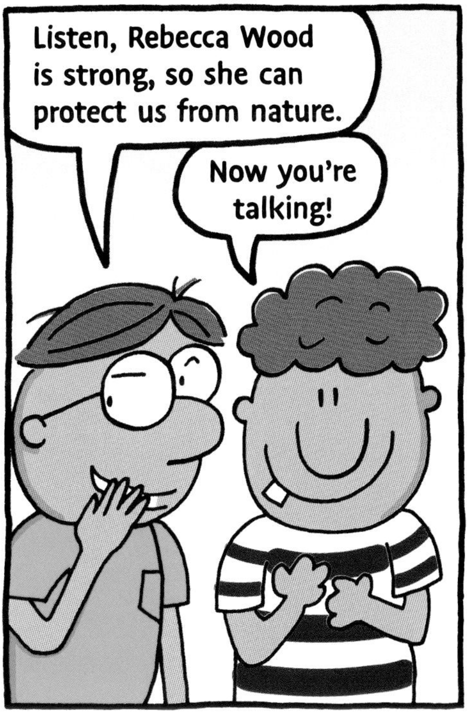
Listen, Rebecca Wood is strong, so she can protect us from nature.
Now you're talking!

CHAPTER 4 - WELCOME TO LEAFY PARK!

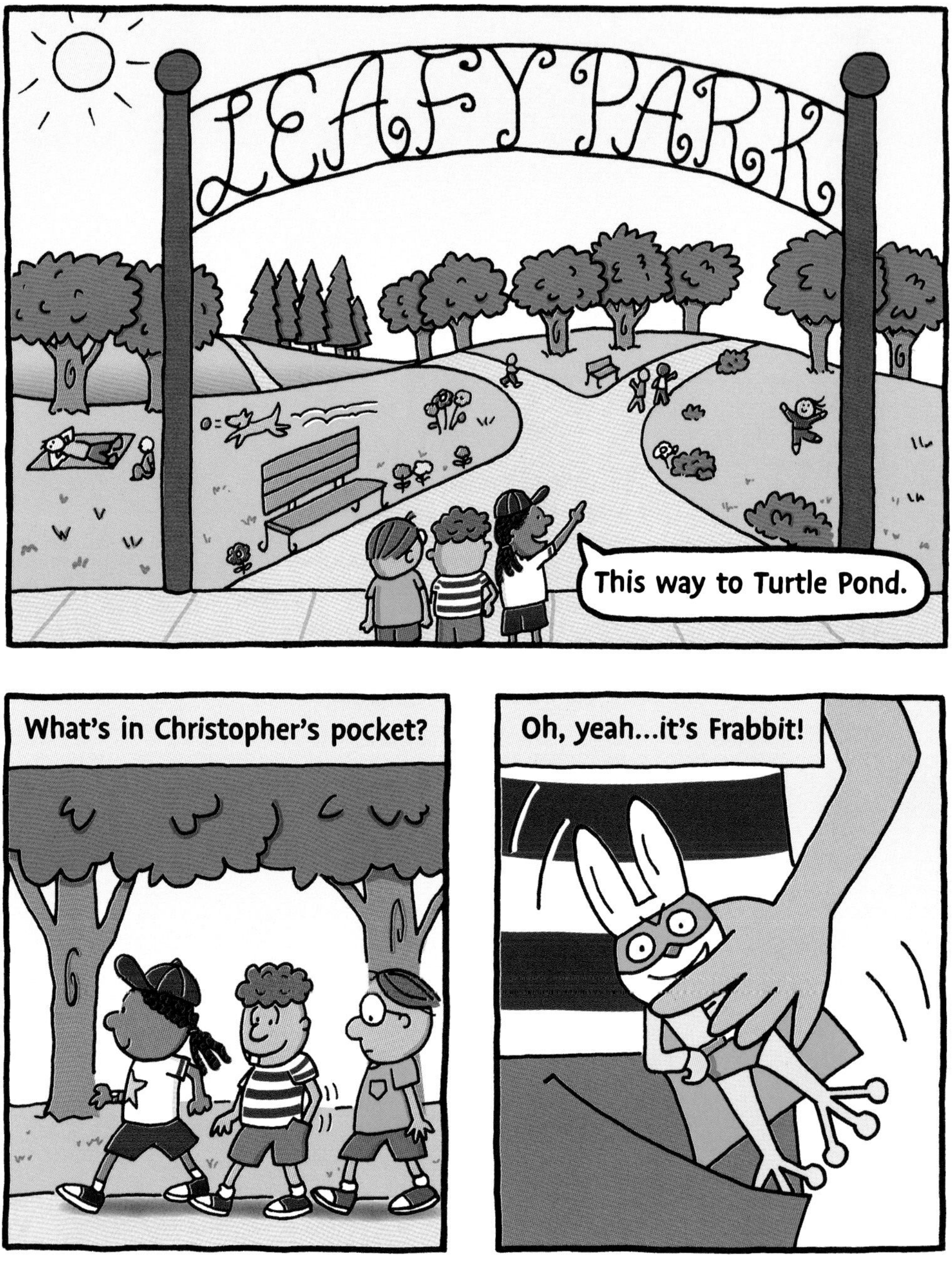
LEAFY PARK
This way to Turtle Pond.
What's in Christopher's pocket?
Oh, yeah...it's Frabbit!

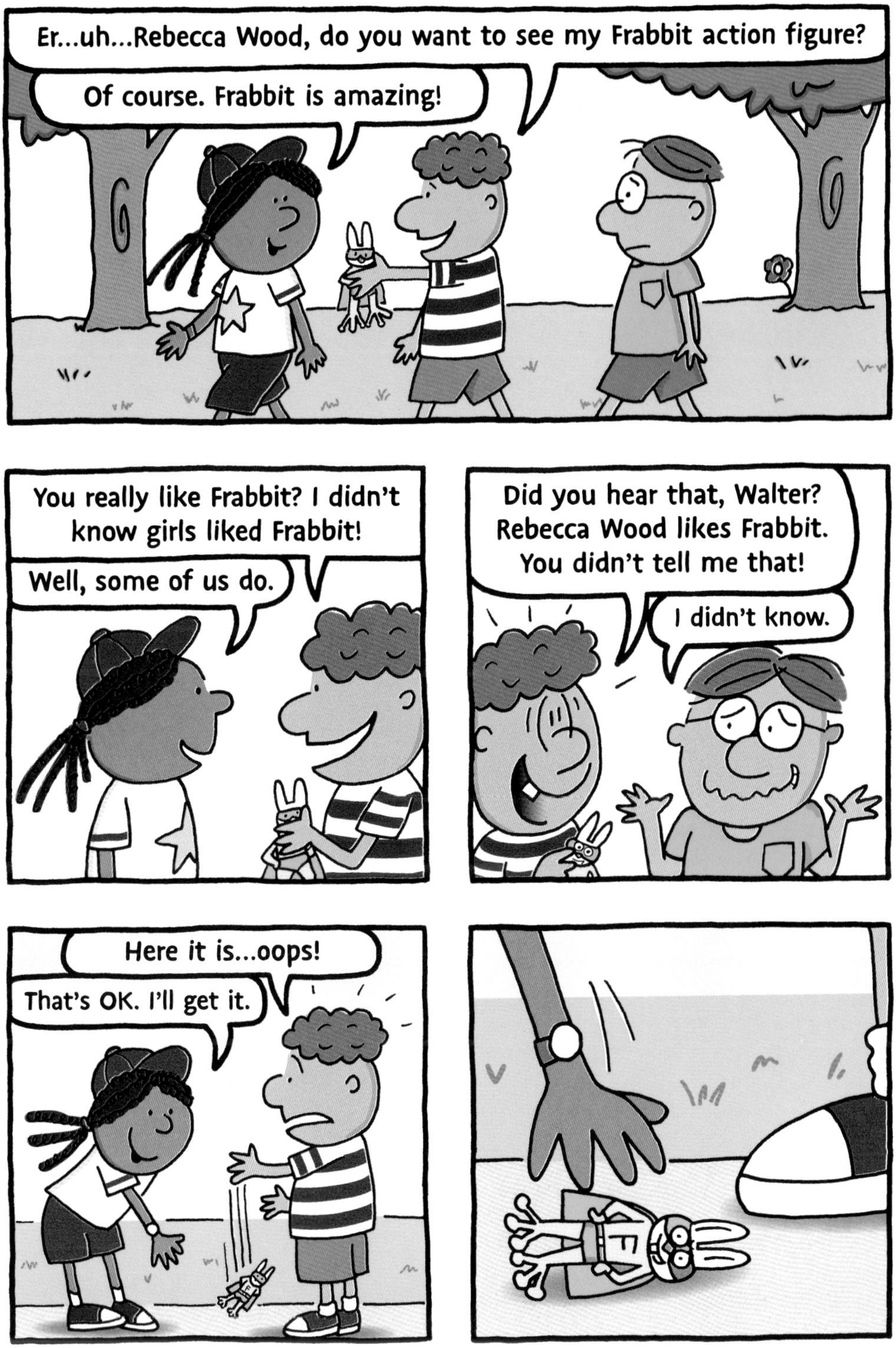
Er...uh...Rebecca Wood, do you want to see my Frabbit action figure?
Of course. Frabbit is amazing!
You really like Frabbit? I didn't know girls liked Frabbit!
Well, some of us do.
Did you hear that, Walter? Rebecca Wood likes Frabbit. You didn't tell me that!
I didn't know.
Here it is...oops!
That's OK. I'll get it.

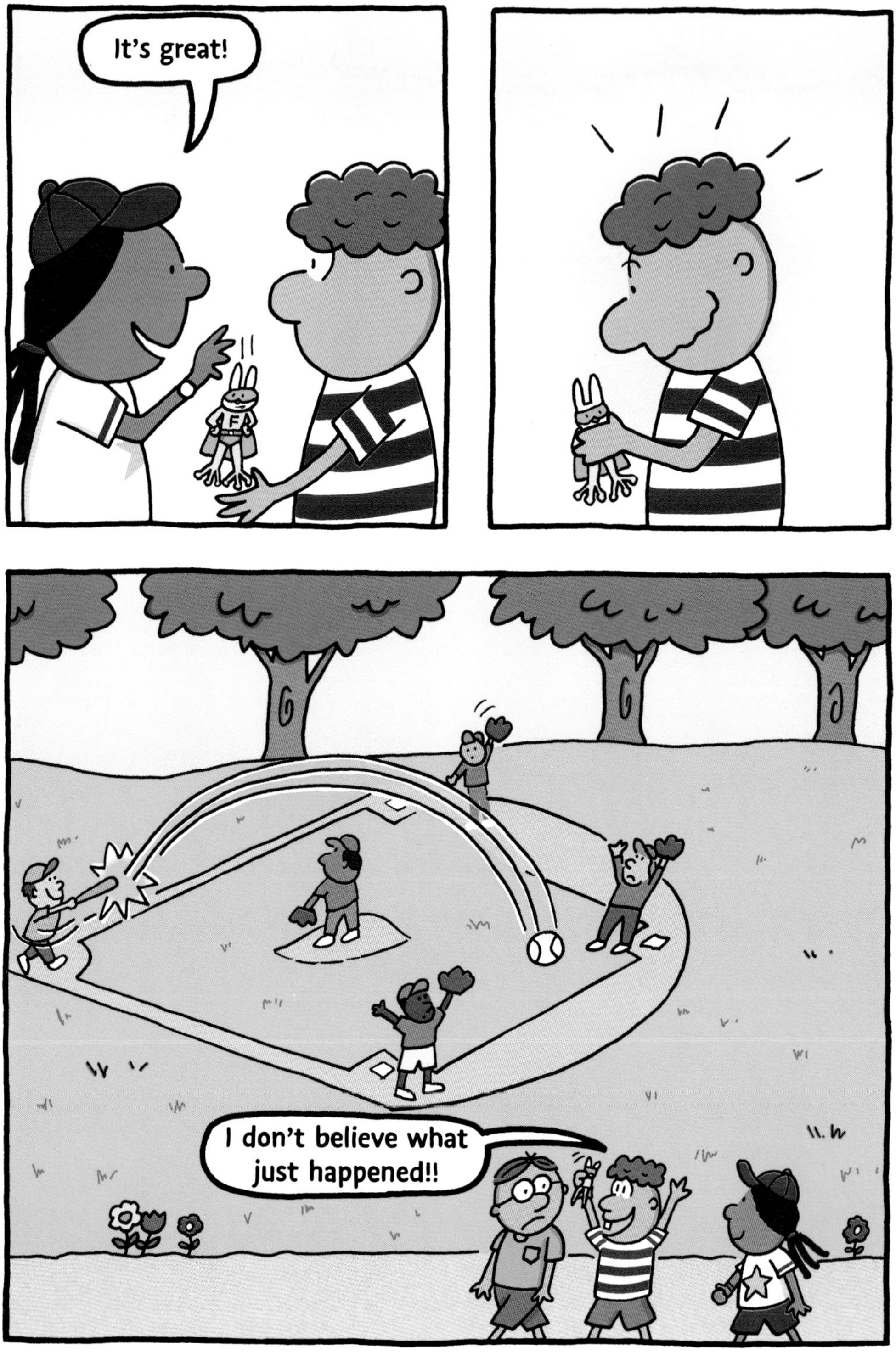
It's great!
F
I don't believe what just happened!!

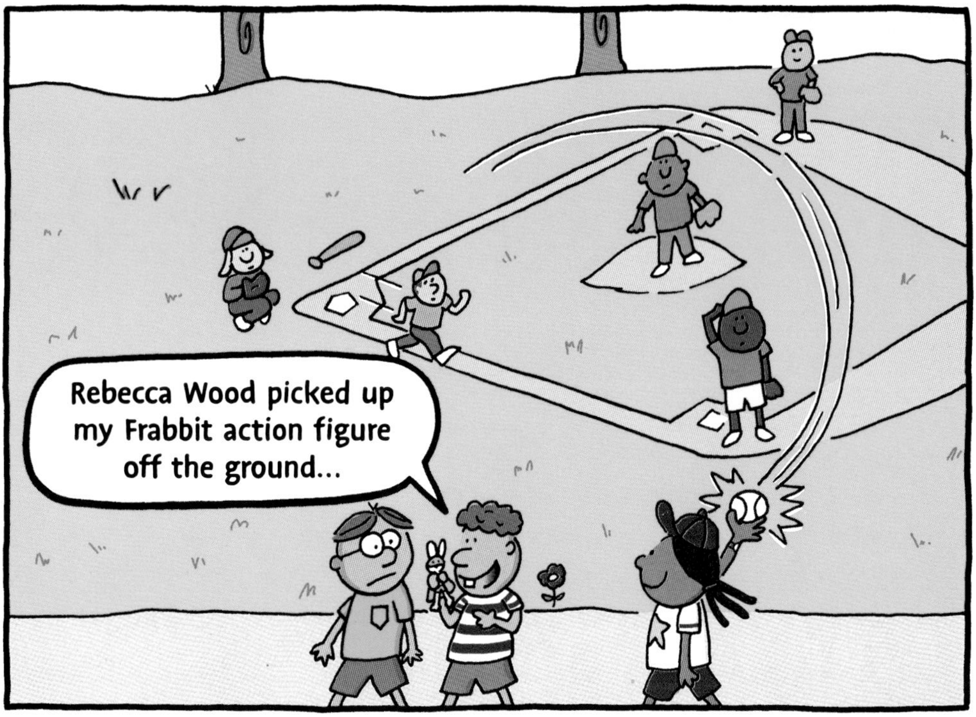
Rebecca Wood picked up my Frabbit action figure off the ground...

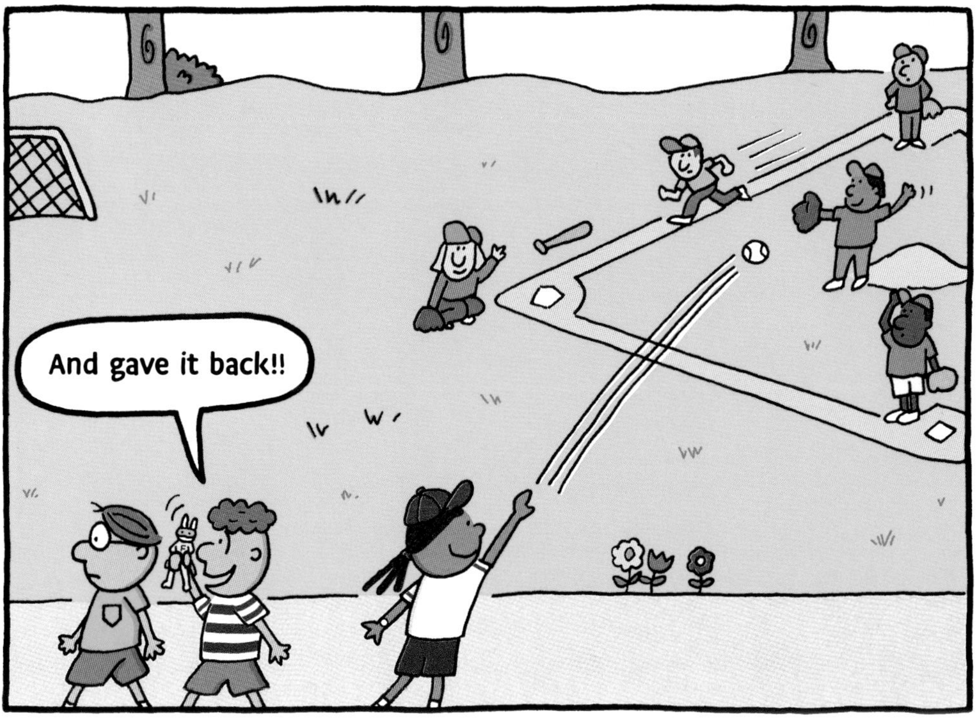
And gave it back!!

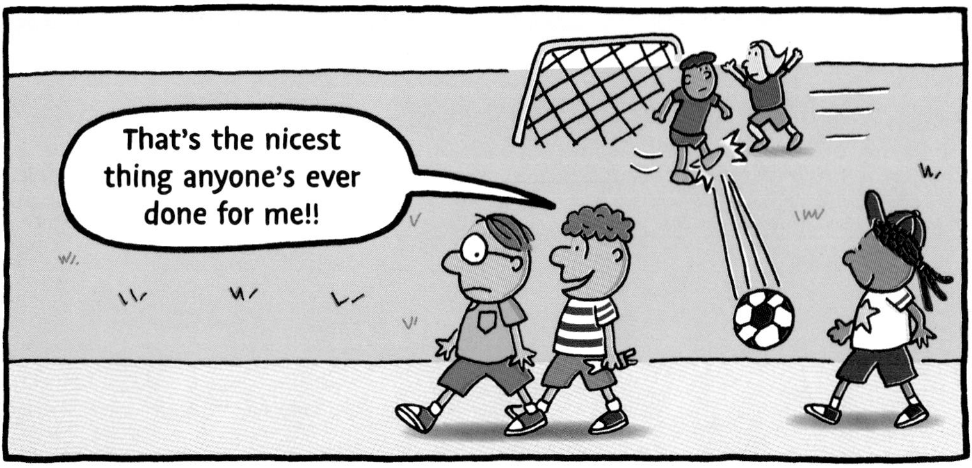
That's the nicest thing anyone's ever done for me!!

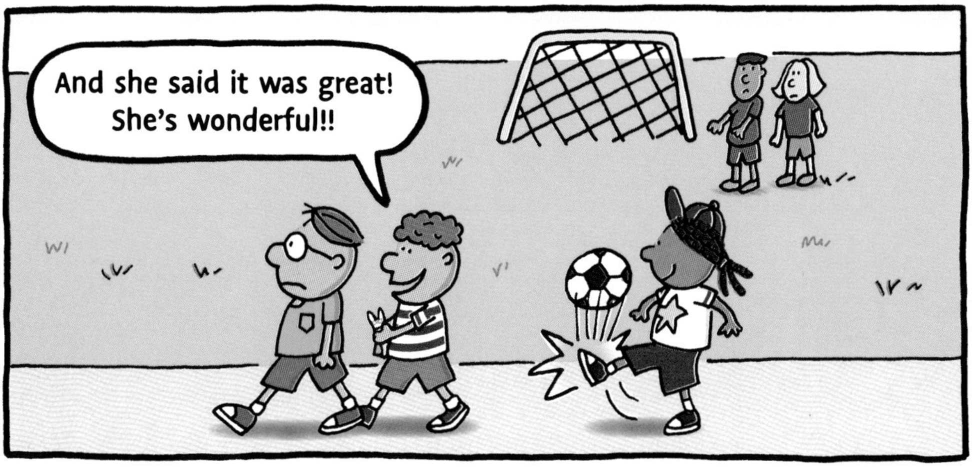
And she said it was great! She's wonderful!!

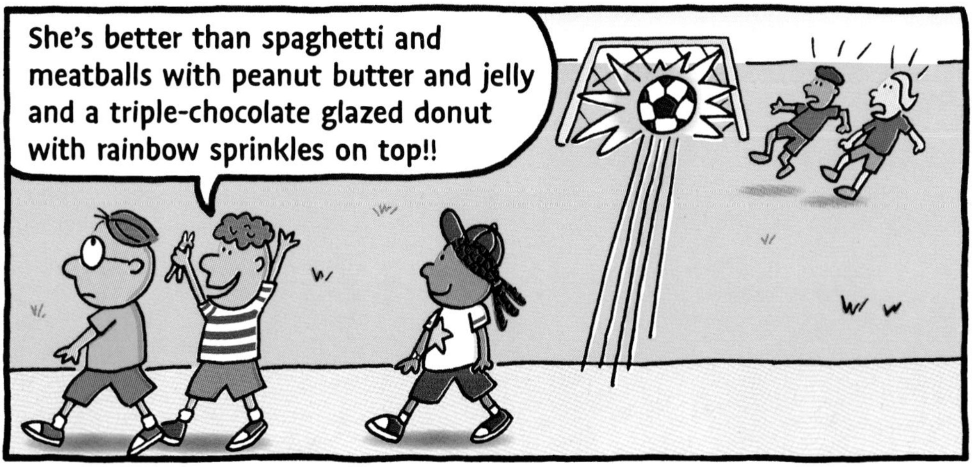
She's better than spaghetti and meatballs with peanut butter and jelly and a triple-chocolate glazed donut with rainbow sprinkles on top!!

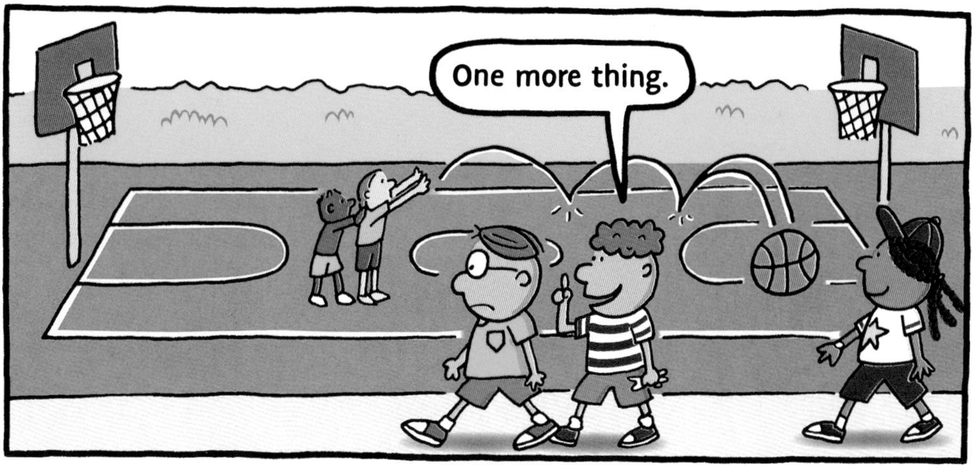
One more thing.

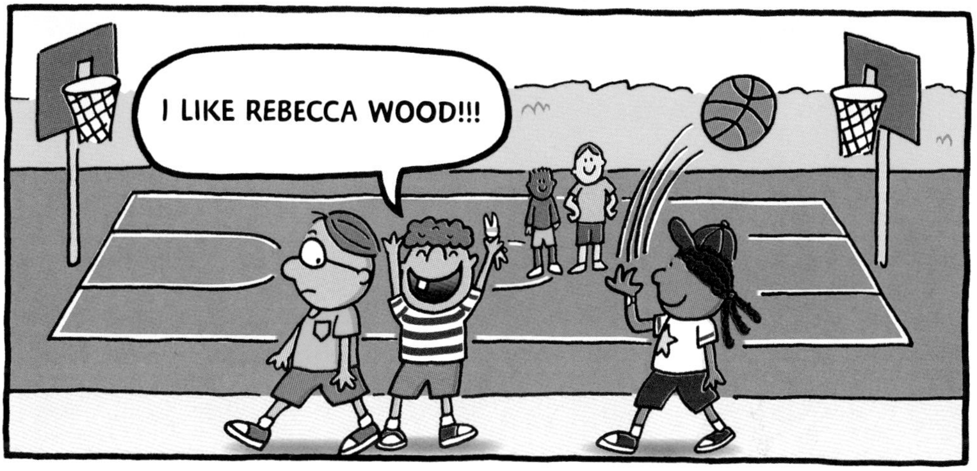
I LIKE REBECCA WOOD!!!

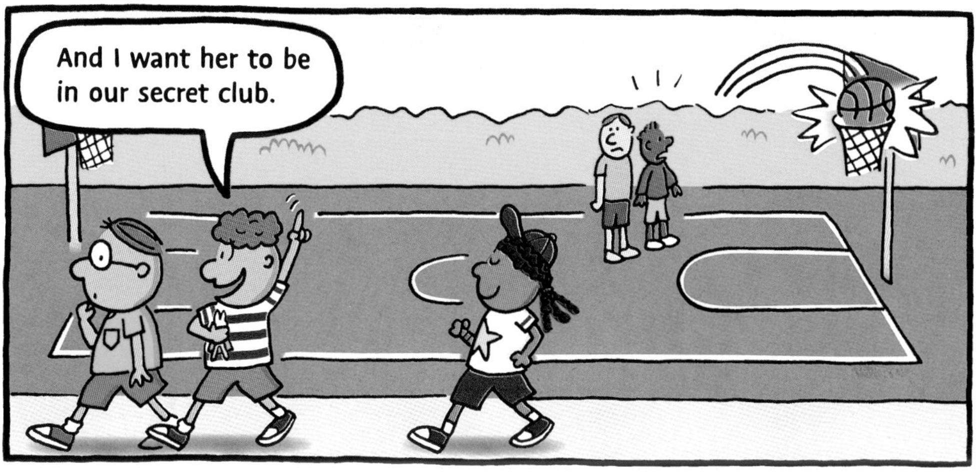
And I want her to be in our secret club.

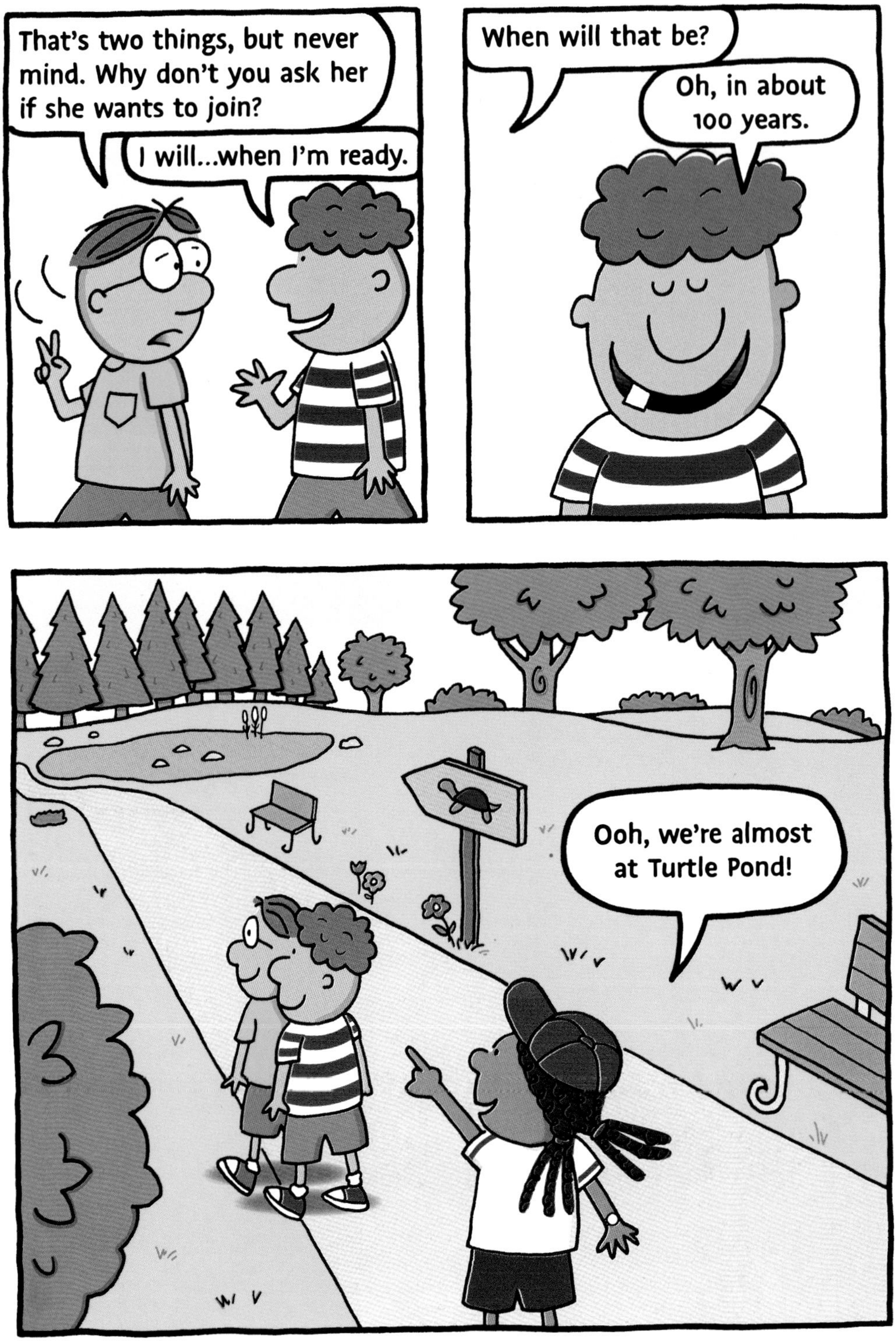
That's two things, but never mind. Why don't you ask her if she wants to join?
I will...when I'm ready.
When will that be?
Oh, in about 100 years.
Ooh, we're almost at Turtle Pond!

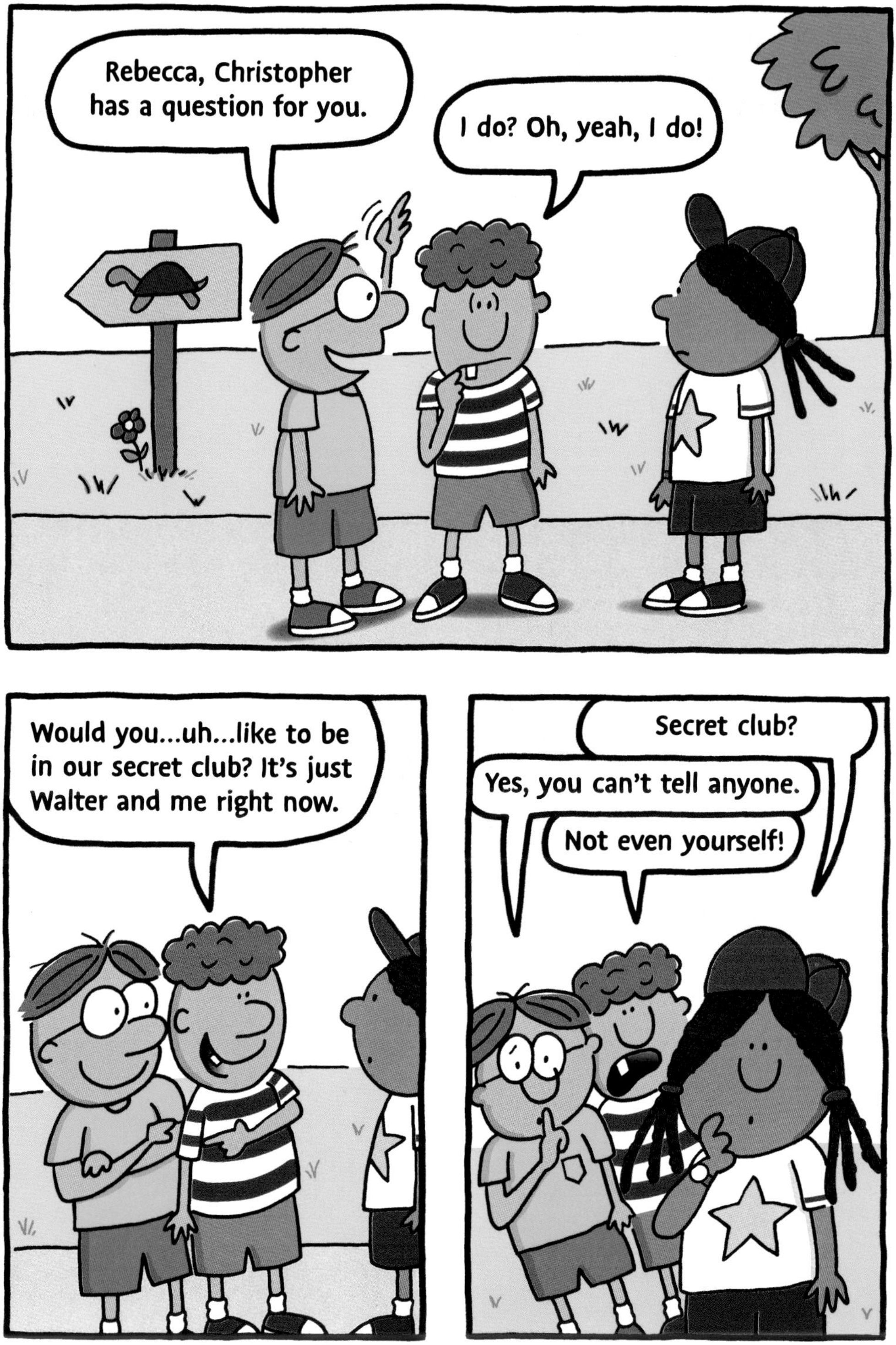
Rebecca, Christopher has a question for you.
I do? Oh, yeah, I do!
Would you...uh...like to be in our secret club? It's just Walter and me right now.
Secret club?
Yes, you can't tell anyone.
Not even yourself!

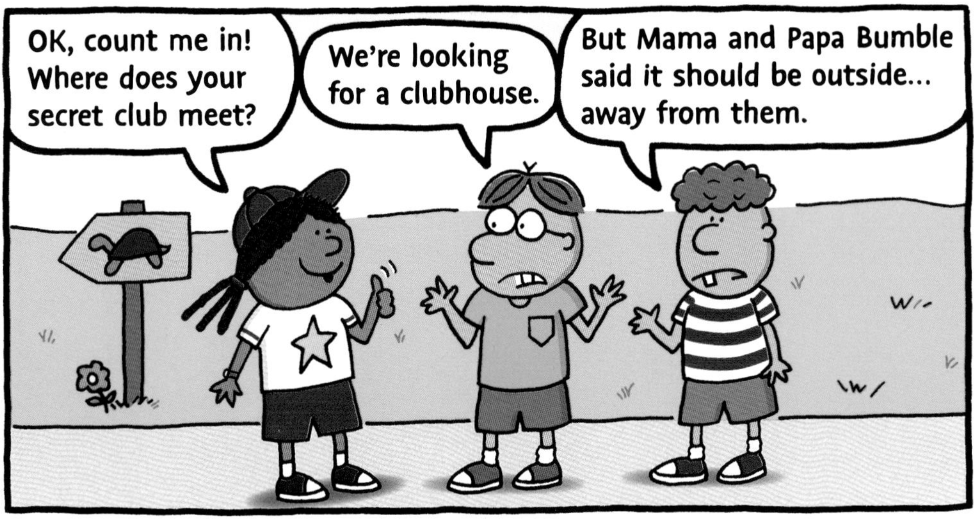
OK, count me in! Where does your secret club meet?
We're looking for a clubhouse.
But Mama and Papa Bumble said it should be outside... away from them.

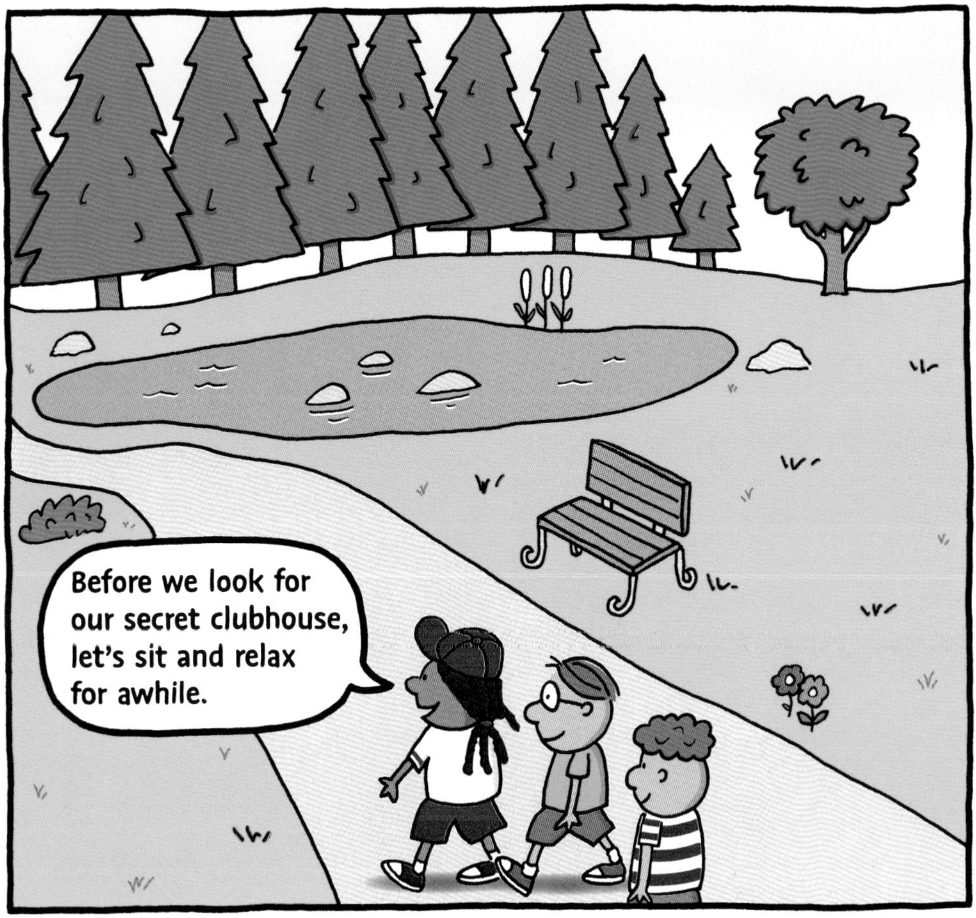
Before we look for our secret clubhouse, let's sit and relax for awhile.

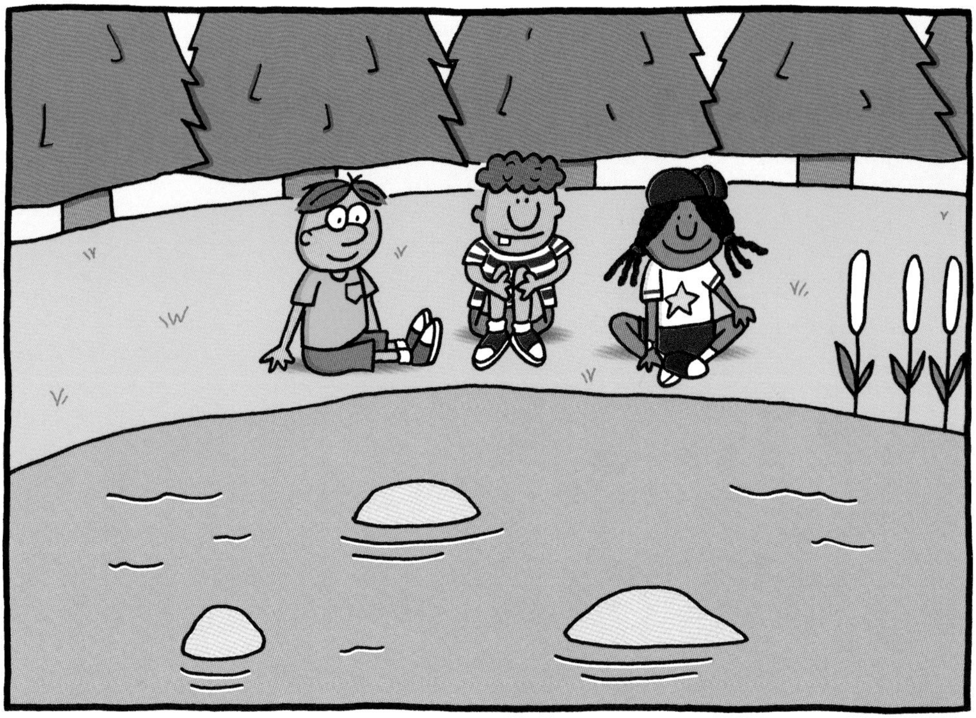

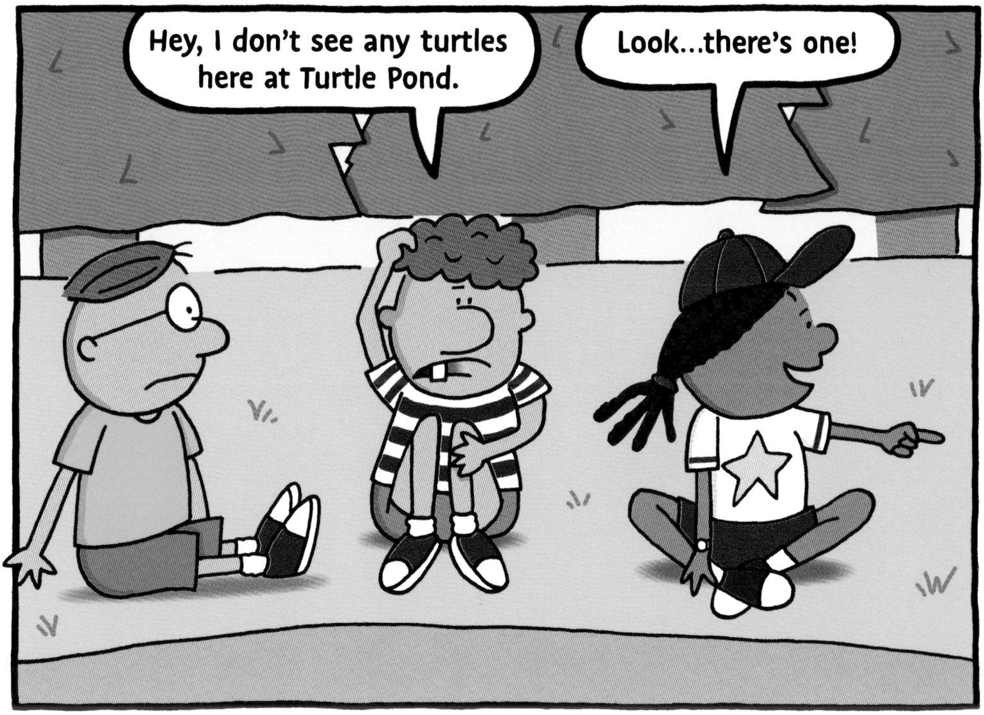
Hey, I don't see any turtles here at Turtle Pond.
Look...there's one!

CHAPTER 5 - THE TURTLE FROM TURTLE POND!

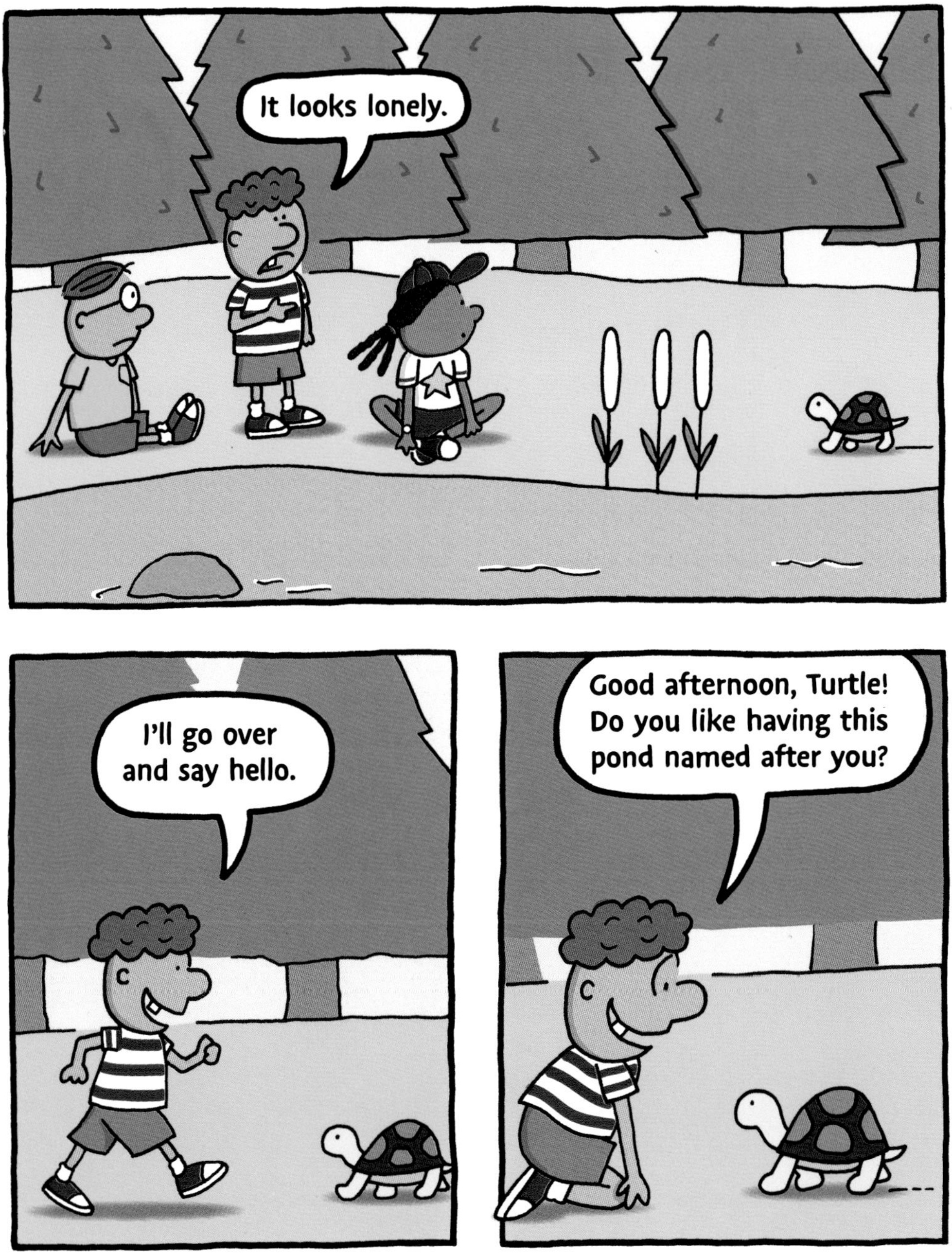
It looks lonely.
I'll go over and say hello.
Good afternoon, Turtle! Do you like having this pond named after you?

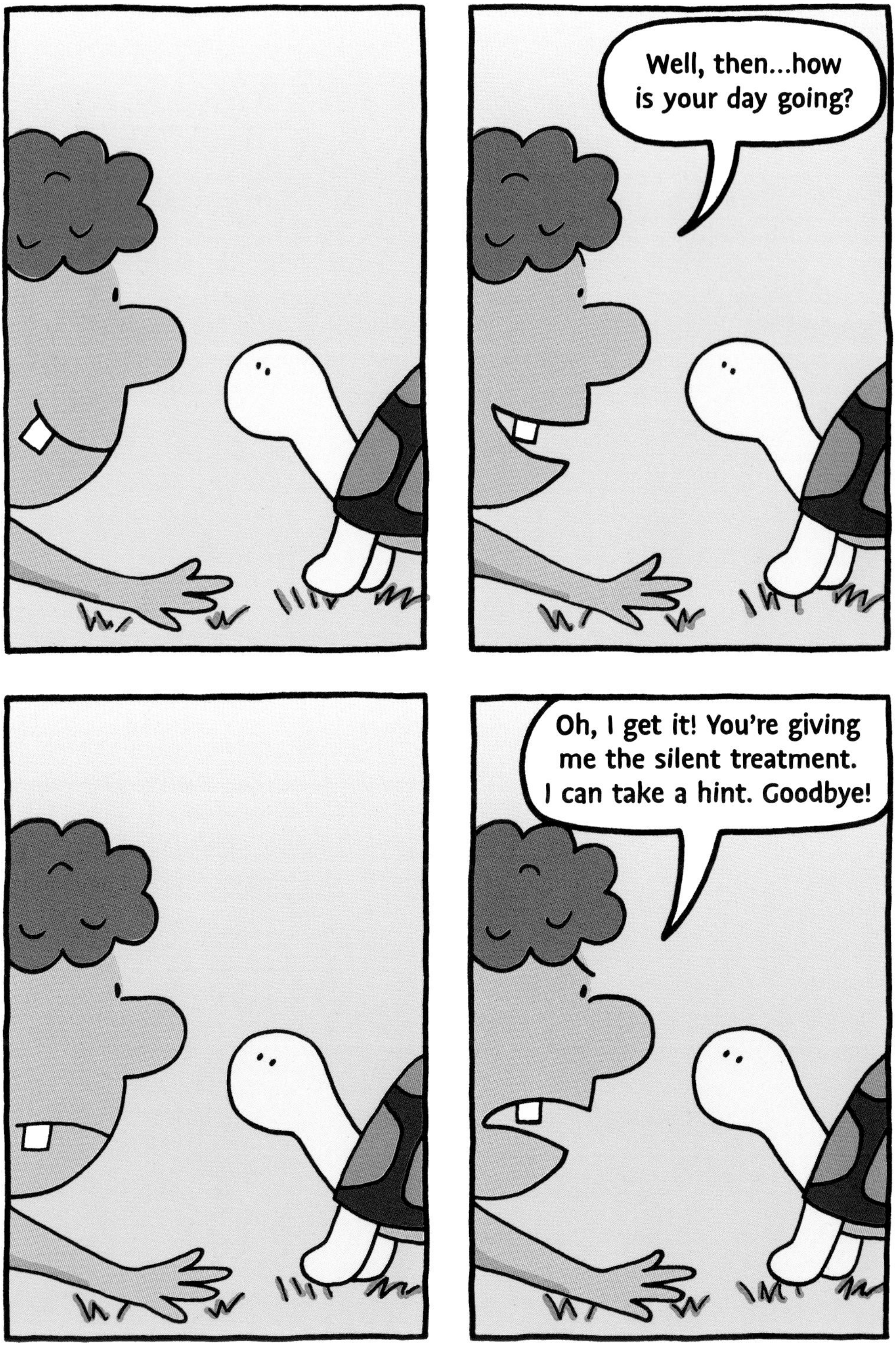
Well, then...how is your day going?
Oh, I get it! You're giving me the silent treatment. I can take a hint. Goodbye!

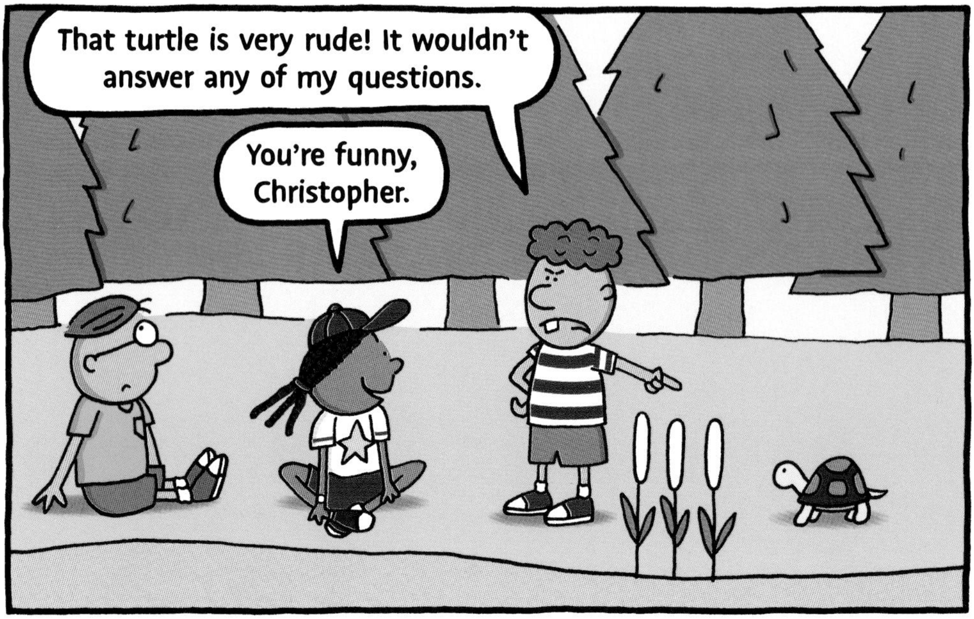
That turtle is very rude! It wouldn't answer any of my questions.
You're funny, Christopher.

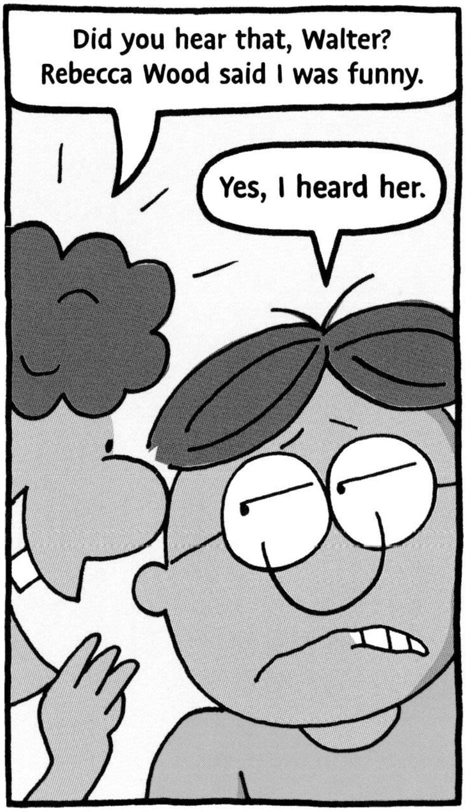
Did you hear that, Walter? Rebecca Wood said I was funny.
Yes, I heard her.

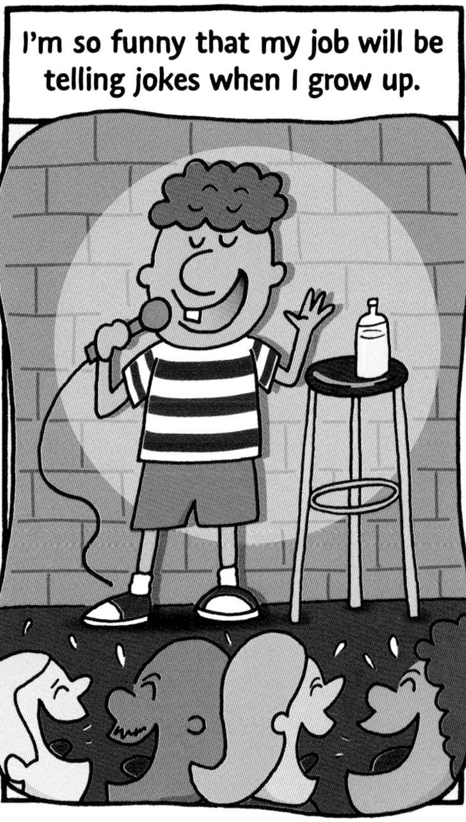
I'm so funny that my job will be telling jokes when I grow up.

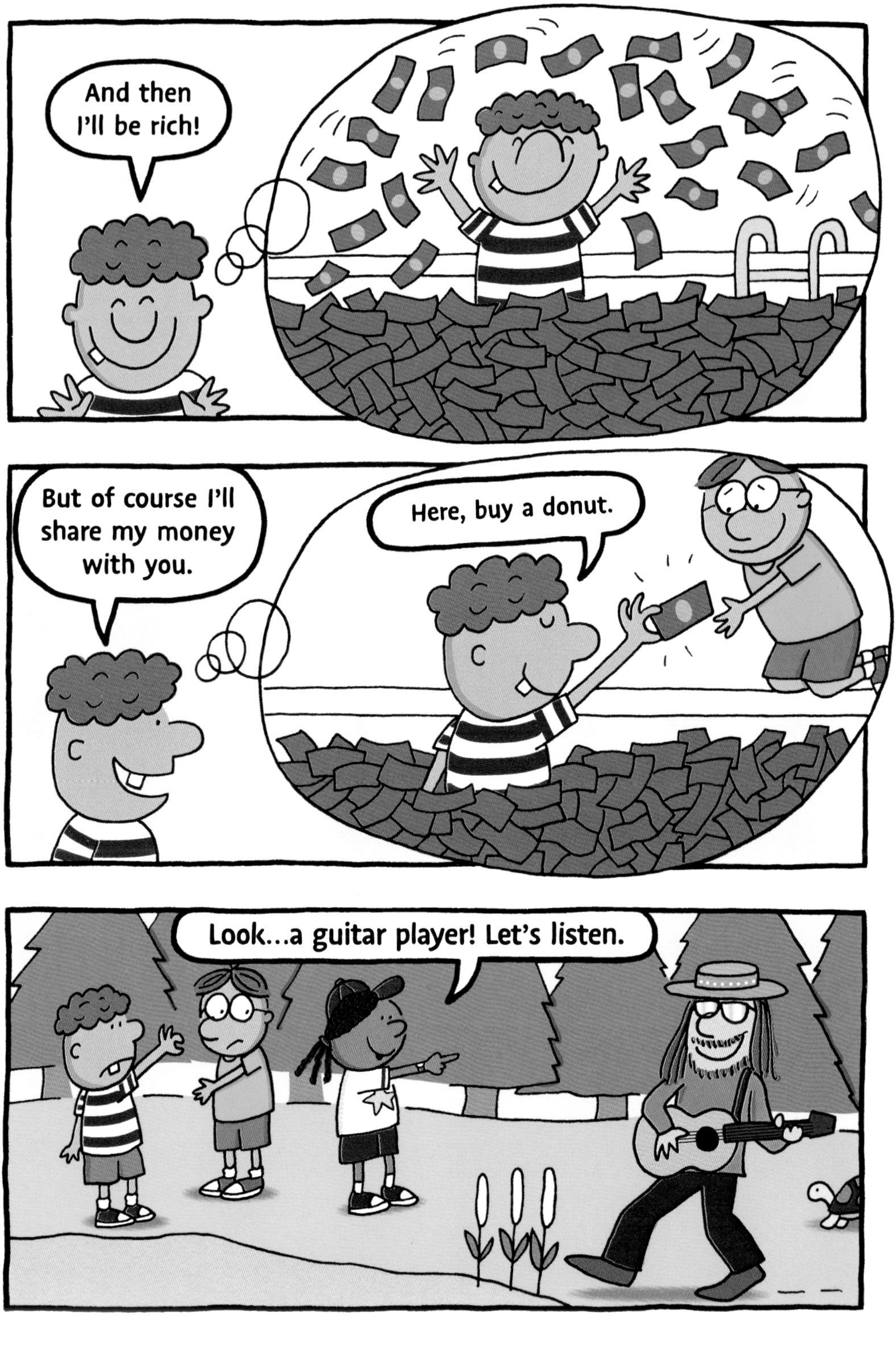
And then I'll be rich!
But of course I'll share my money with you.
Here, buy a donut.
Look...a guitar player! Let's listen.

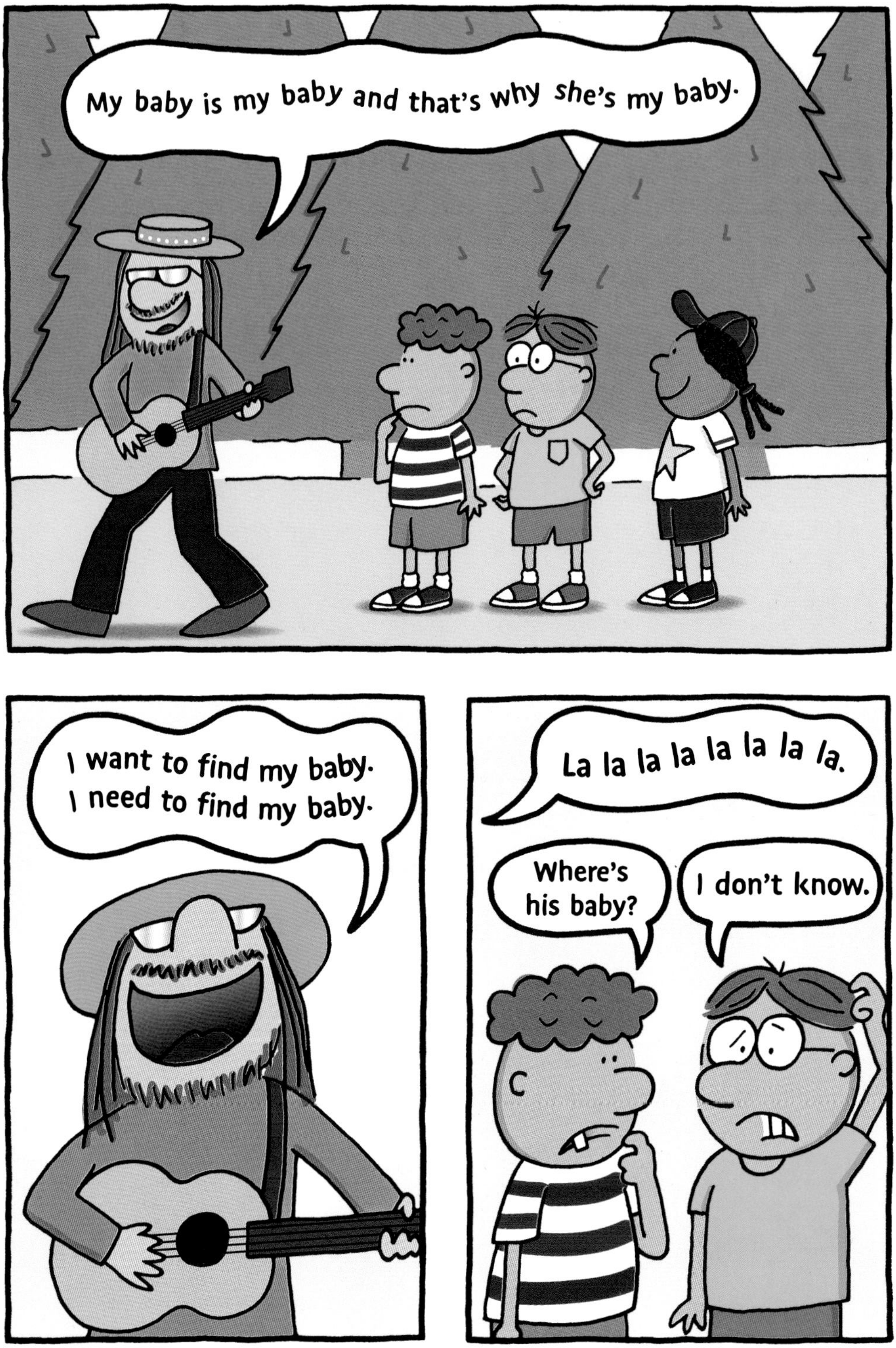

My baby is my baby and that's why *she's* my baby.
I want to find my baby. I need to find my baby.
La la la la la la la la.
Where's his baby?
I don't know.

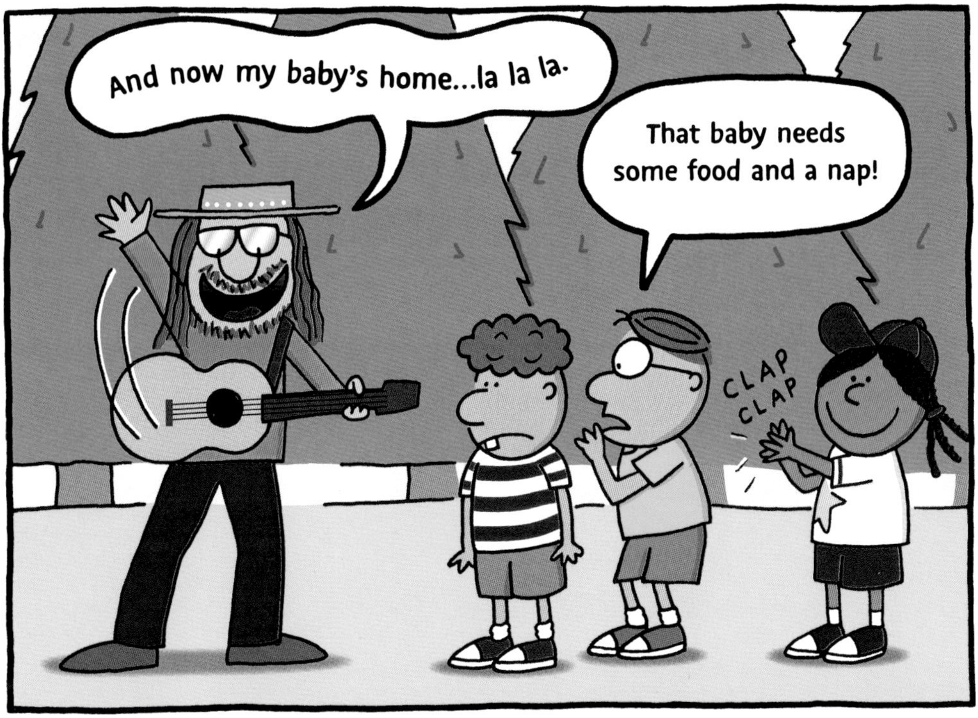
And now my baby's home...la la la.
That baby needs some food and a nap!
CLAP CLAP

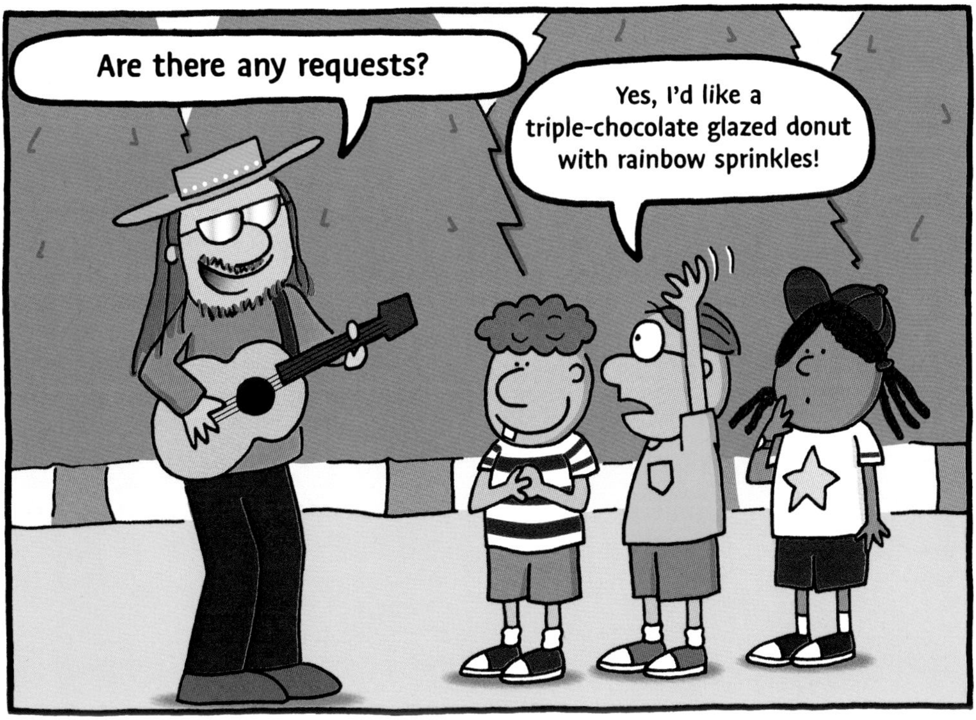
Are there any requests?
Yes, I'd like a triple-chocolate glazed donut with rainbow sprinkles!

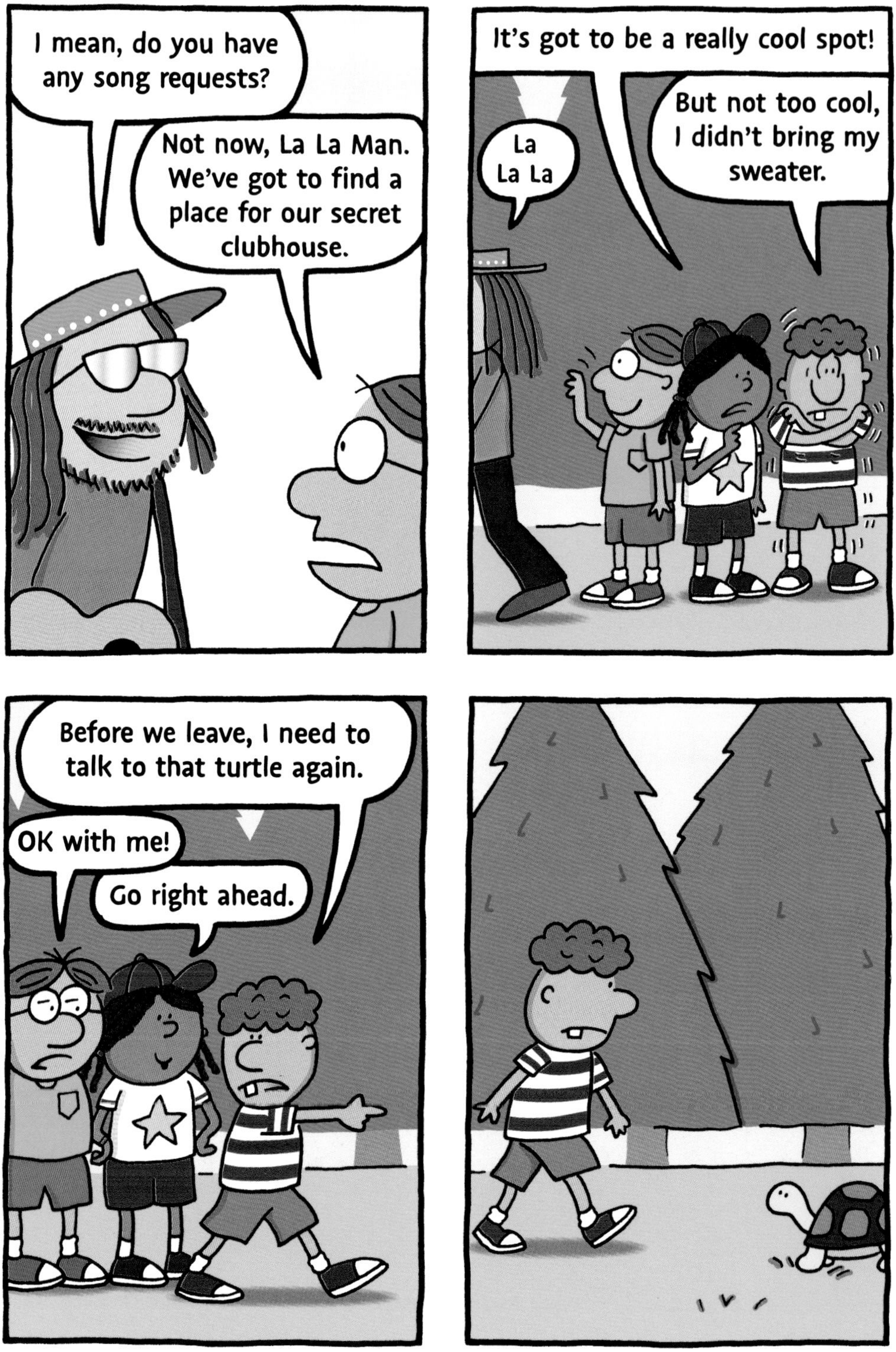
I mean, do you have any song requests?
Not now, La La Man. We've got to find a place for our secret clubhouse.
It's got to be a really cool spot!
La La La
But not too cool, I didn't bring my sweater.
Before we leave, I need to talk to that turtle again.
OK with me!
Go right ahead.

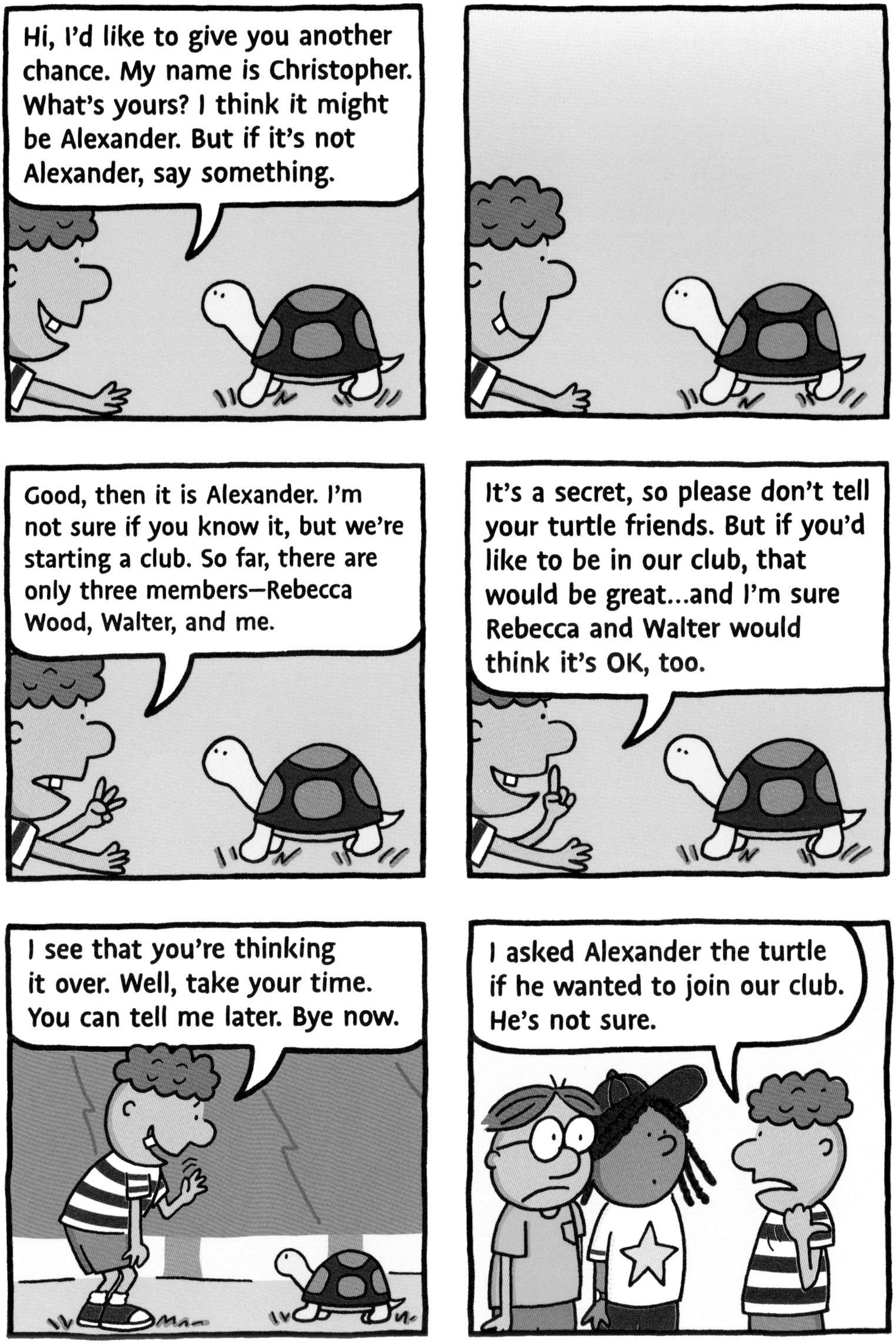
Hi, I'd like to give you another chance. My name is Christopher. What's yours? I think it might be Alexander. But if it's not Alexander, say something.
Good, then it is Alexander. I'm not sure if you know it, but we're starting a club. So far, there are only three members—Rebecca Wood, Walter, and me.
It's a secret, so please don't tell your turtle friends. But if you'd like to be in our club, that would be great...and I'm sure Rebecca and Walter would think it's OK, too.
I see that you're thinking it over. Well, take your time. You can tell me later. Bye now.
I asked Alexander the turtle if he wanted to join our club. He's not sure.

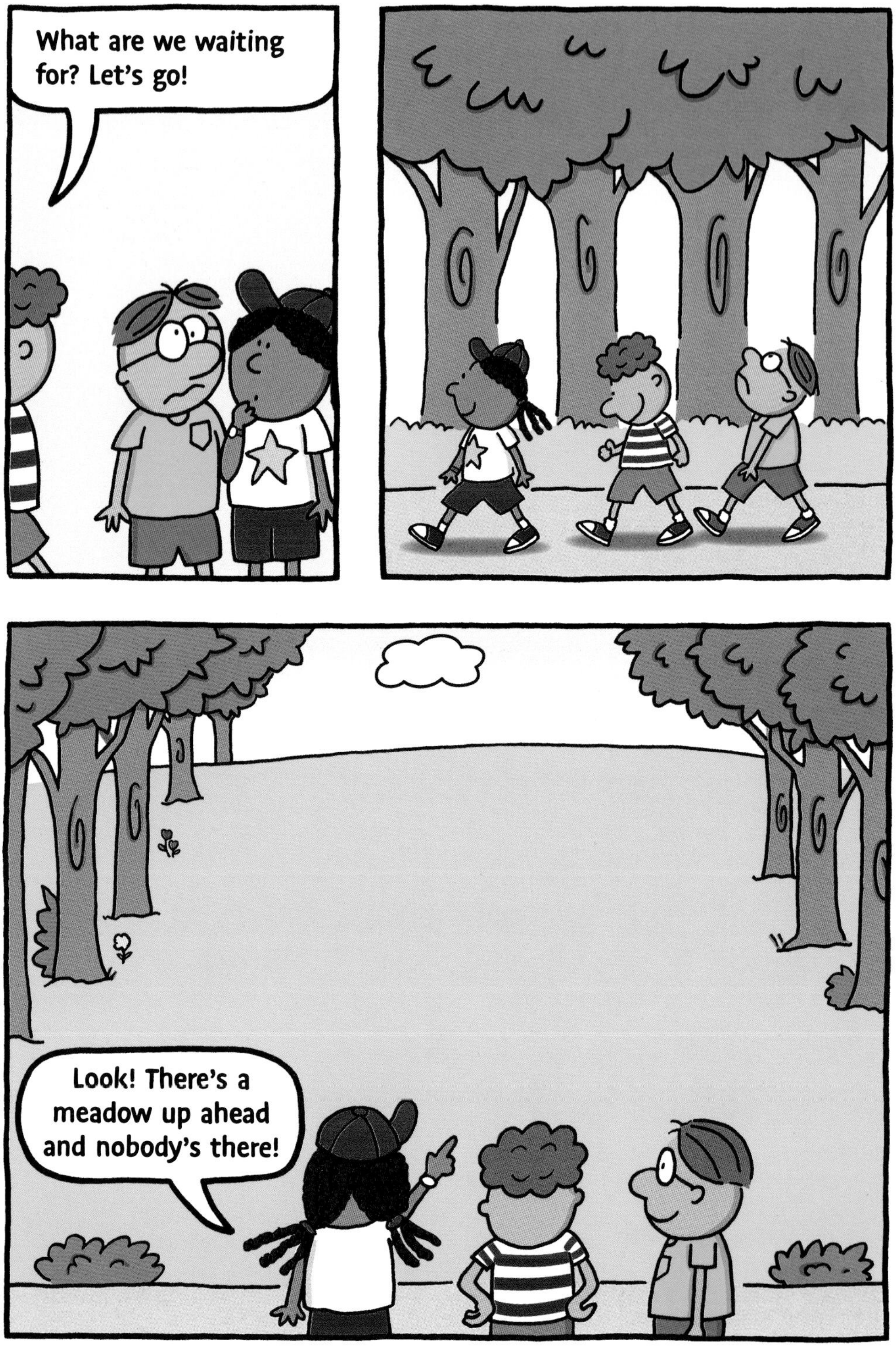
What are we waiting for? Let's go!
Look! There's a meadow up ahead and nobody's there!

CHAPTER 6 - WHAT'S THE SECRET PASSWORD?

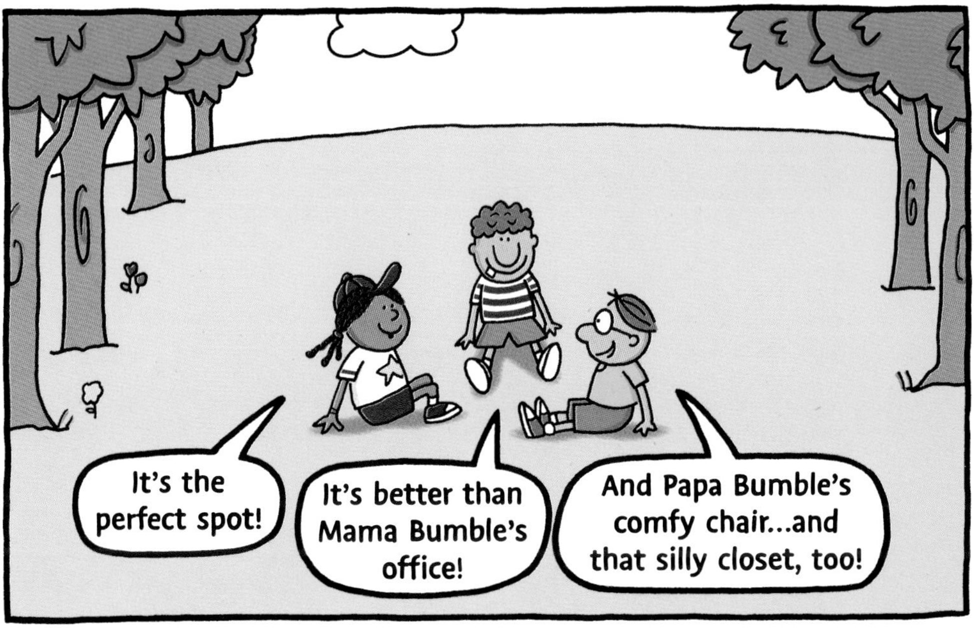
It's the perfect spot!
It's better than Mama Bumble's office!
And Papa Bumble's comfy chair...and that silly closet, too!

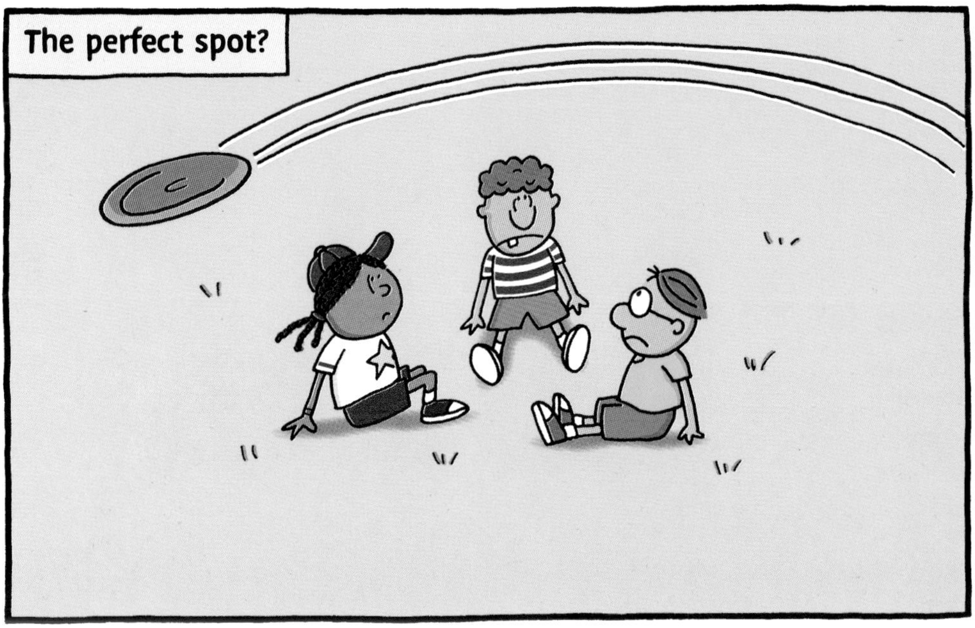
The perfect spot?

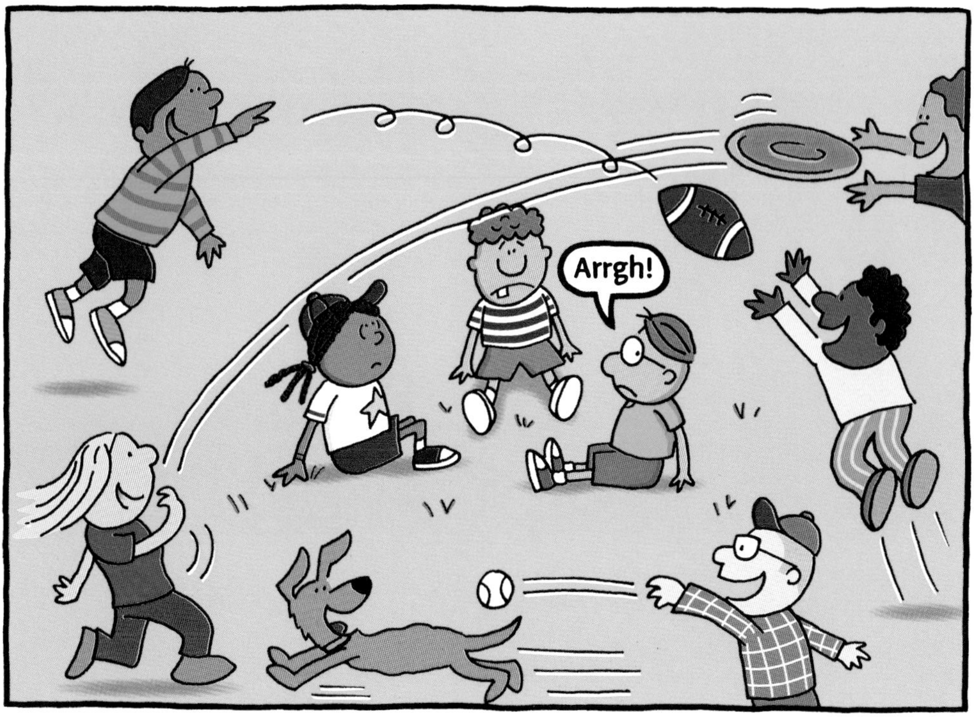
Arrgh!

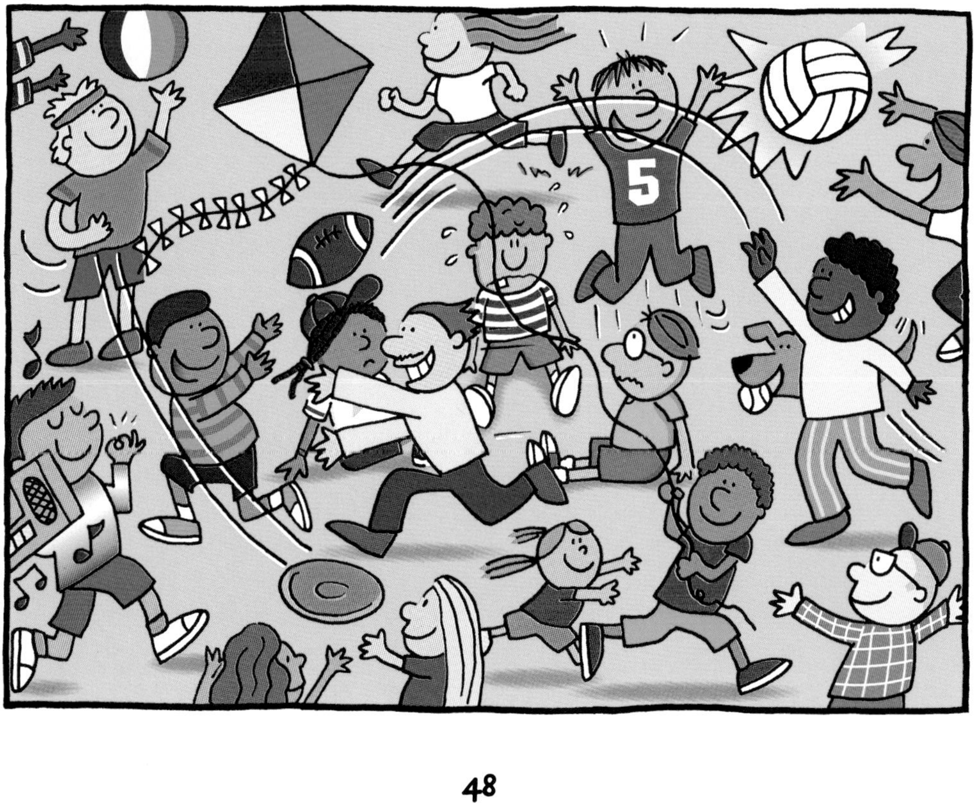
5

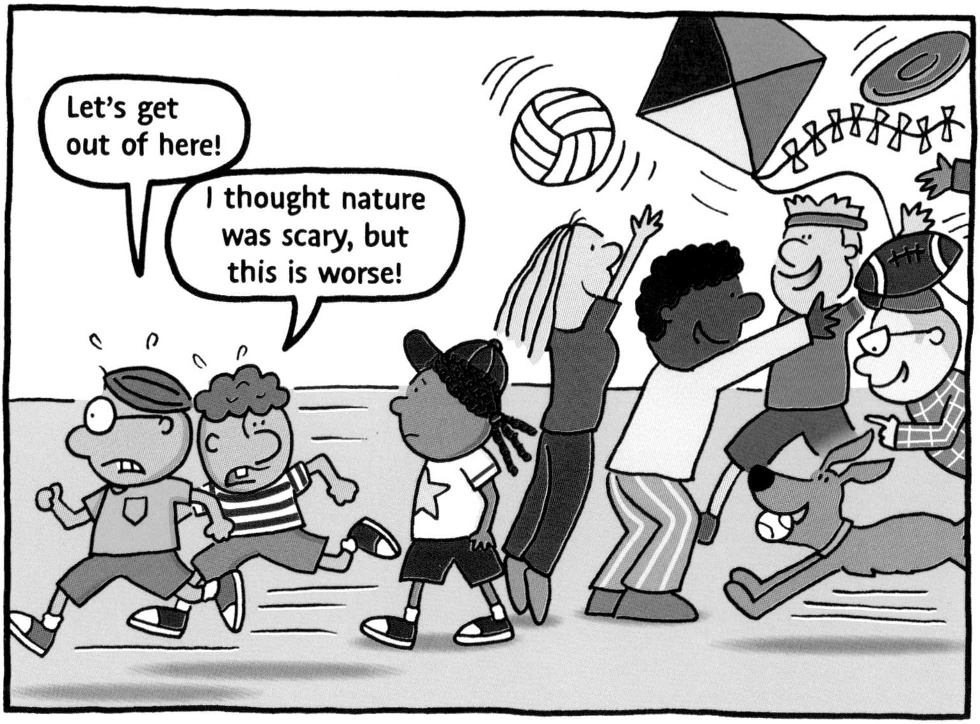
Let's get out of here!
I thought nature was scary, but this is worse!

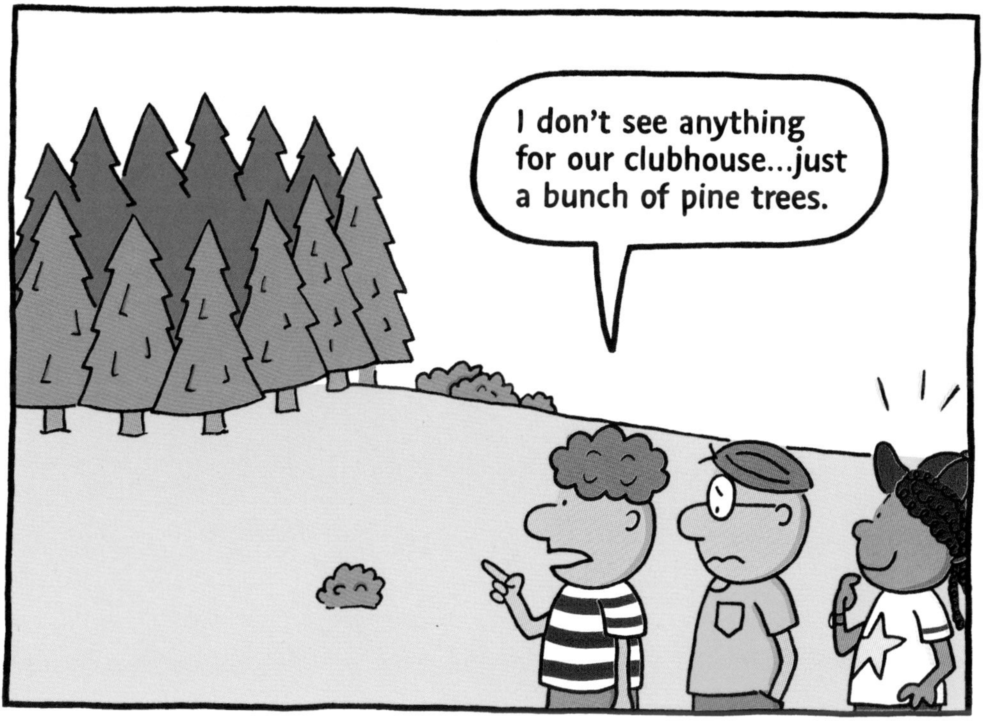
I don't see anything for our clubhouse...just a bunch of pine trees.

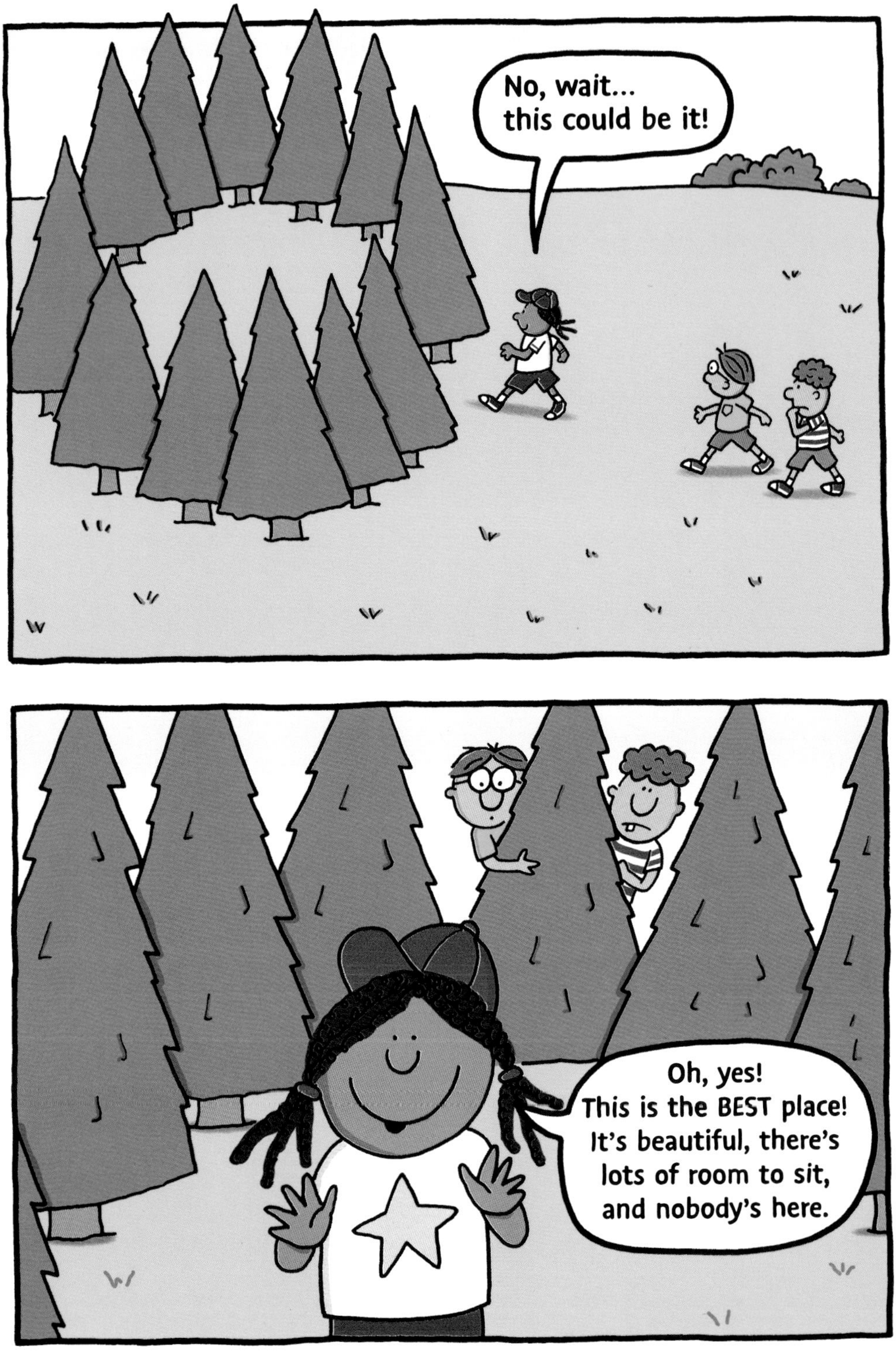
No, wait...
this could be it!
Oh, yes!
This is the BEST place!
It's beautiful, there's
lots of room to sit,
and nobody's here.

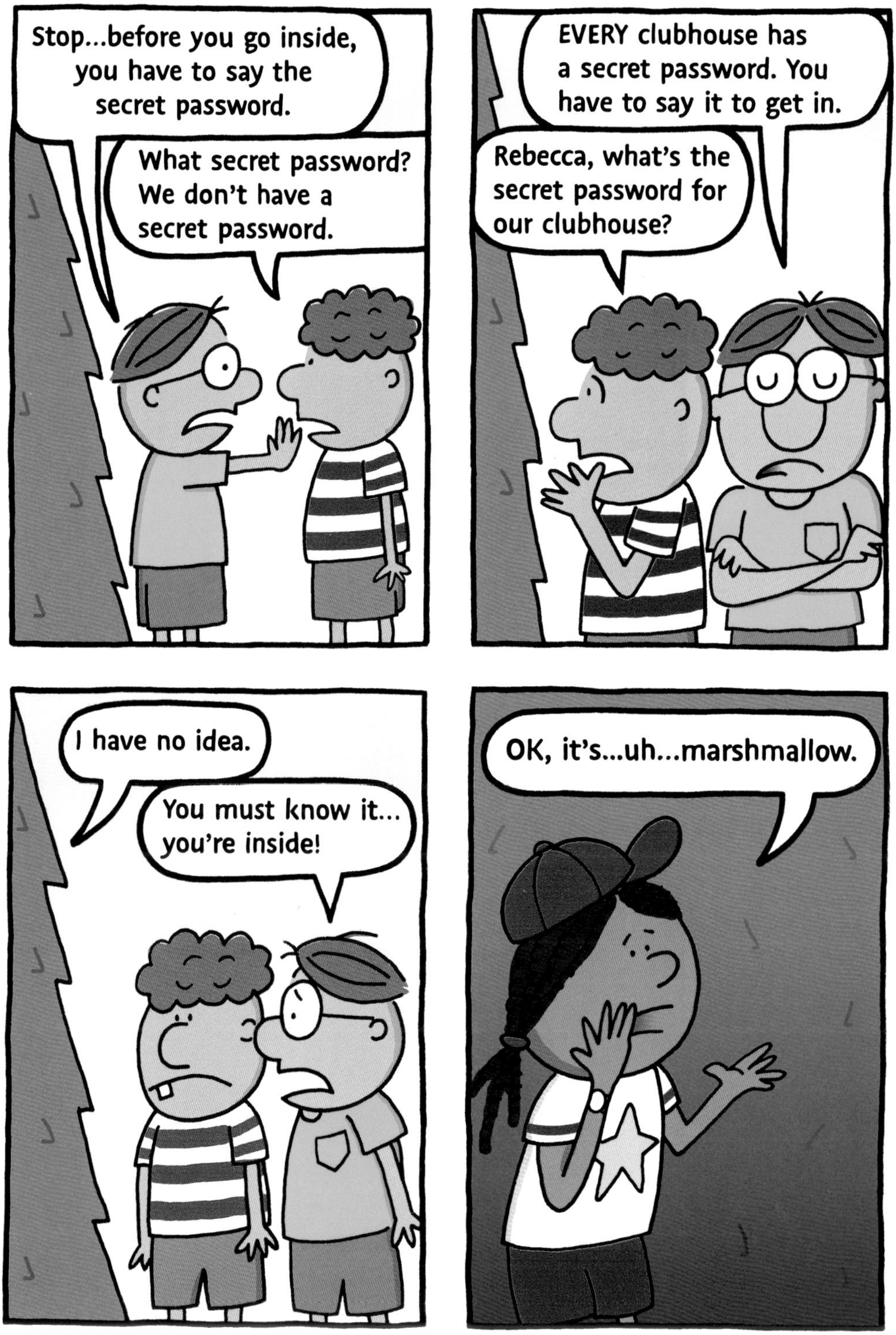
Stop...before you go inside, you have to say the secret password.
What secret password? We don't have a secret password.
EVERY clubhouse has a secret password. You have to say it to get in.
Rebecca, what's the secret password for our clubhouse?
I have no idea.
You must know it... you're inside!
OK, it's...uh...marshmallow.

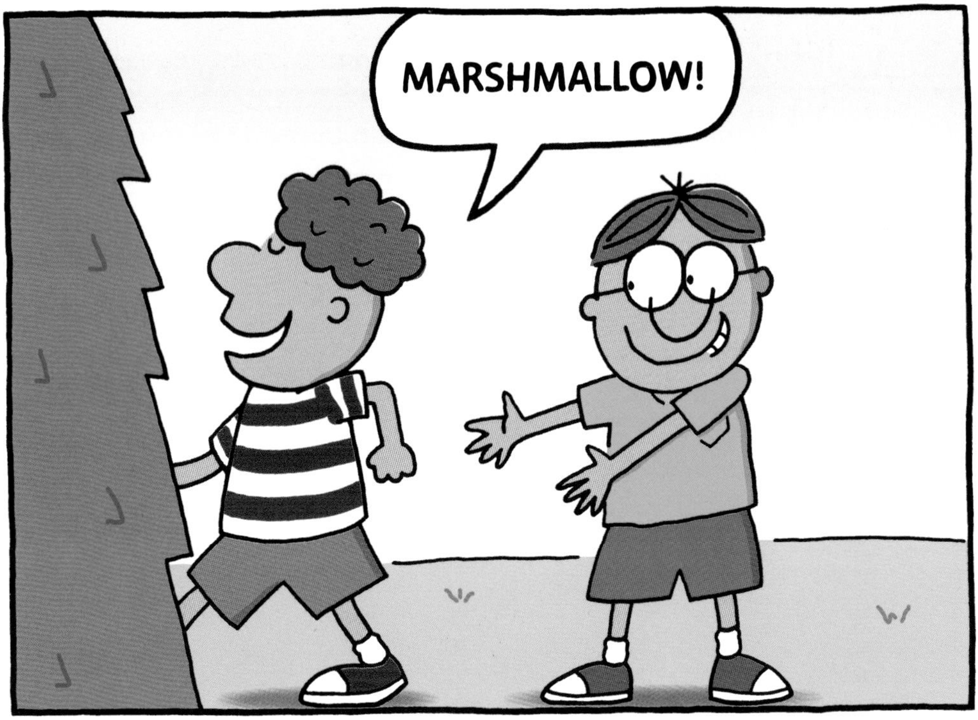
MARSHMALLOW!

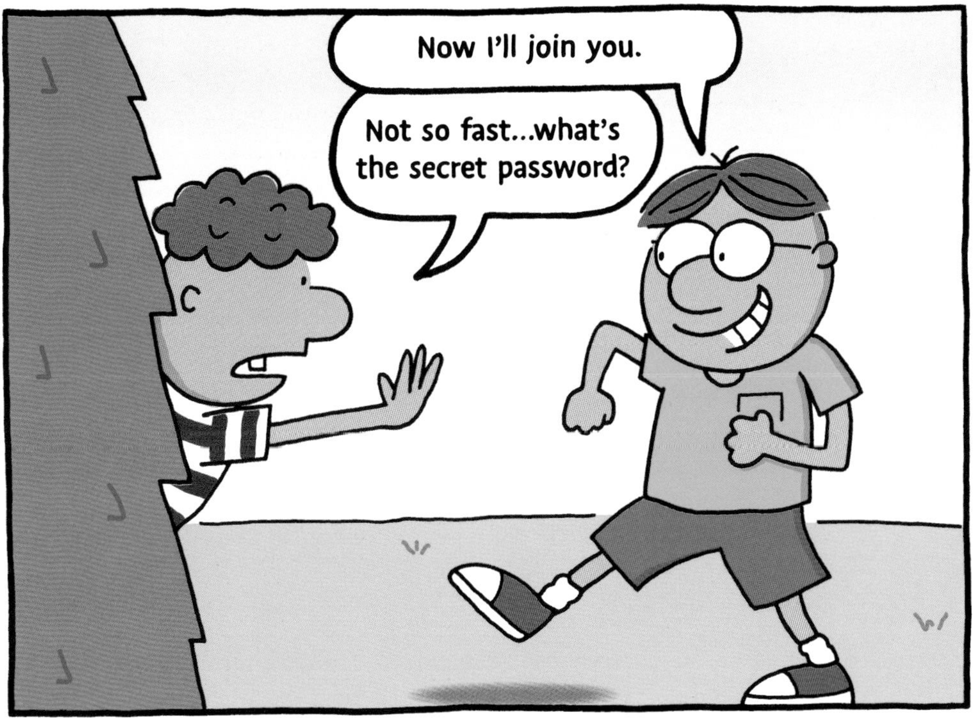
Now I'll join you.
Not so fast...what's the secret password?

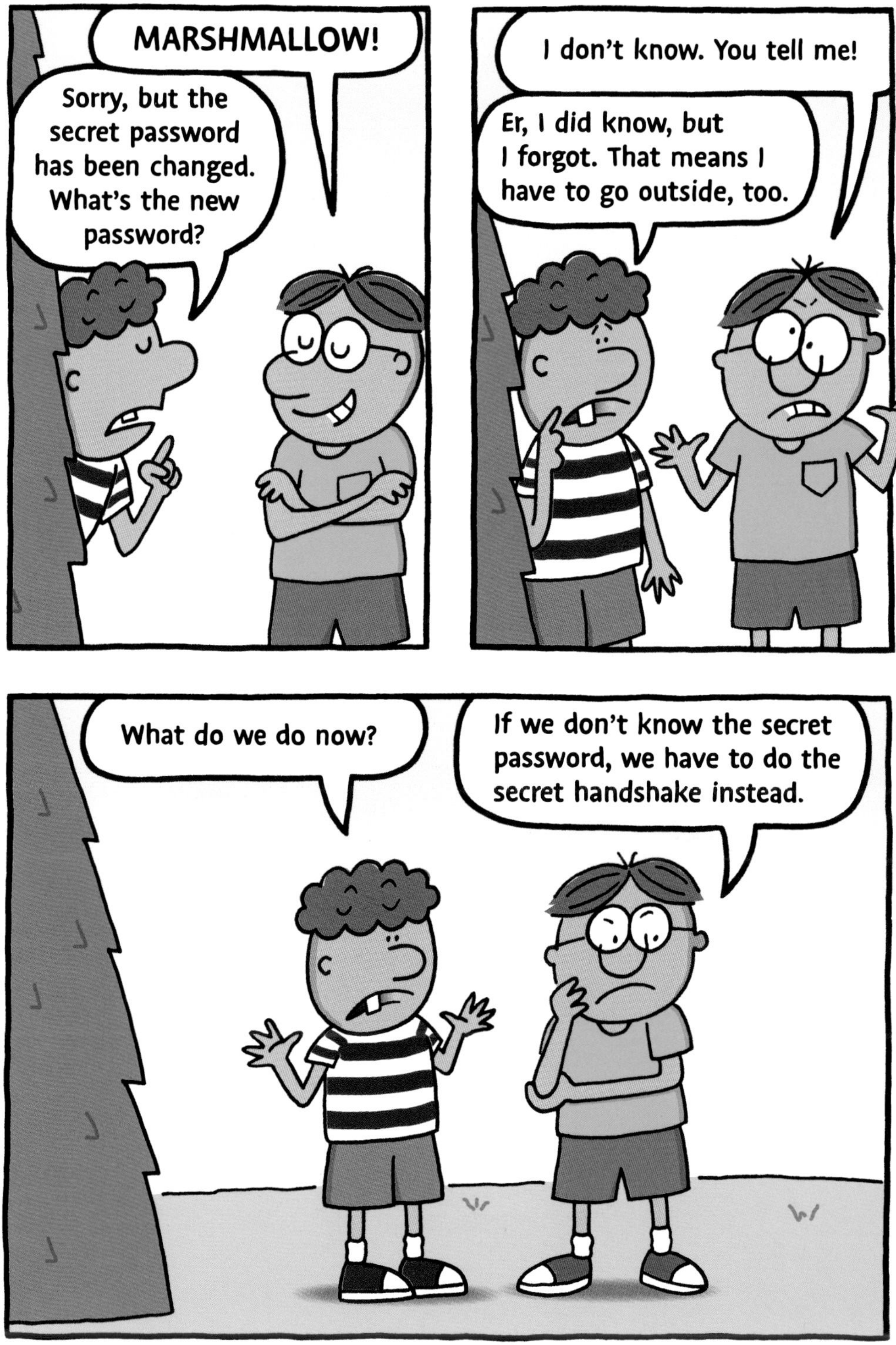
MARSHMALLOW!
Sorry, but the secret password has been changed. What's the new password?
I don't know. You tell me!
Er, I did know, but I forgot. That means I have to go outside, too.
What do we do now?
If we don't know the secret password, we have to do the secret handshake instead.

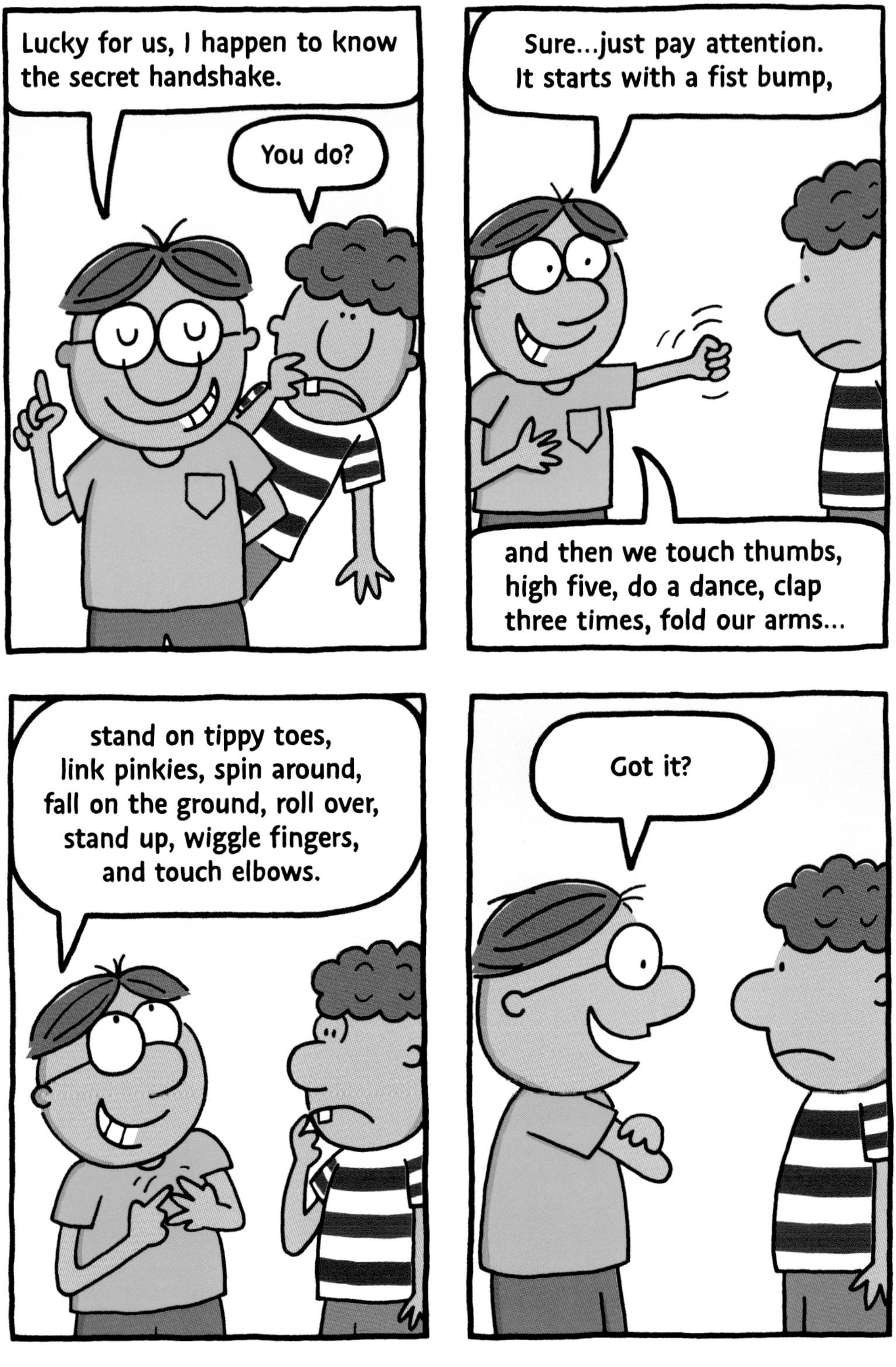
Lucky for us, I happen to know the secret handshake.
You do?
Sure...just pay attention. It starts with a fist bump,
and then we touch thumbs, high five, do a dance, clap three times, fold our arms...
stand on tippy toes, link pinkies, spin around, fall on the ground, roll over, stand up, wiggle fingers, and touch elbows.
Got it?

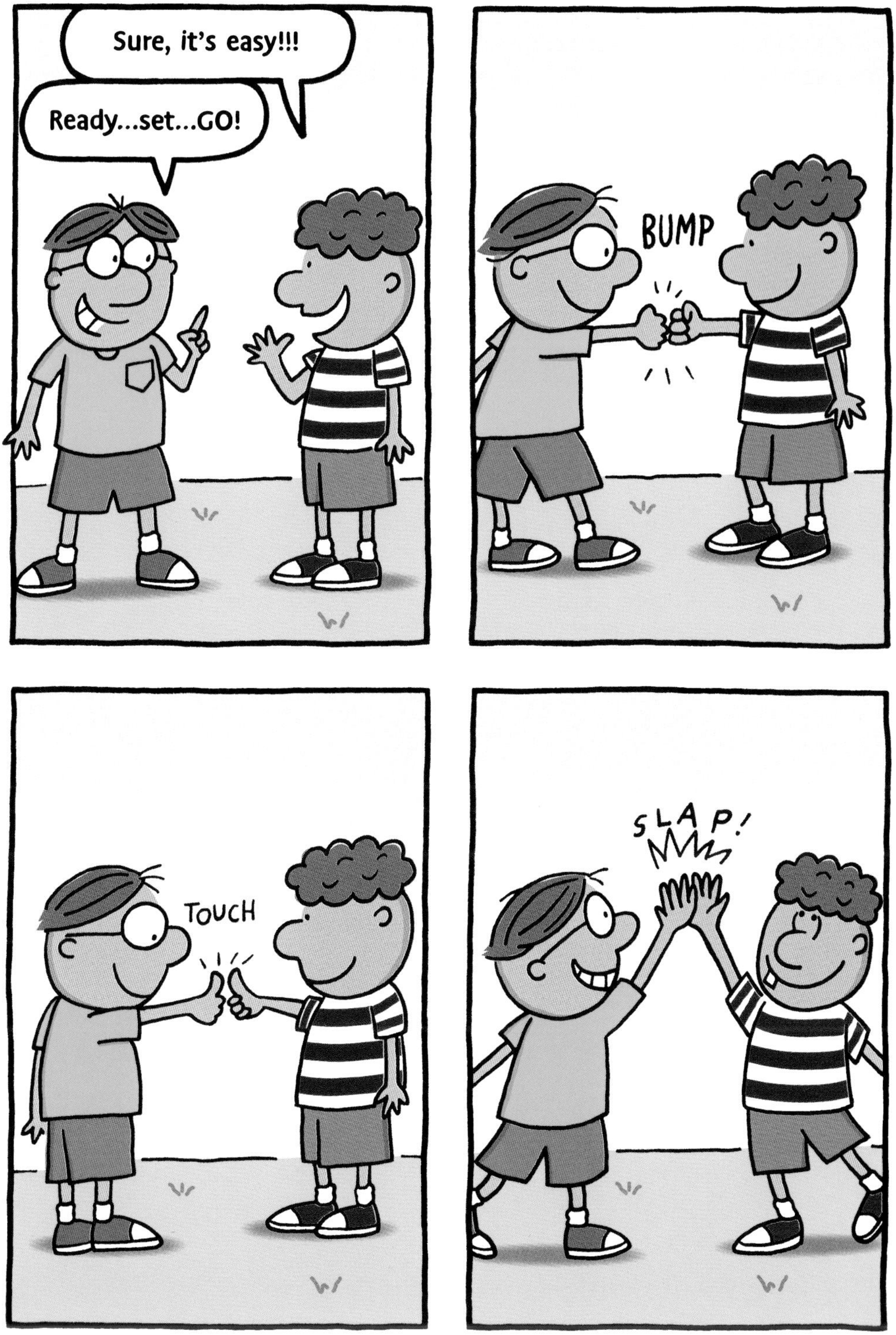
Sure, it's easy!!!
Ready...set...GO!
BUMP
TOUCH
SLAP!

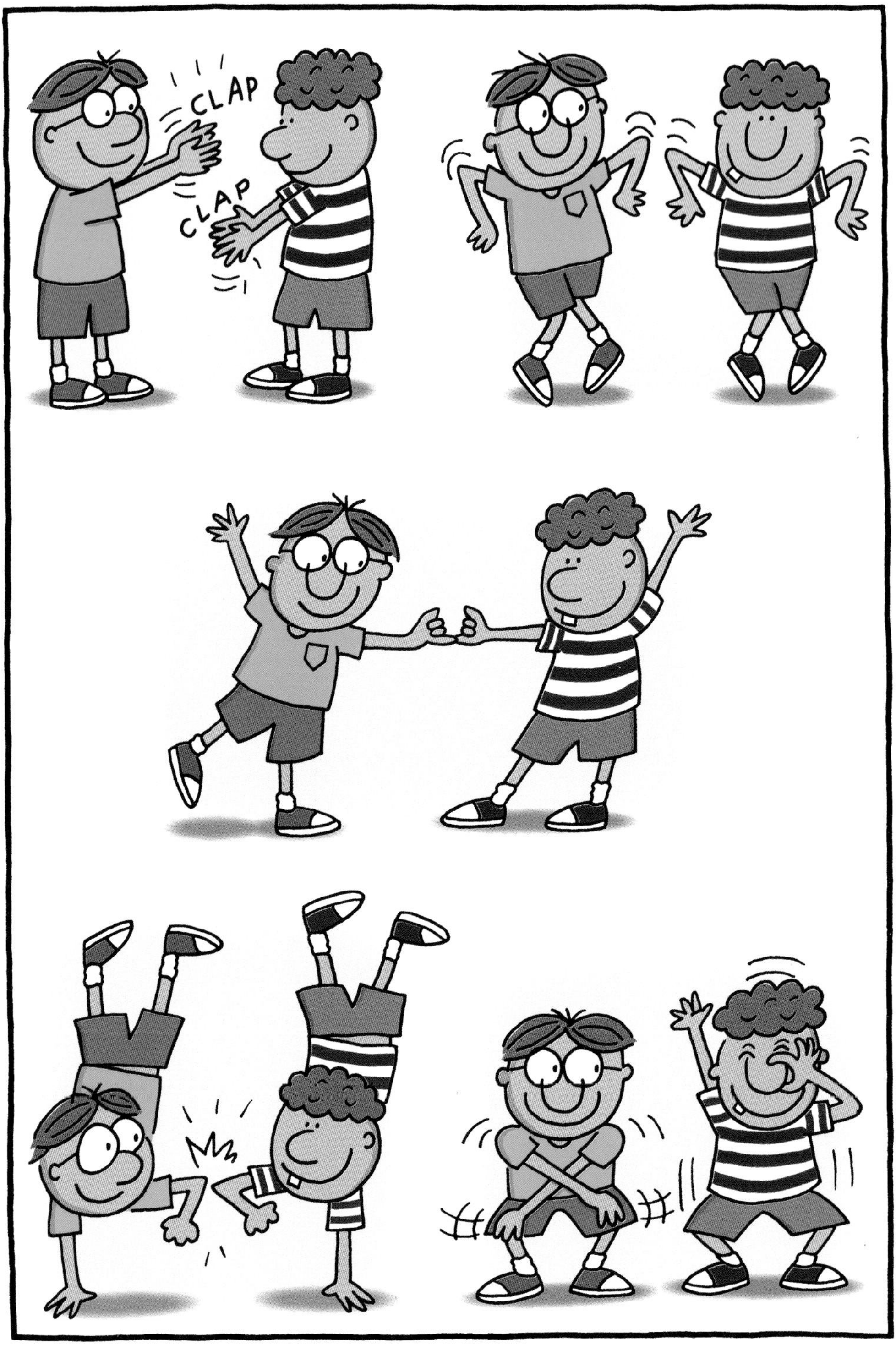
CLAP
CLAP

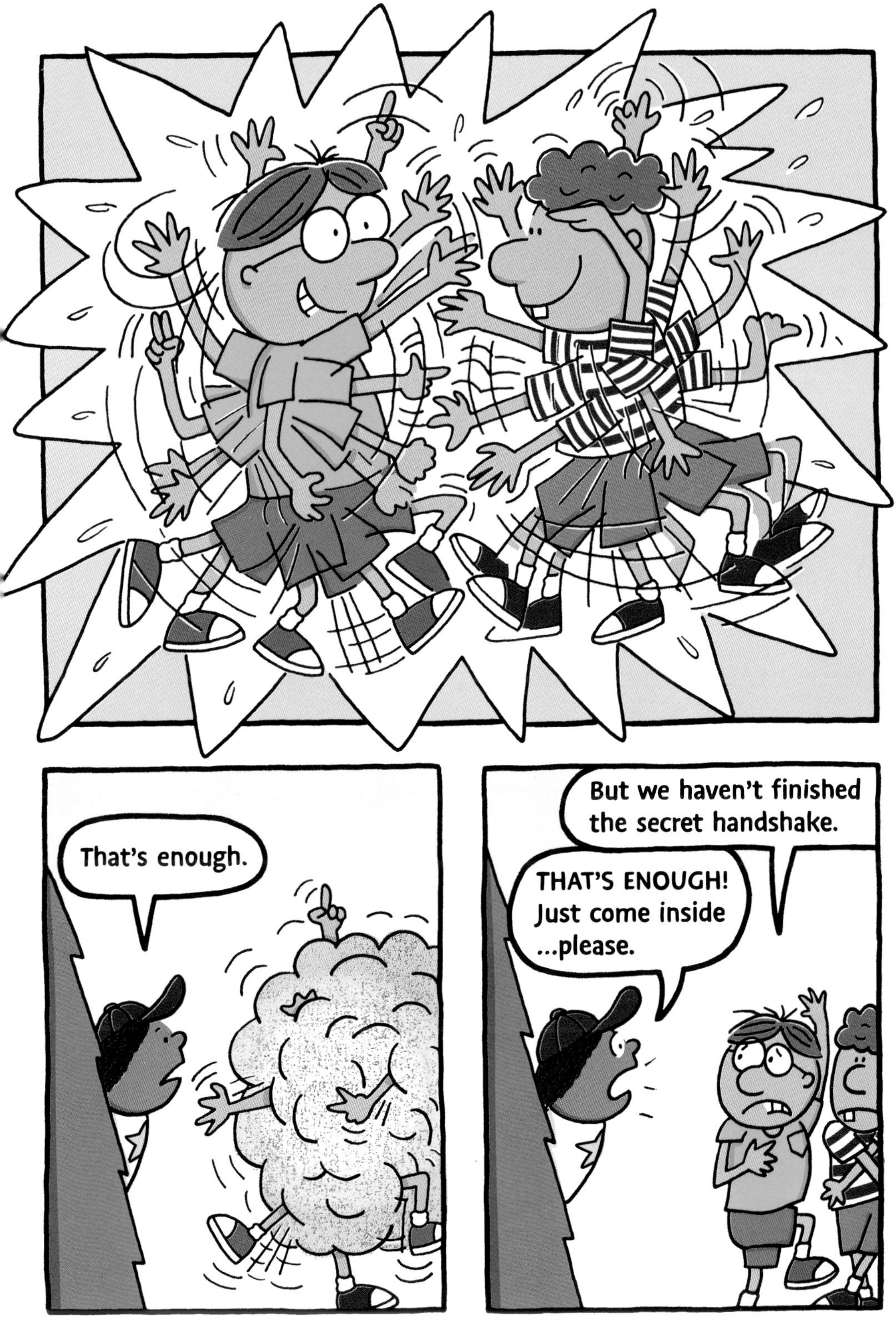
That's enough.
But we haven't finished the secret handshake.
THAT'S ENOUGH! Just come inside ...please.

CHAPTER 7 - THE NOT-SO-SECRET CLUBHOUSE!

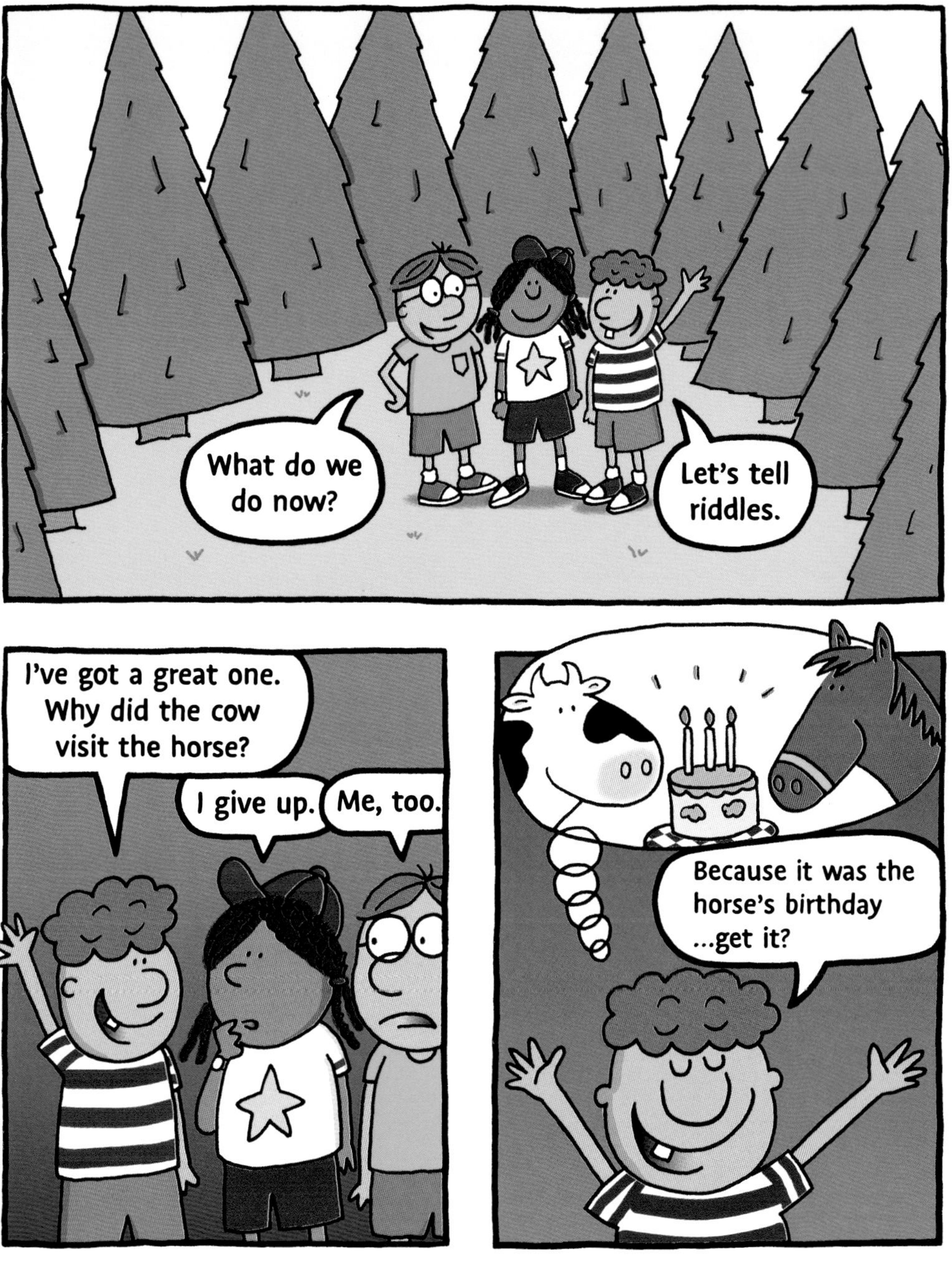

What do we do now?
Let's tell riddles.
I've got a great one. Why did the cow visit the horse?
I give up.
Me, too.
Because it was the horse's birthday ...get it?

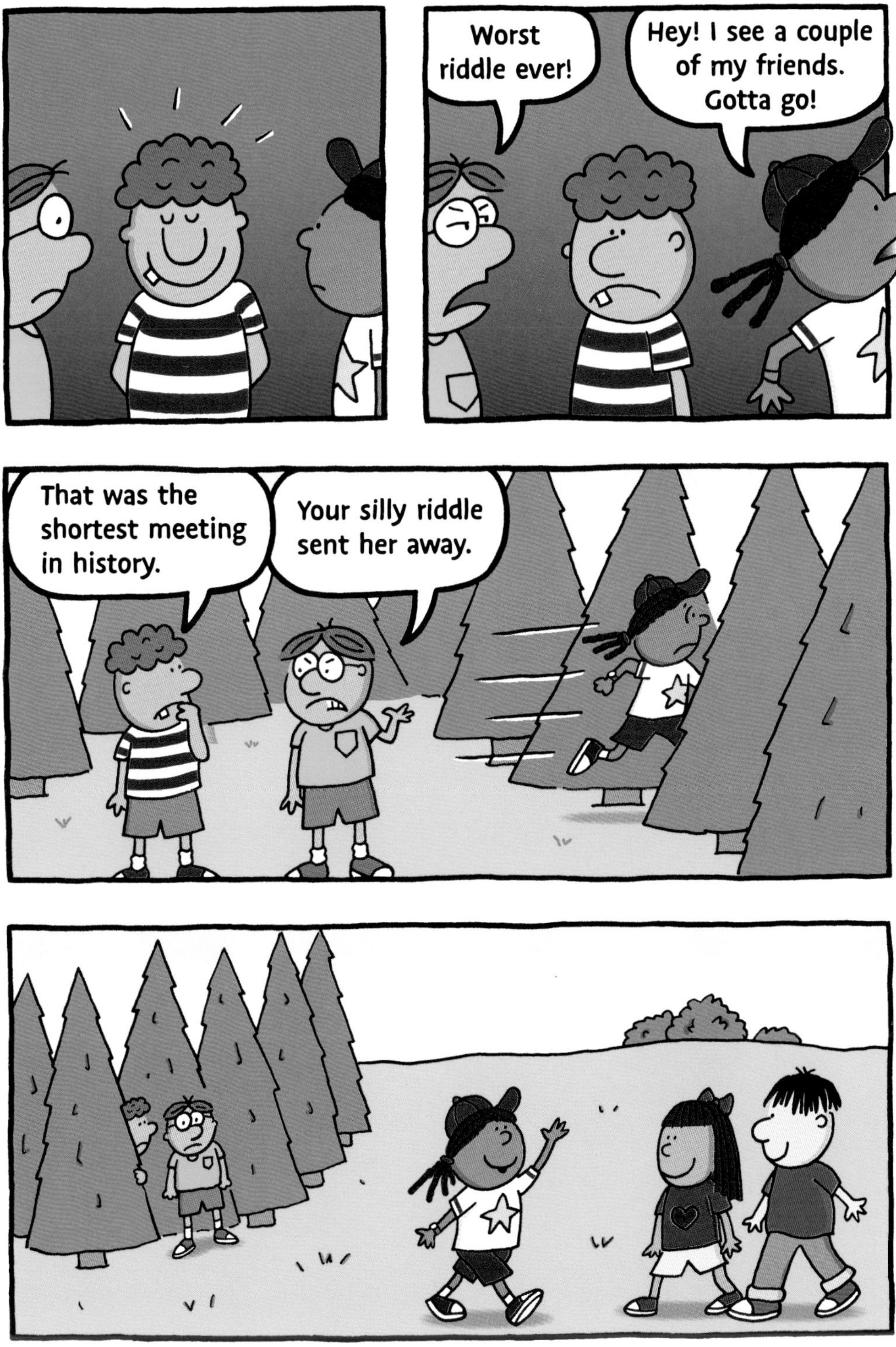
Worst riddle ever!
Hey! I see a couple of my friends. Gotta go!
That was the shortest meeting in history.
Your silly riddle sent her away.

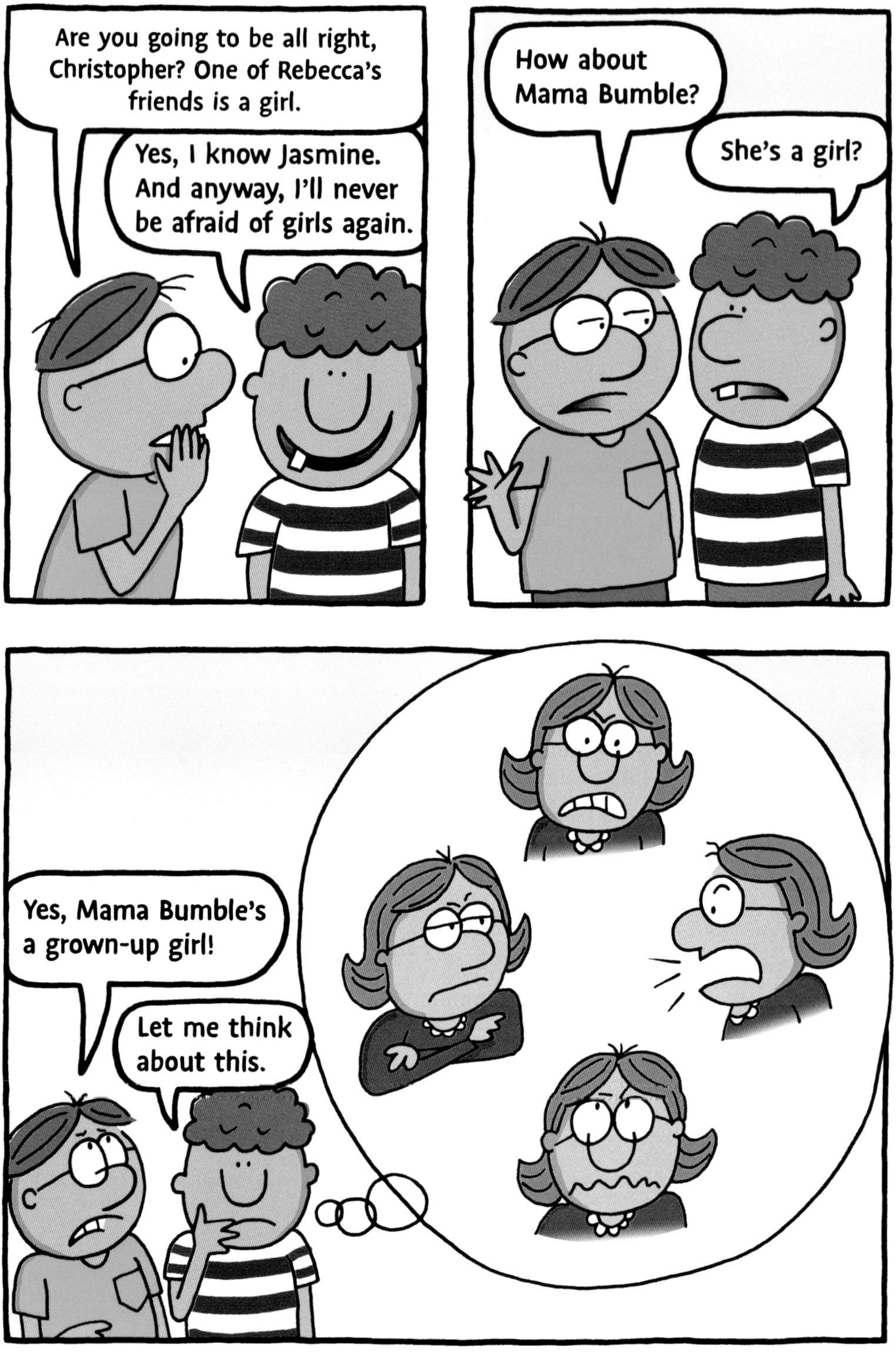
Are you going to be all right, Christopher? One of Rebecca's friends is a girl.
Yes, I know Jasmine. And anyway, I'll never be afraid of girls again.
How about Mama Bumble?
She's a girl?
Yes, Mama Bumble's a grown-up girl!
Let me think about this.

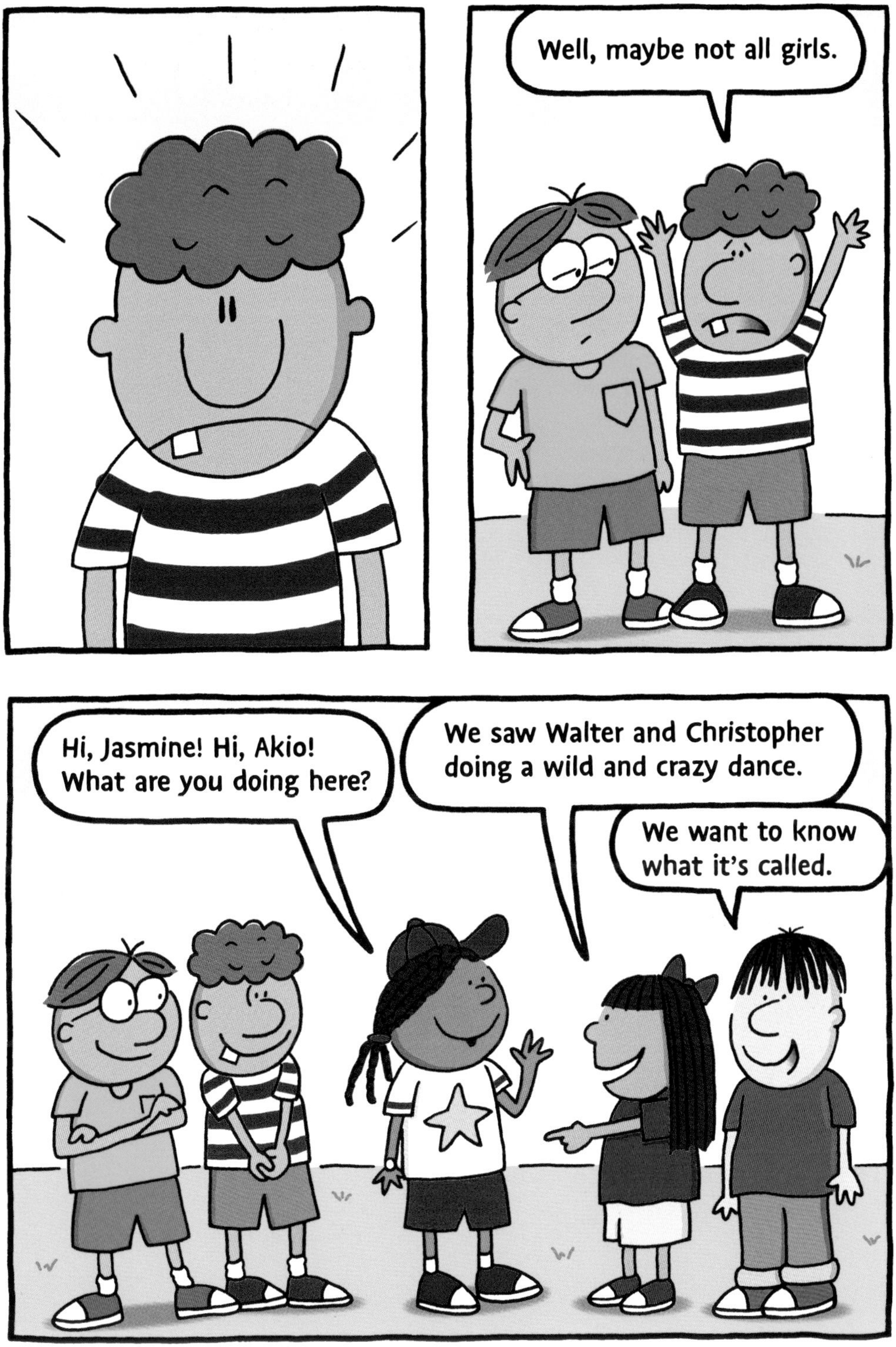
Well, maybe not all girls.
Hi, Jasmine! Hi, Akio!
What are you doing here?
We saw Walter and Christopher
doing a wild and crazy dance.
We want to know
what it's called.

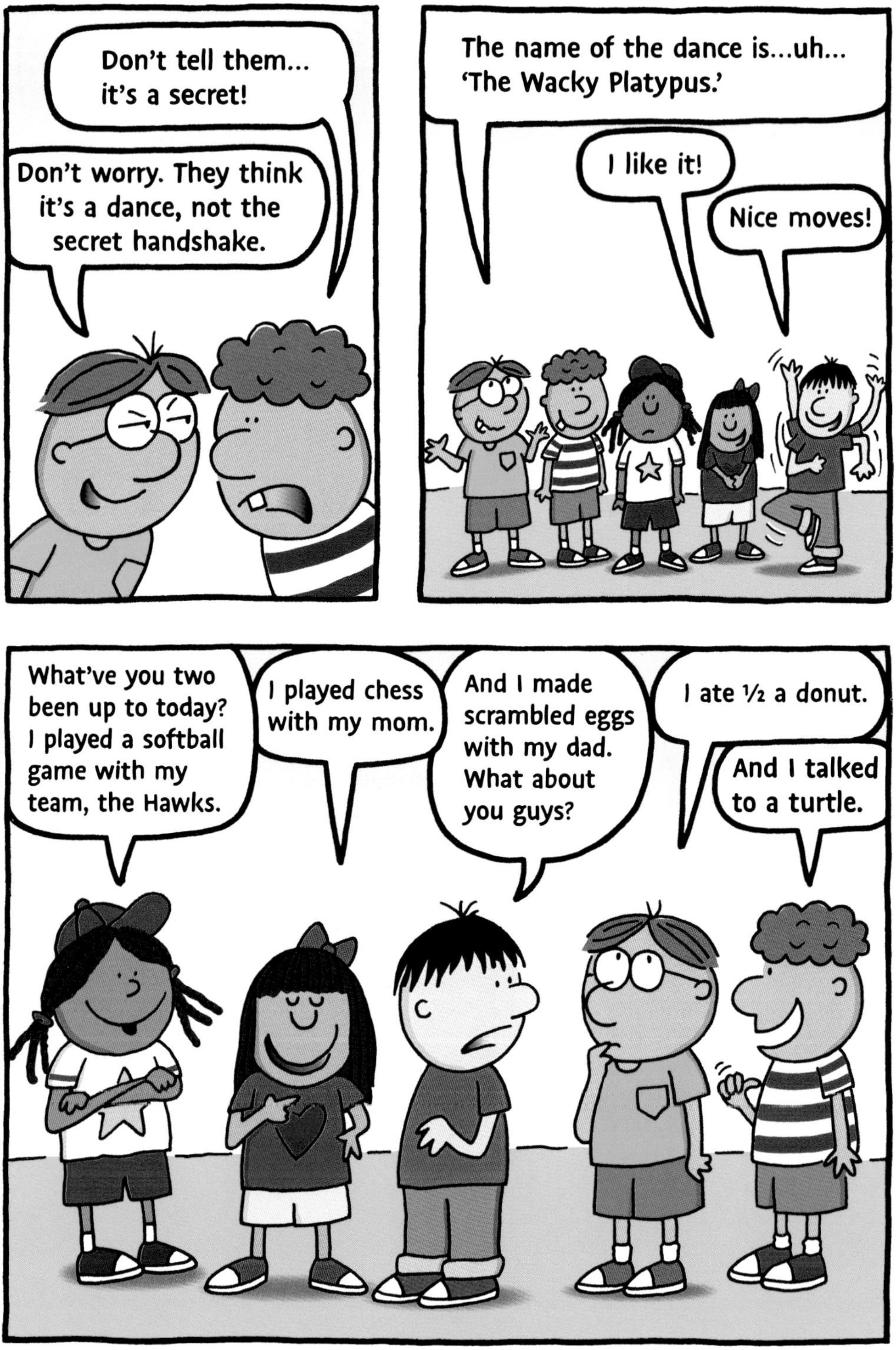
Don't tell them...
it's a secret!
Don't worry. They think it's a dance, not the secret handshake.
The name of the dance is...uh... 'The Wacky Platypus.'
I like it!
Nice moves!
What've you two been up to today? I played a softball game with my team, the Hawks.
I played chess with my mom.
And I made scrambled eggs with my dad. What about you guys?
I ate ½ a donut.
And I talked to a turtle.

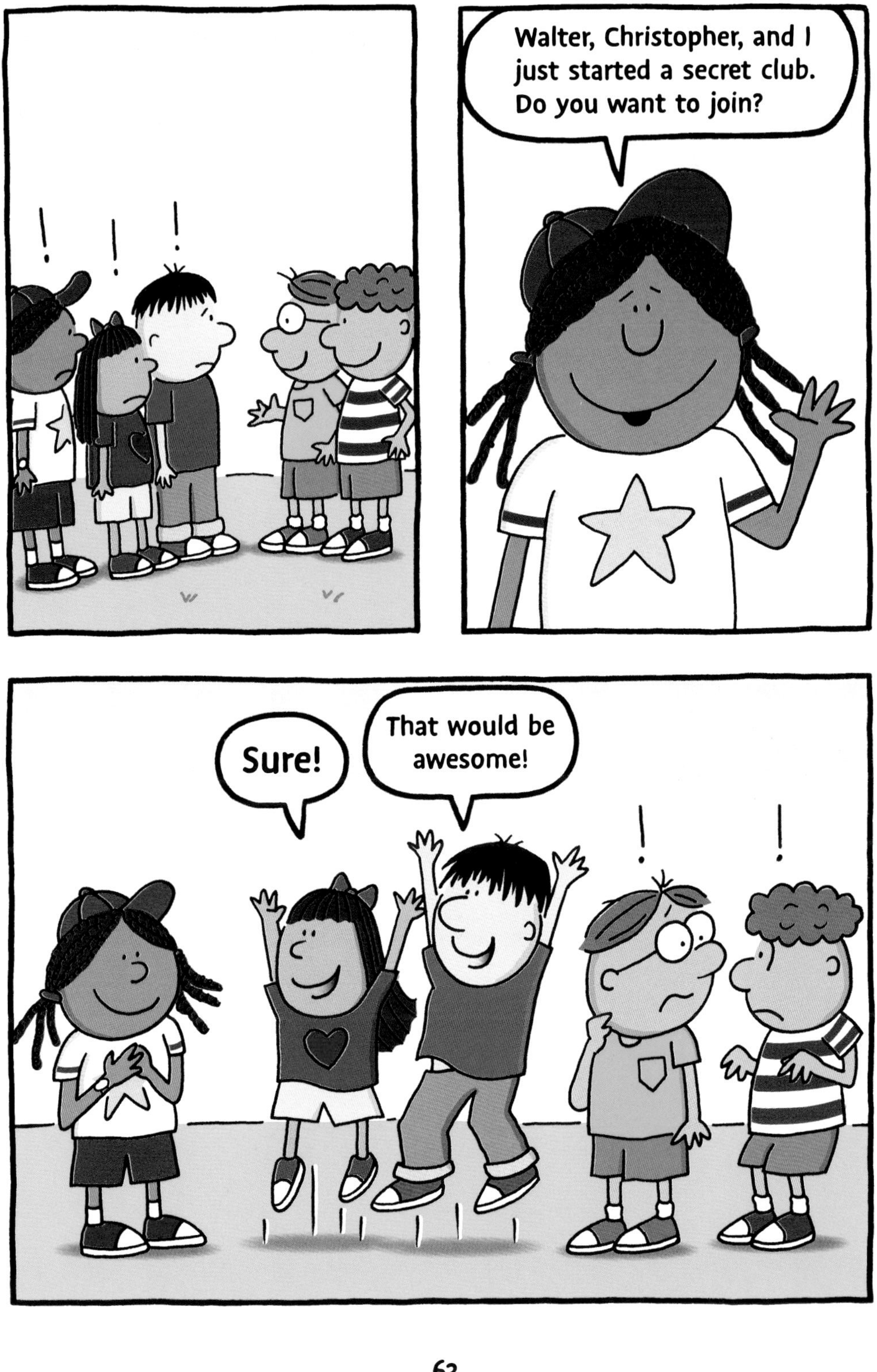
Walter, Christopher, and I just started a secret club. Do you want to join?
Sure!
That would be awesome!

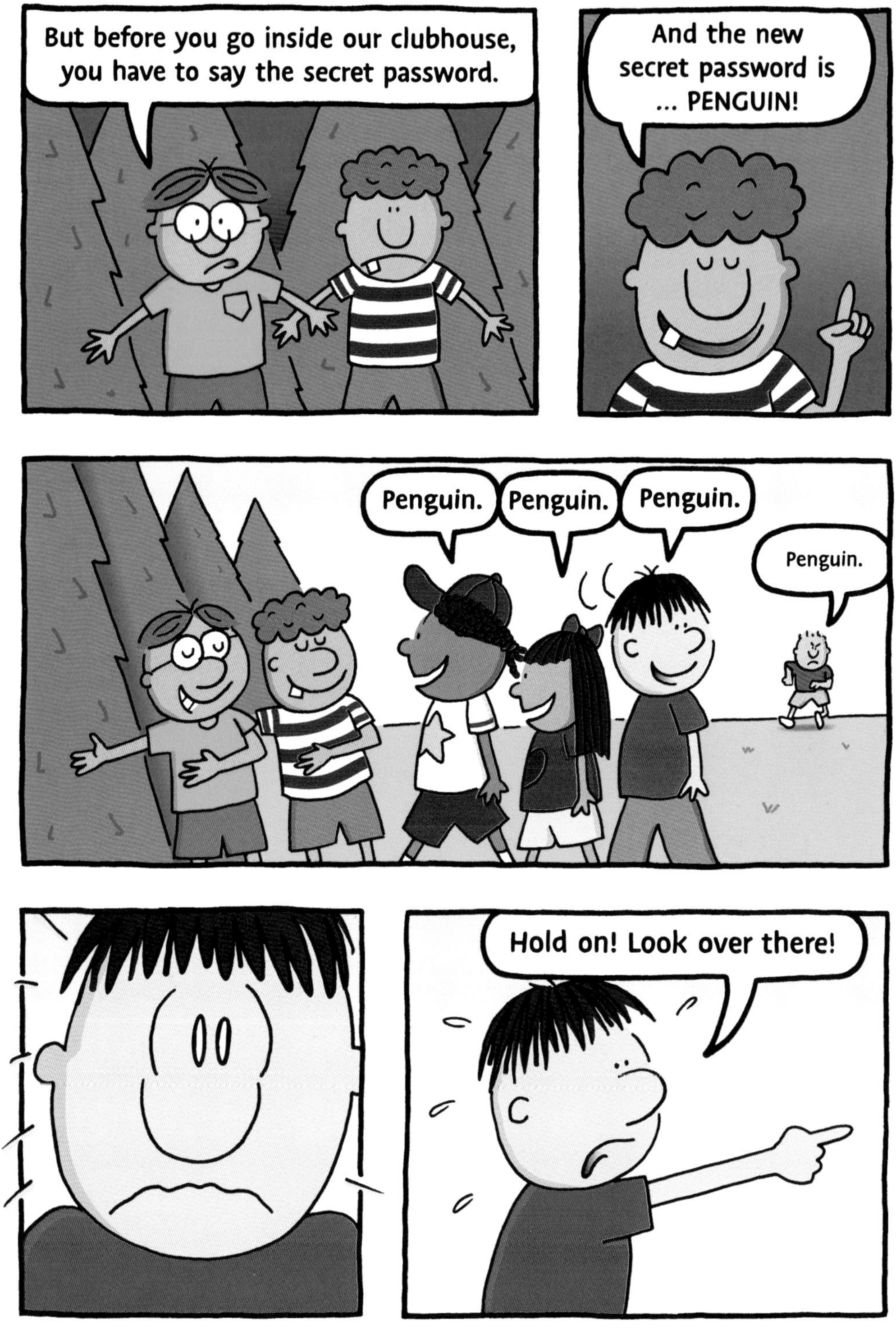
But before you go inside our clubhouse, you have to say the secret password.
And the new secret password is ... PENGUIN!
Penguin.
Penguin.
Penguin.
Penguin.
Hold on! Look over there!

CHAPTER 8 - IS HAROLD THE BULLY SCARY?

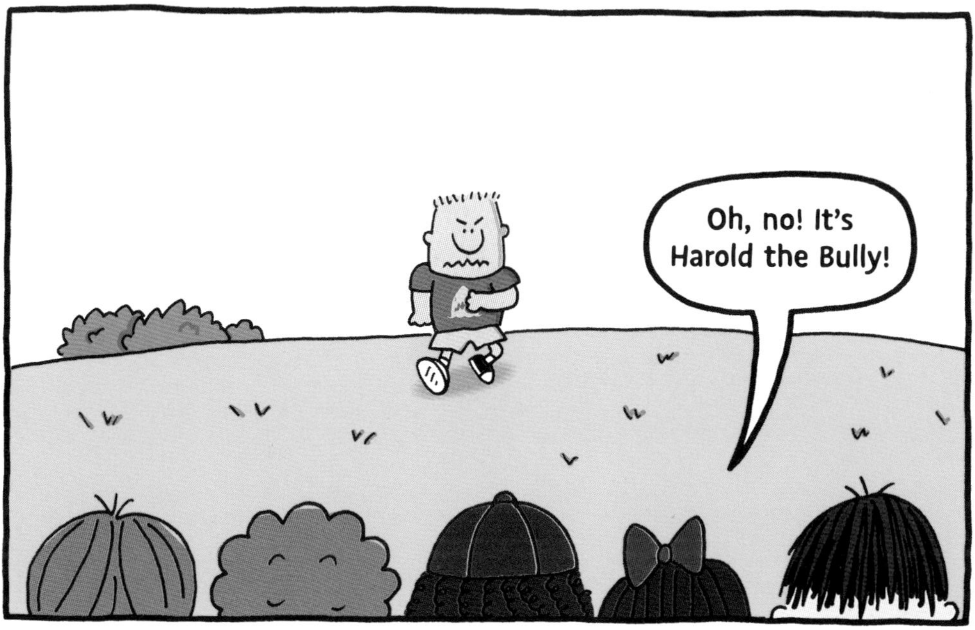
Oh, no! It's Harold the Bully!

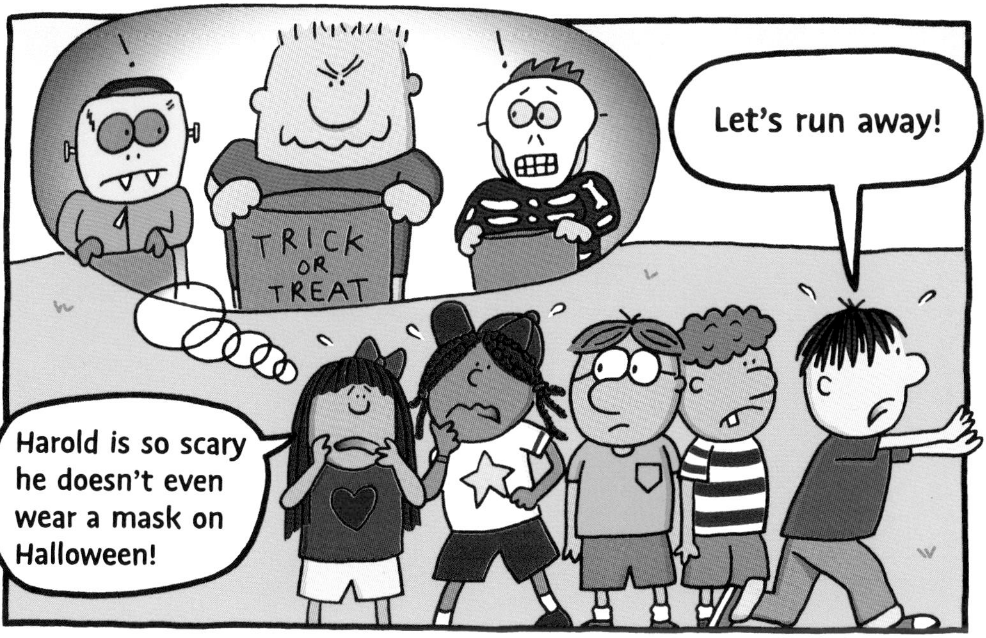
TRICK OR TREAT
Let's run away!
Harold is so scary he doesn't even wear a mask on Halloween!

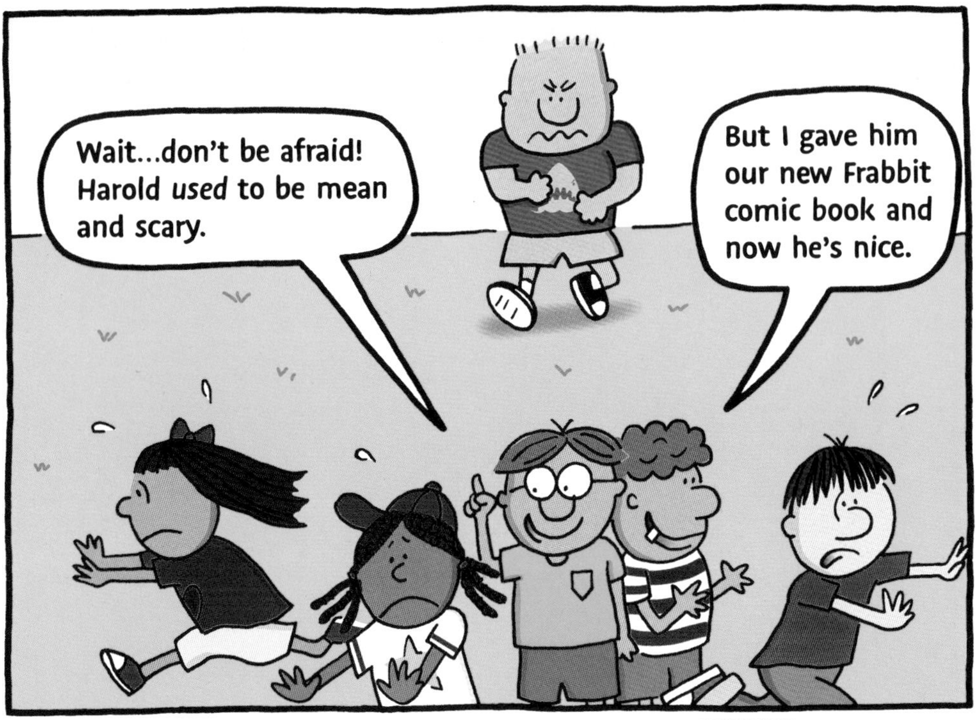
Wait...don't be afraid! Harold *used* to be mean and scary.
But I gave him our new Frabbit comic book and now he's nice.

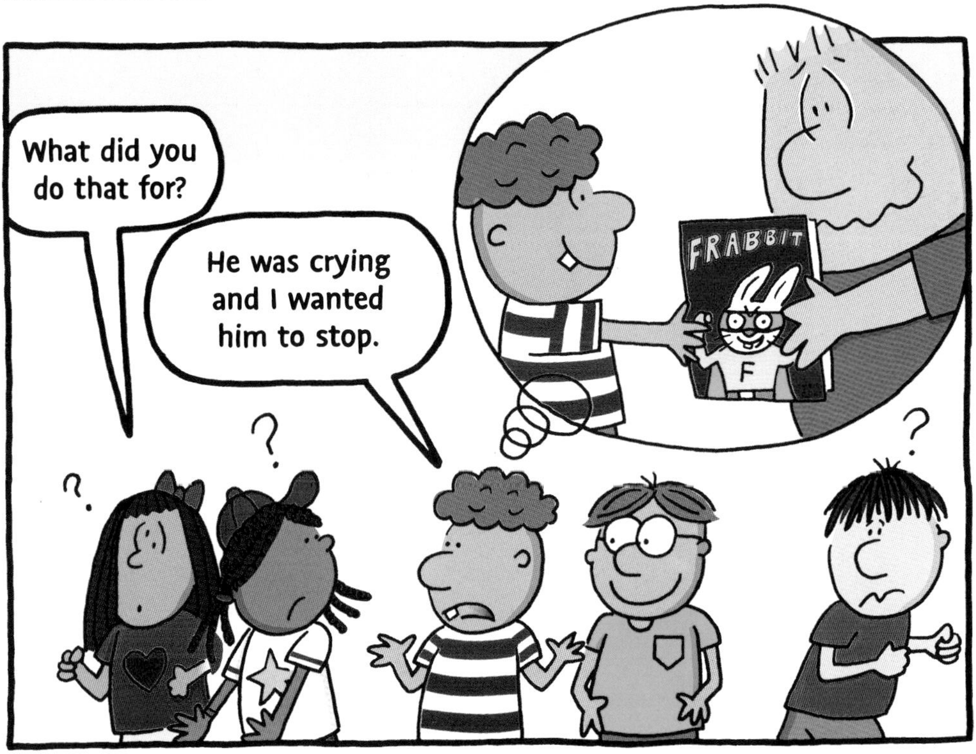
What did you do that for?
He was crying and I wanted him to stop.
FRABBIT
F

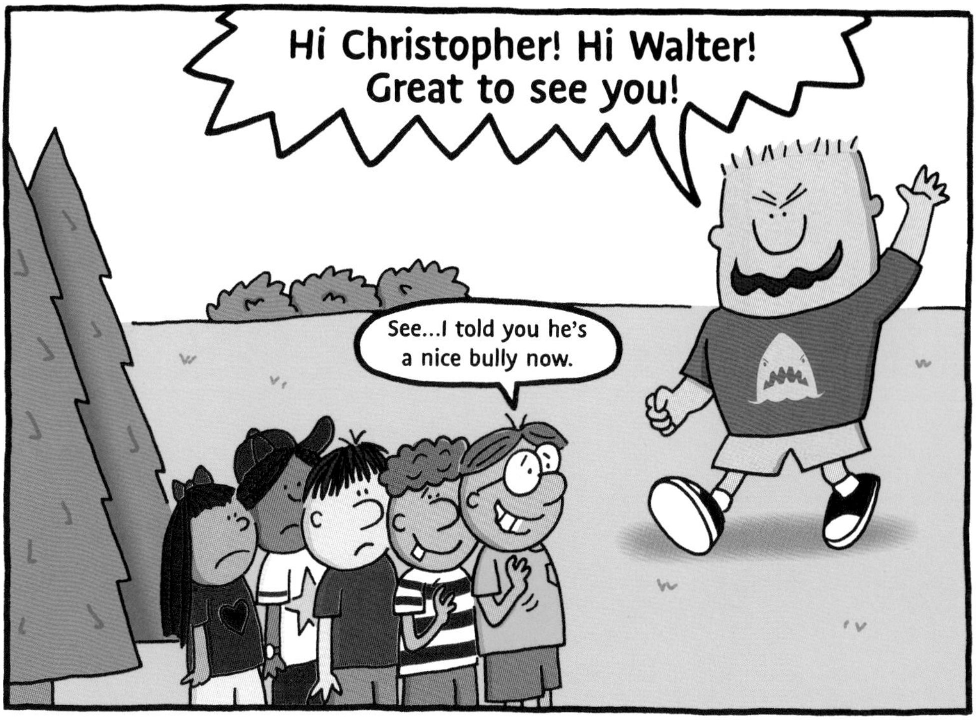
Hi Christopher! Hi Walter! Great to see you!
See...I told you he's a nice bully now.

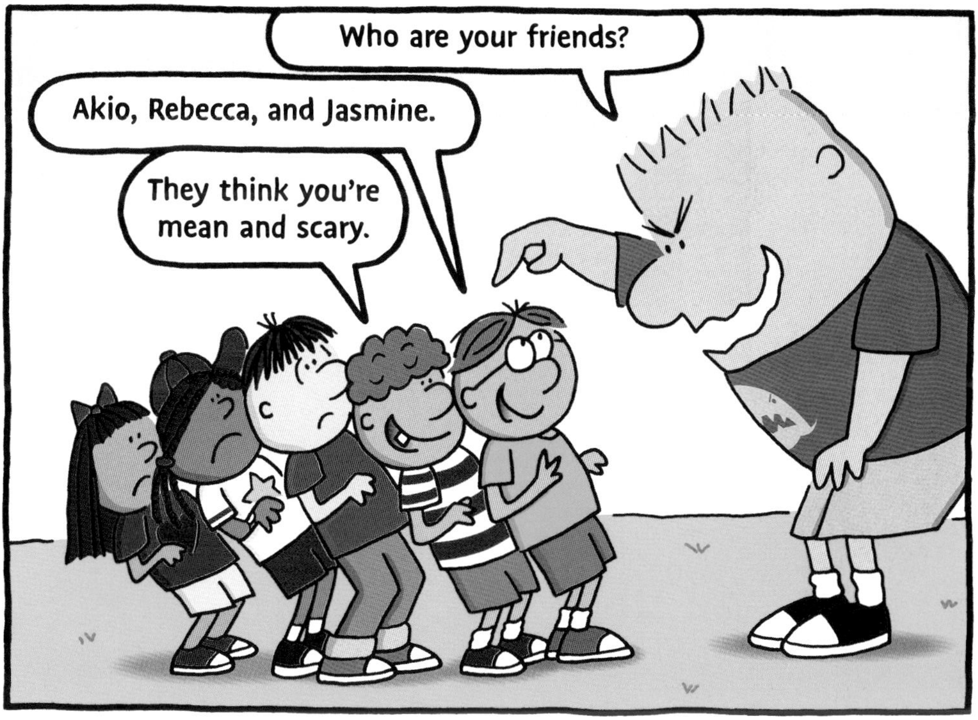
Who are your friends?
Akio, Rebecca, and Jasmine.
They think you're mean and scary.

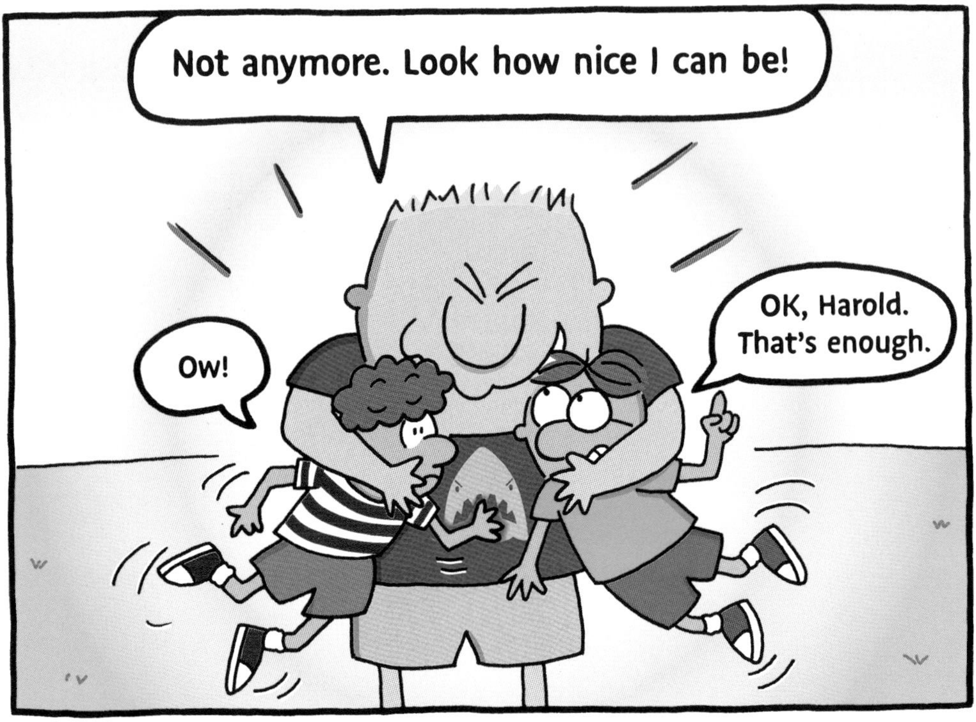
Not anymore. Look how nice I can be!
Ow!
OK, Harold. That's enough.

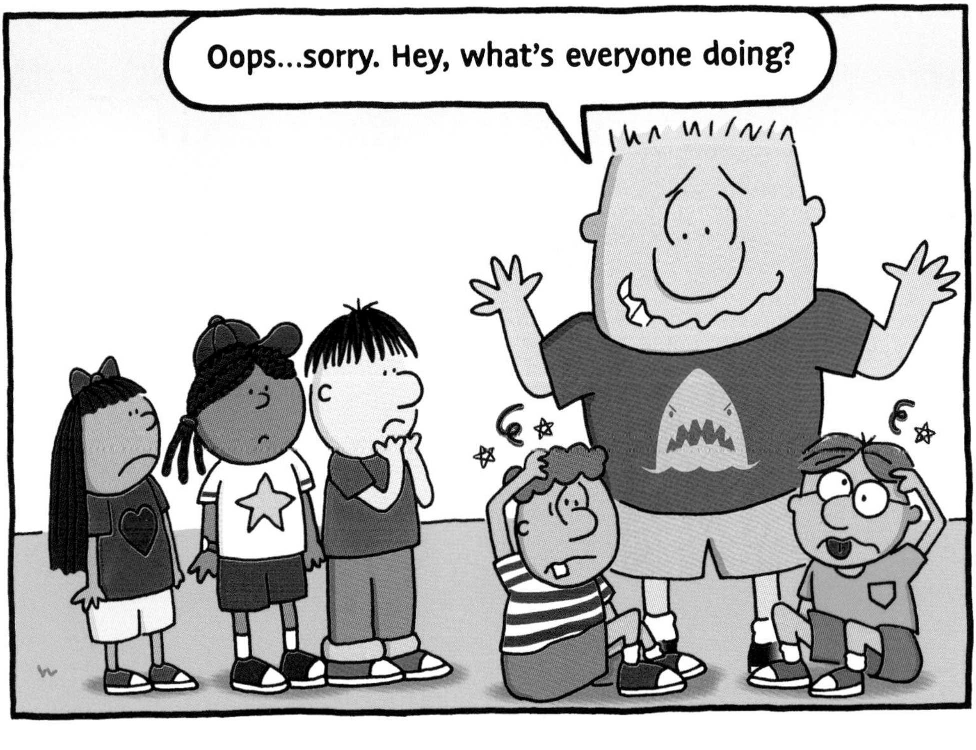
Oops...sorry. Hey, what's everyone doing?

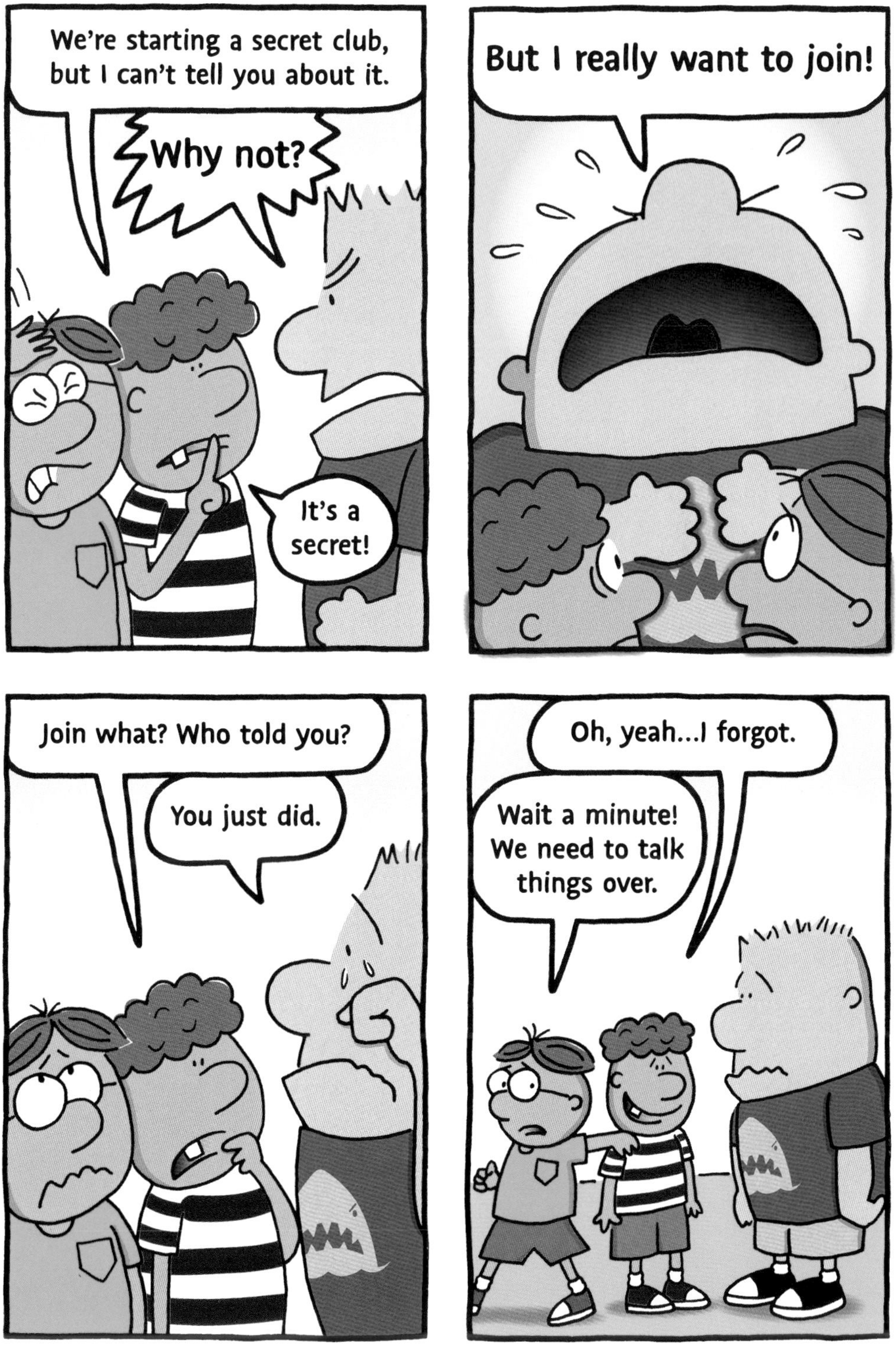
We're starting a secret club, but I can't tell you about it.
Why not?
It's a secret!
But I really want to join!
Join what? Who told you?
You just did.
Oh, yeah...I forgot.
Wait a minute! We need to talk things over.

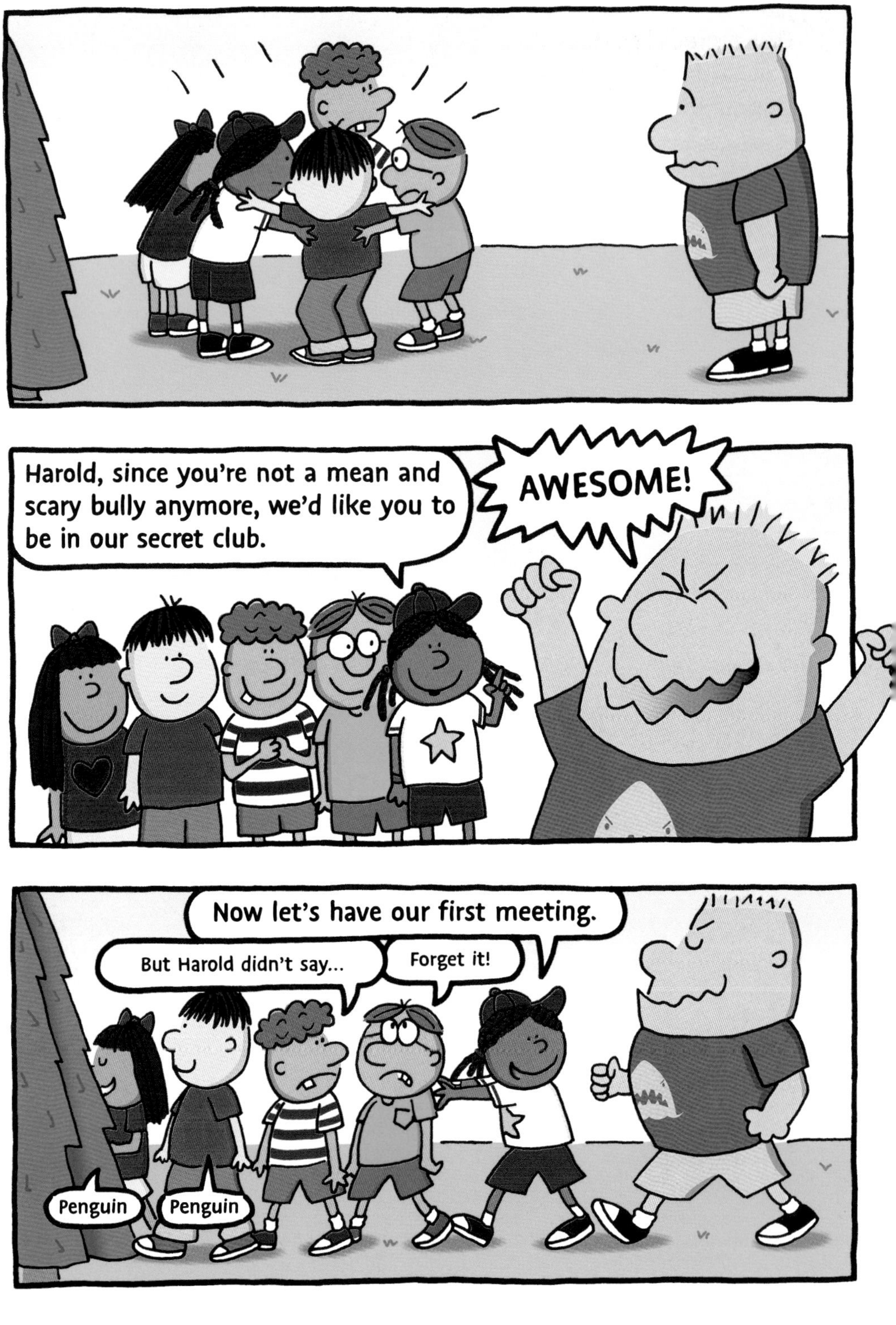
Harold, since you're not a mean and scary bully anymore, we'd like you to be in our secret club.
AWESOME!
Now let's have our first meeting.
But Harold didn't say...
Forget it!
Penguin
Penguin

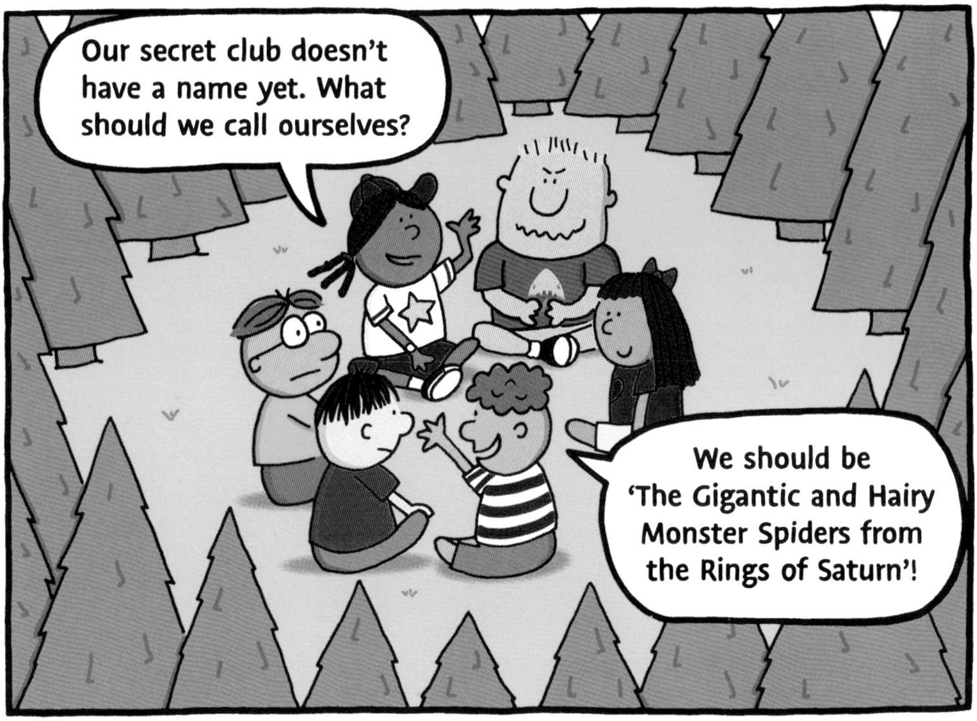
Our secret club doesn't have a name yet. What should we call ourselves?
We should be 'The Gigantic and Hairy Monster Spiders from the Rings of Saturn'!

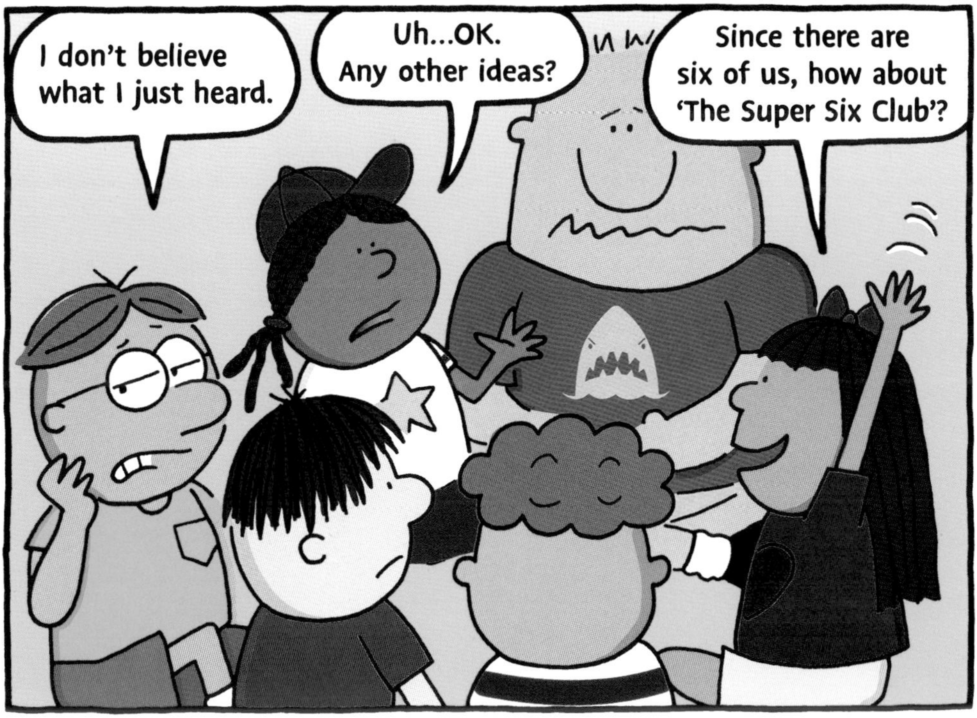
I don't believe what I just heard.
Uh...OK. Any other ideas?
Since there are six of us, how about 'The Super Six Club'?

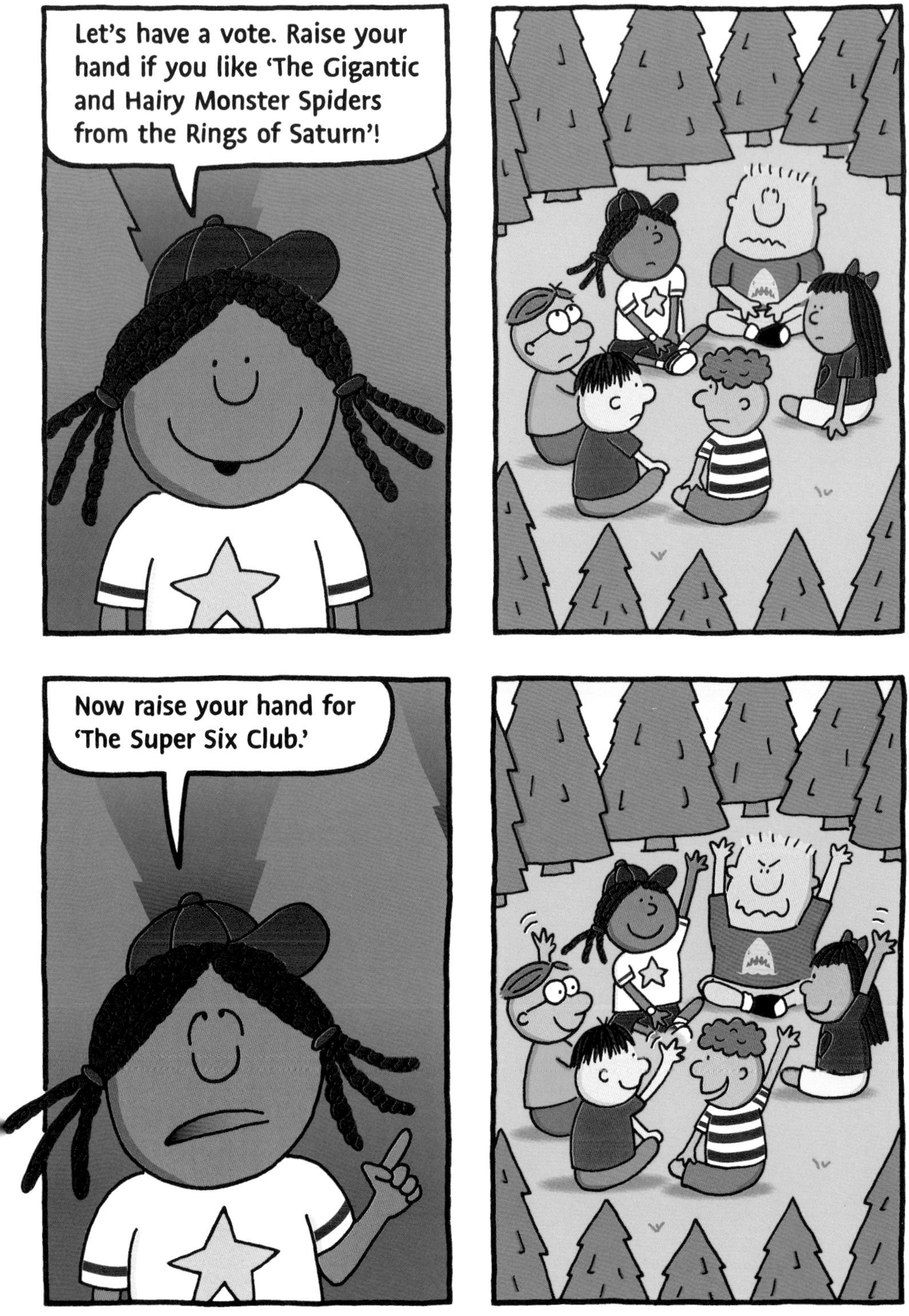
Let's have a vote. Raise your hand if you like 'The Gigantic and Hairy Monster Spiders from the Rings of Saturn'!
Now raise your hand for 'The Super Six Club.'

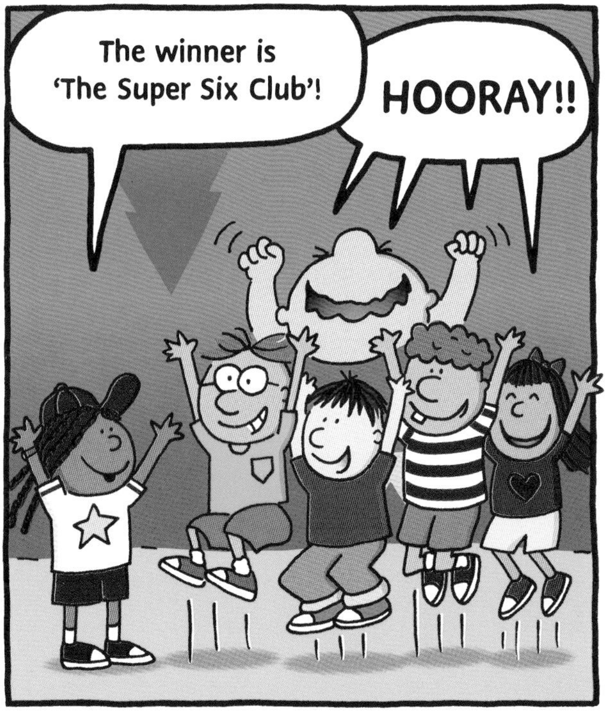
The winner is 'The Super Six Club'!
HOORAY!!

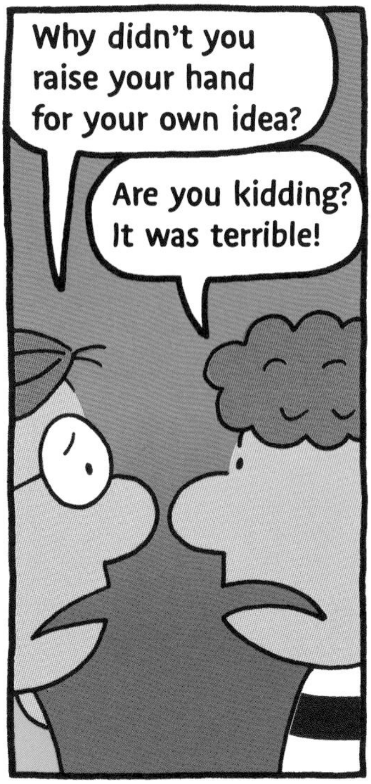
Why didn't you raise your hand for your own idea?
Are you kidding? It was terrible!

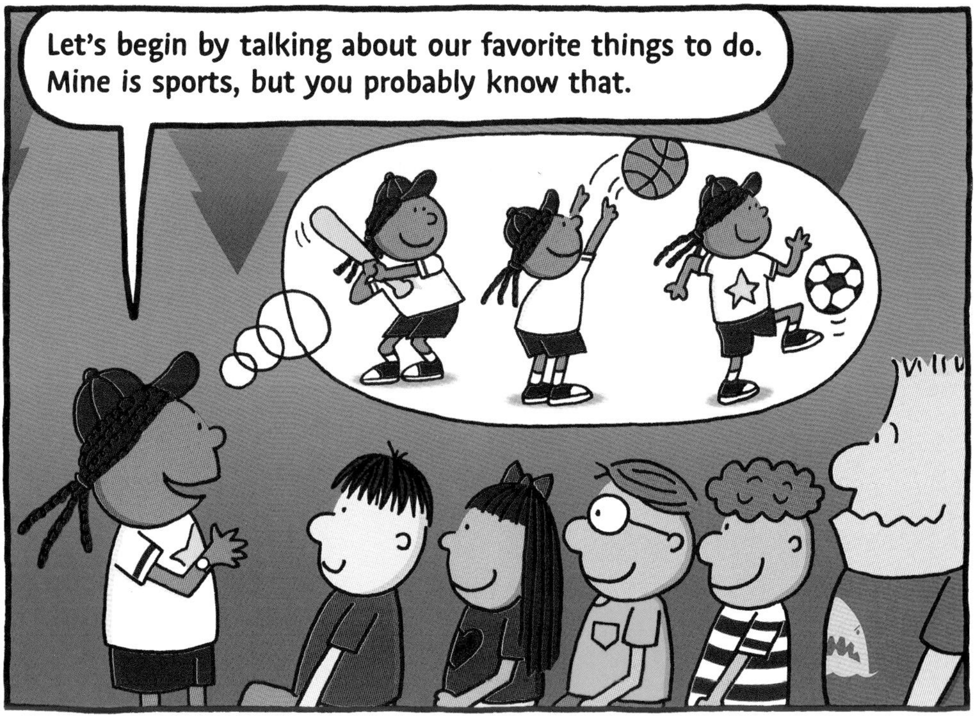
Let's begin by talking about our favorite things to do. Mine is sports, but you probably know that.

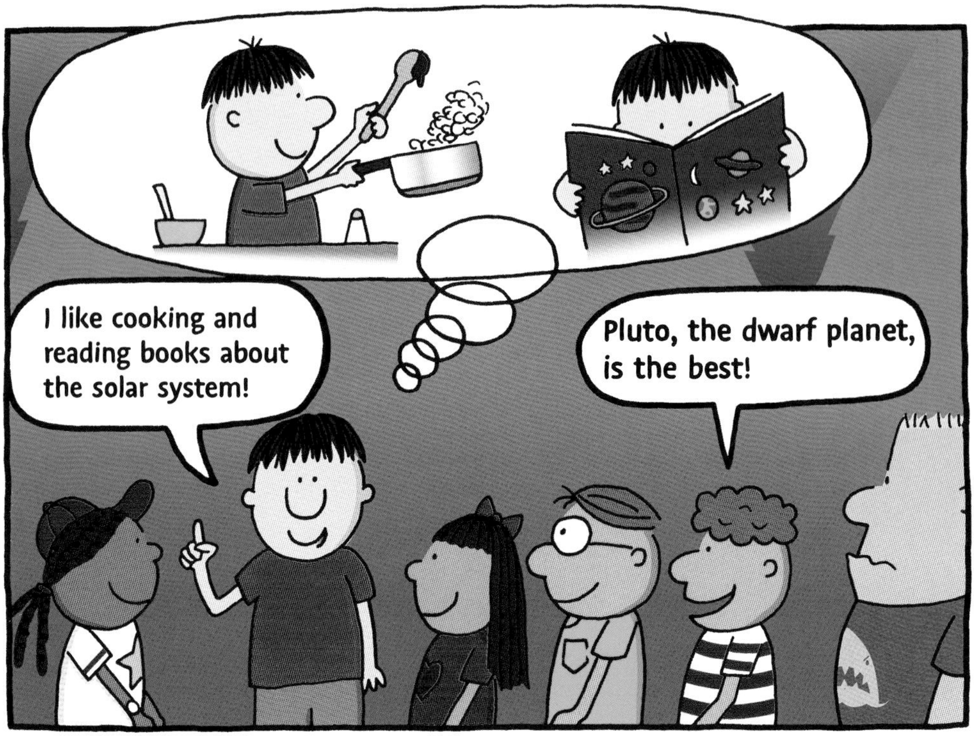
I like cooking and reading books about the solar system!
Pluto, the dwarf planet, is the best!

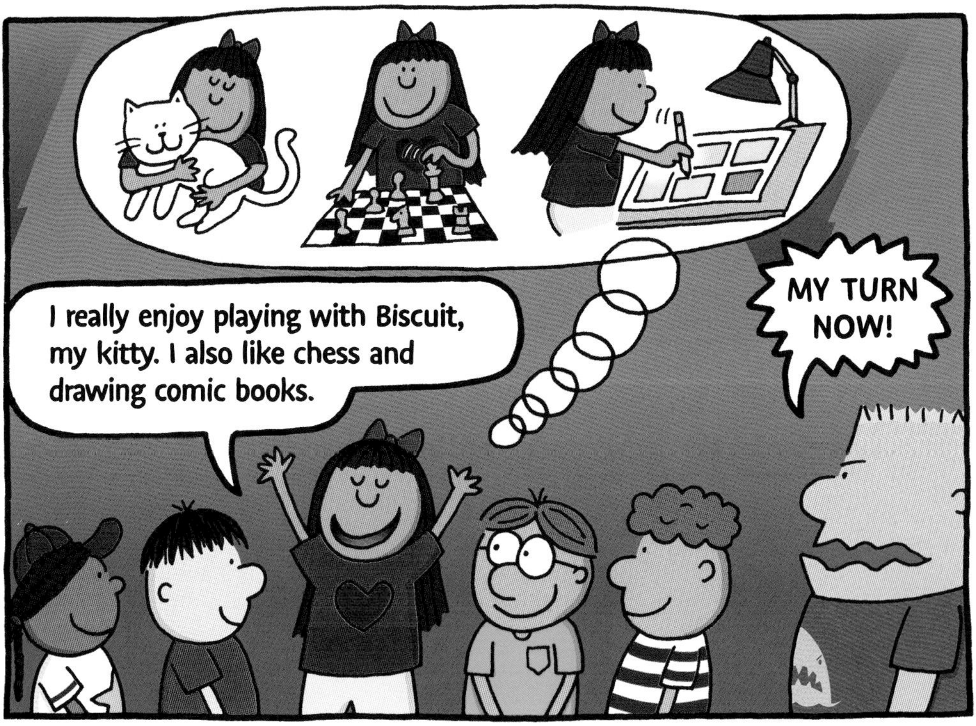
I really enjoy playing with Biscuit, my kitty. I also like chess and drawing comic books.
MY TURN NOW!

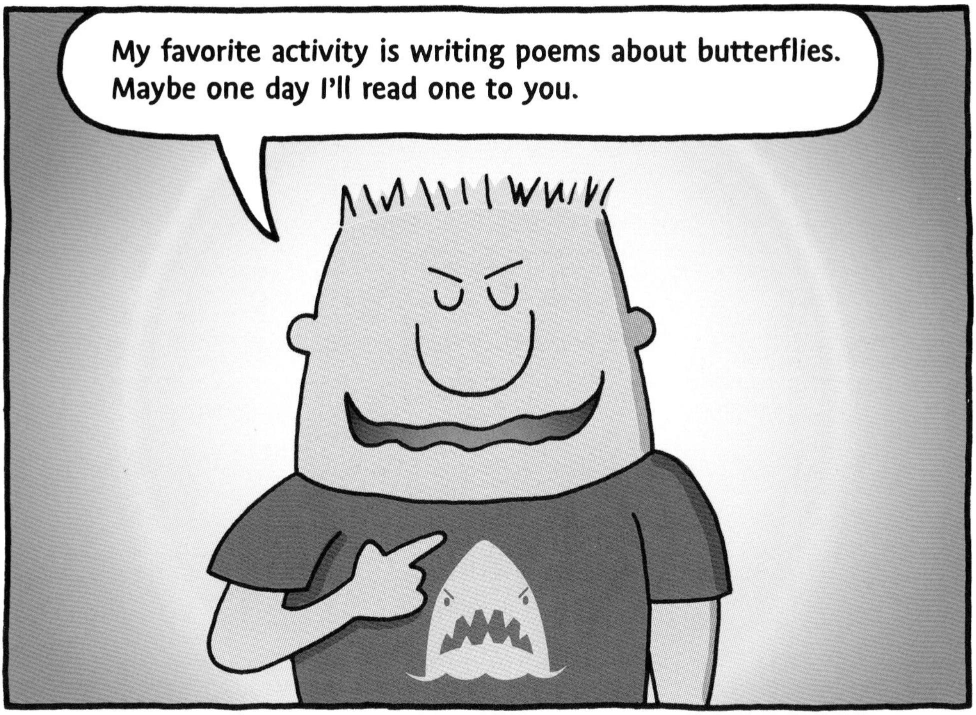
My favorite activity is writing poems about butterflies. Maybe one day I'll read one to you.

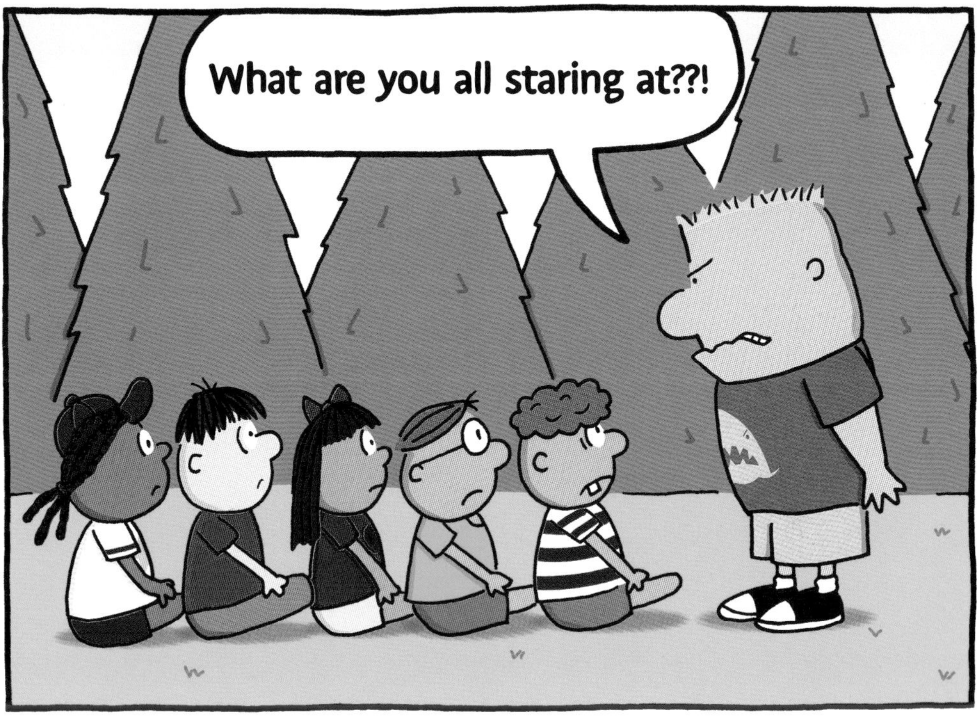
What are you all staring at??!

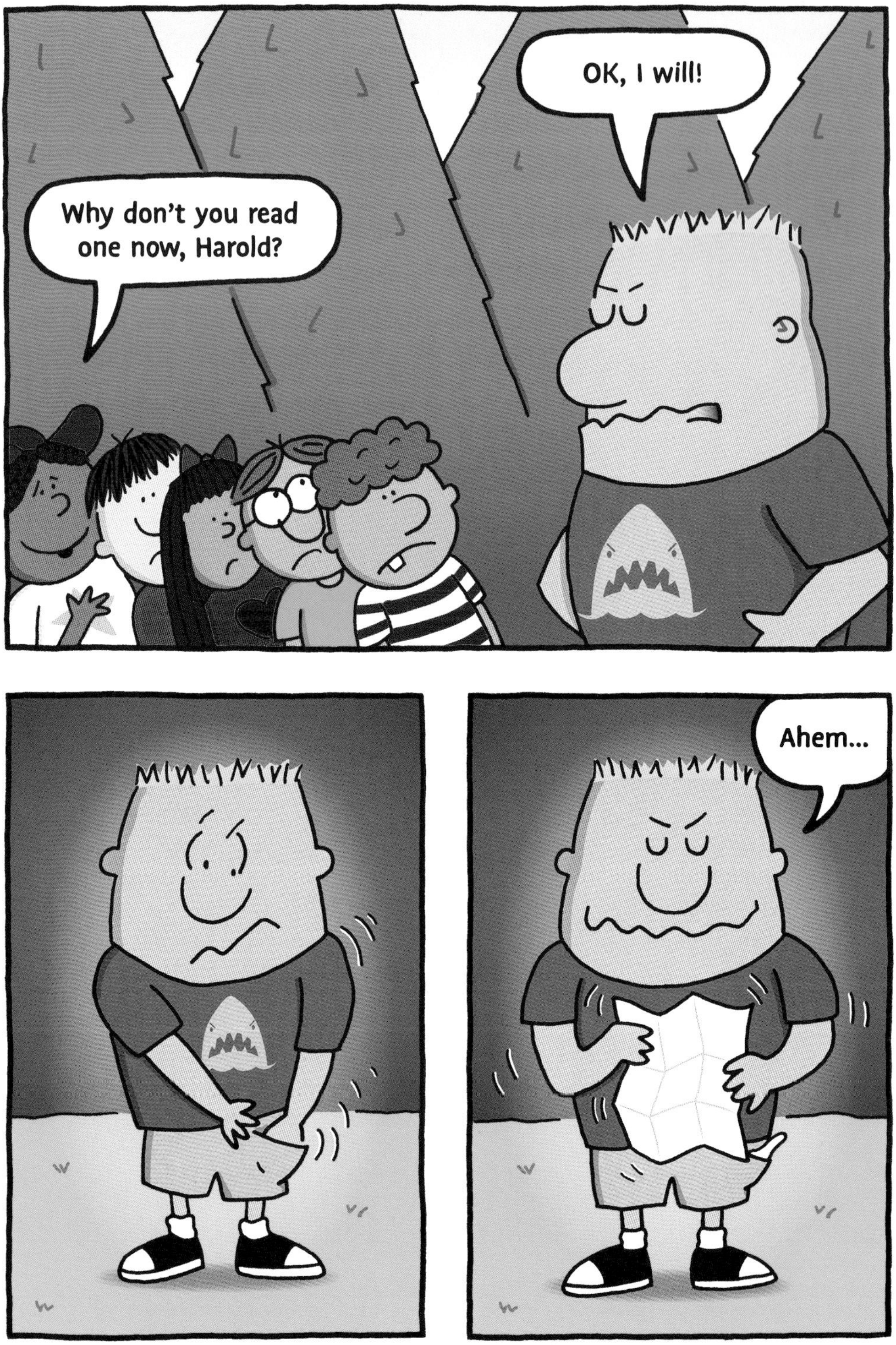
OK, I will!
Why don't you read one now, Harold?
Ahem...

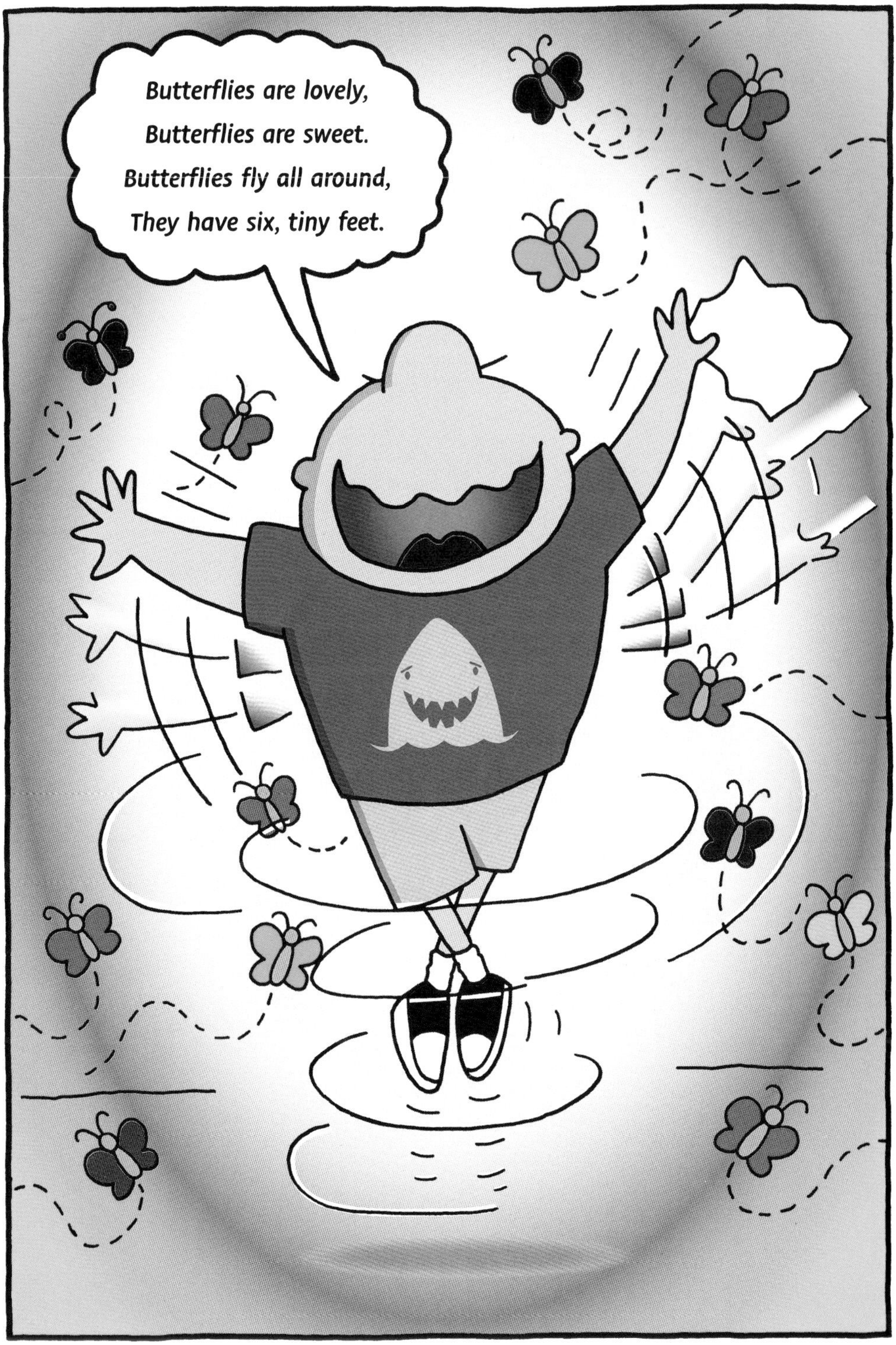
Butterflies are lovely,
Butterflies are sweet.
Butterflies fly all around,
They have six, tiny feet.

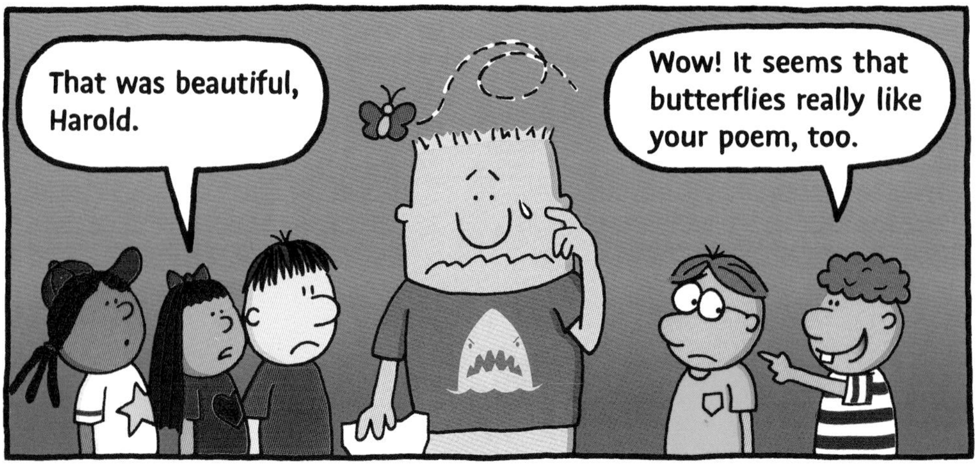
That was beautiful, Harold.
Wow! It seems that butterflies really like your poem, too.

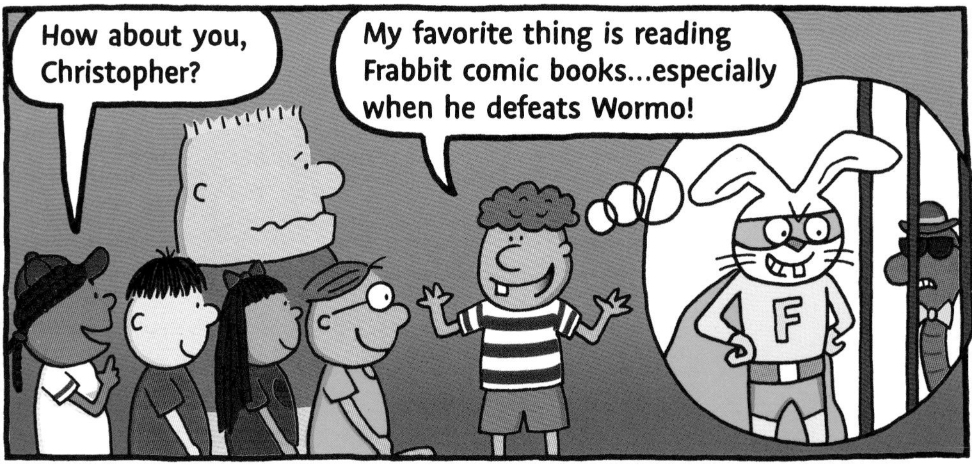
How about you, Christopher?
My favorite thing is reading Frabbit comic books...especially when he defeats Wormo!
F

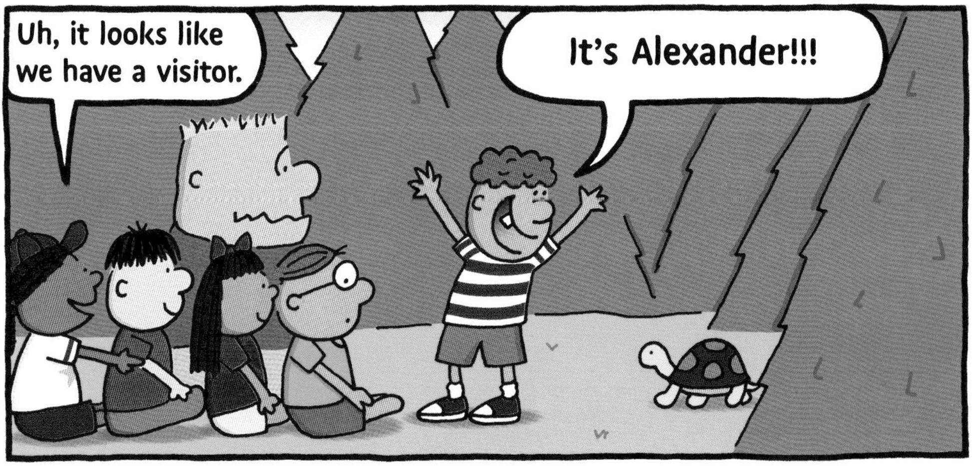
Uh, it looks like we have a visitor.
It's Alexander!!!

Chapter 9 - The New Secret Club Member!

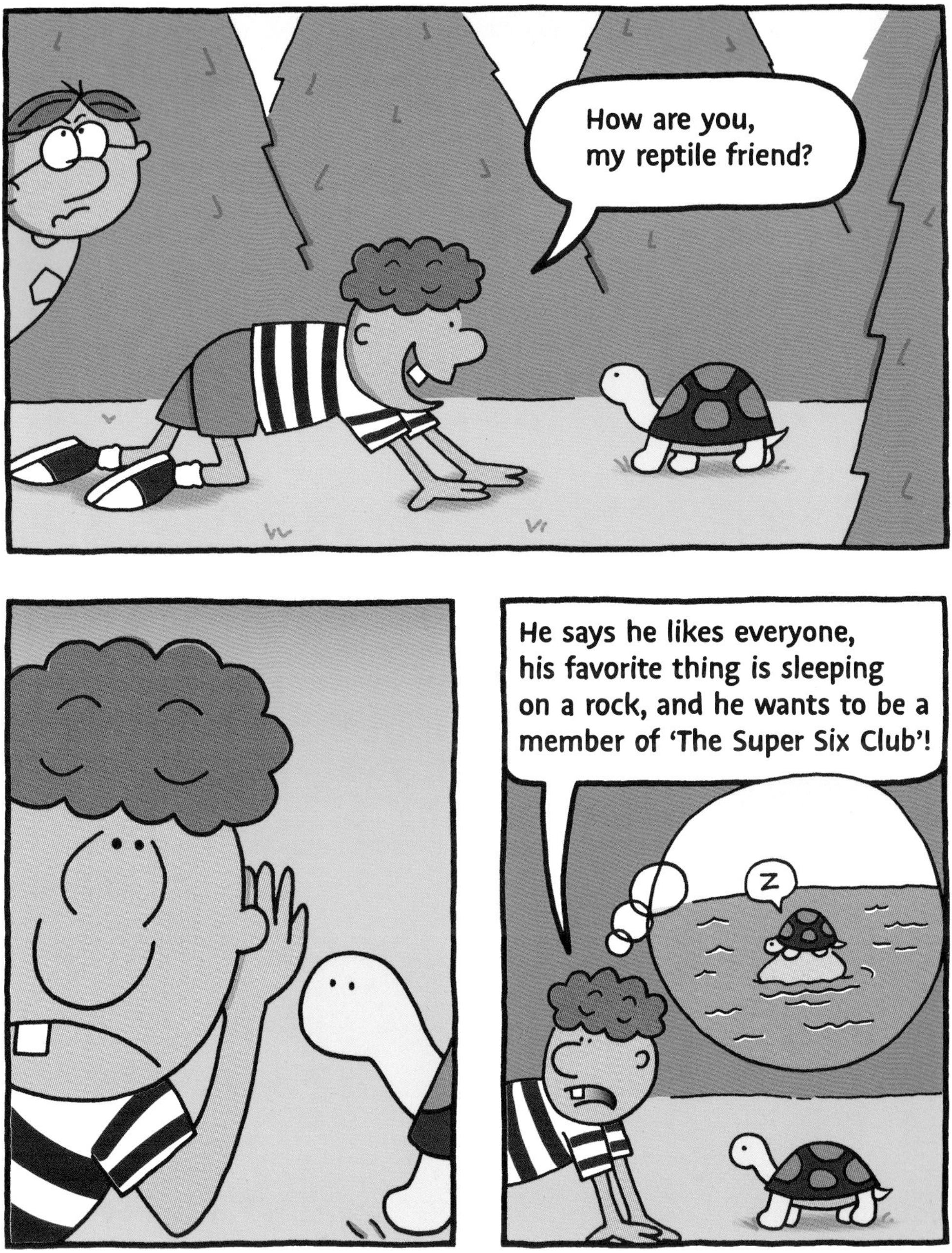
How are you, my reptile friend?
He says he likes everyone, his favorite thing is sleeping on a rock, and he wants to be a member of 'The Super Six Club'!
Z

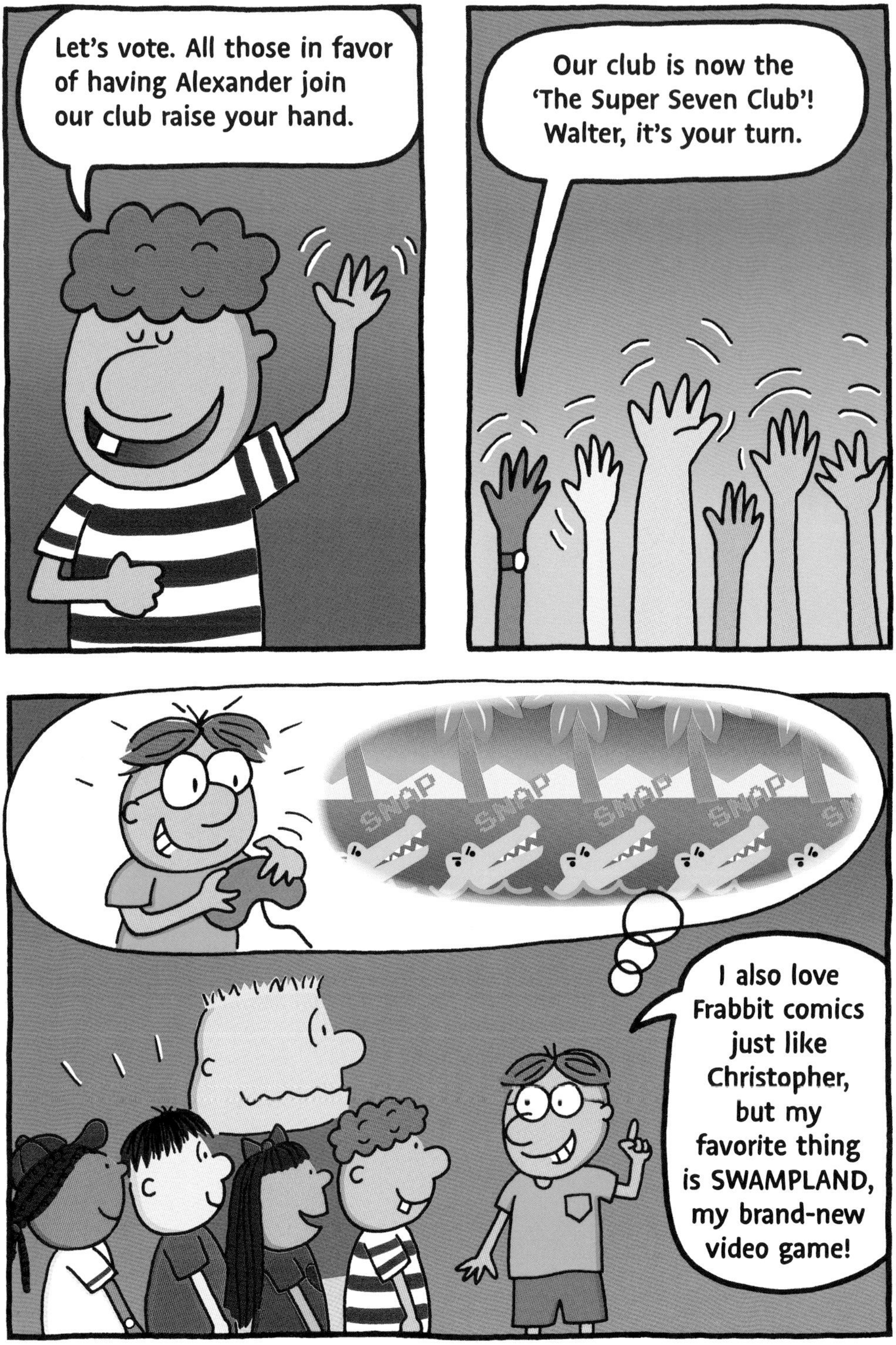
Let's vote. All those in favor of having Alexander join our club raise your hand.
Our club is now the 'The Super Seven Club'! Walter, it's your turn.
SNAP
I also love Frabbit comics just like Christopher, but my favorite thing is SWAMPLAND, my brand-new video game!

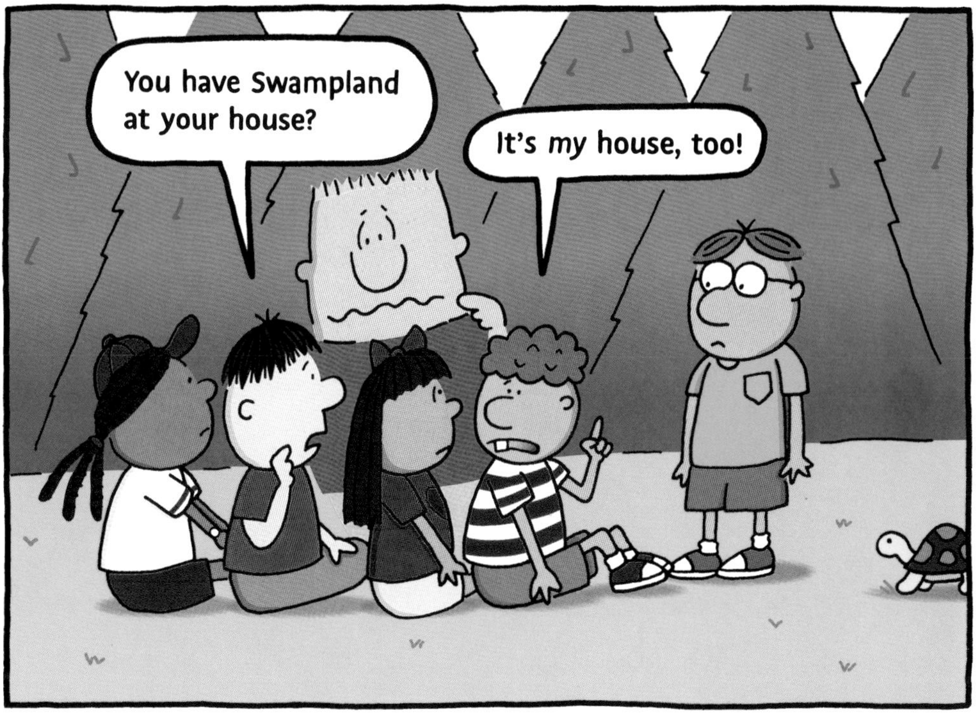
You have Swampland at your house?
It's *my* house, too!

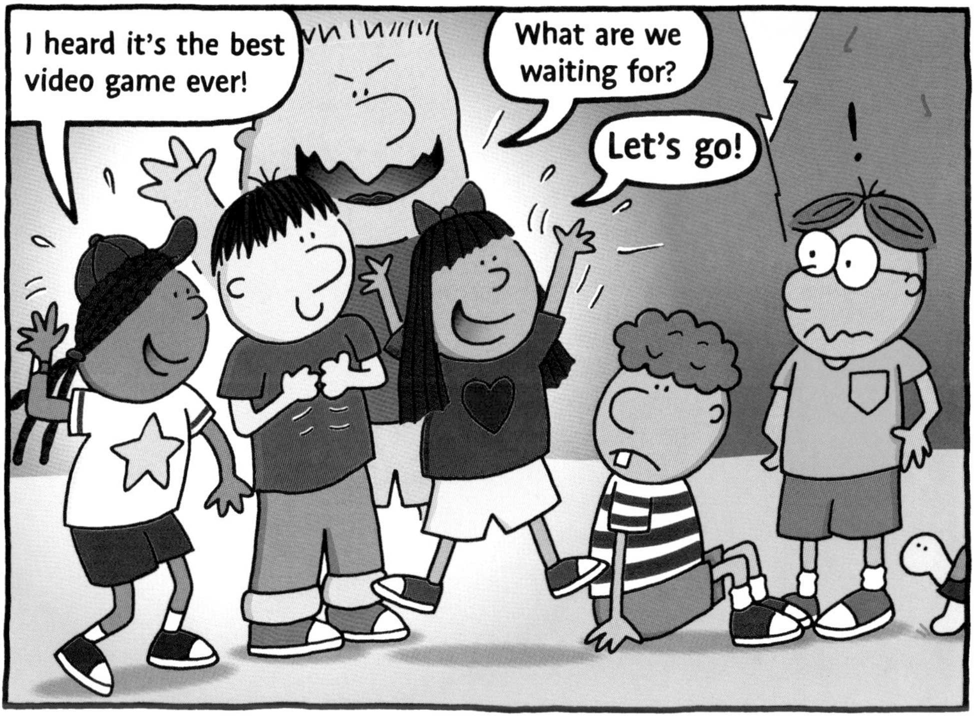
I heard it's the best video game ever!
What are we waiting for?
Let's go!
!

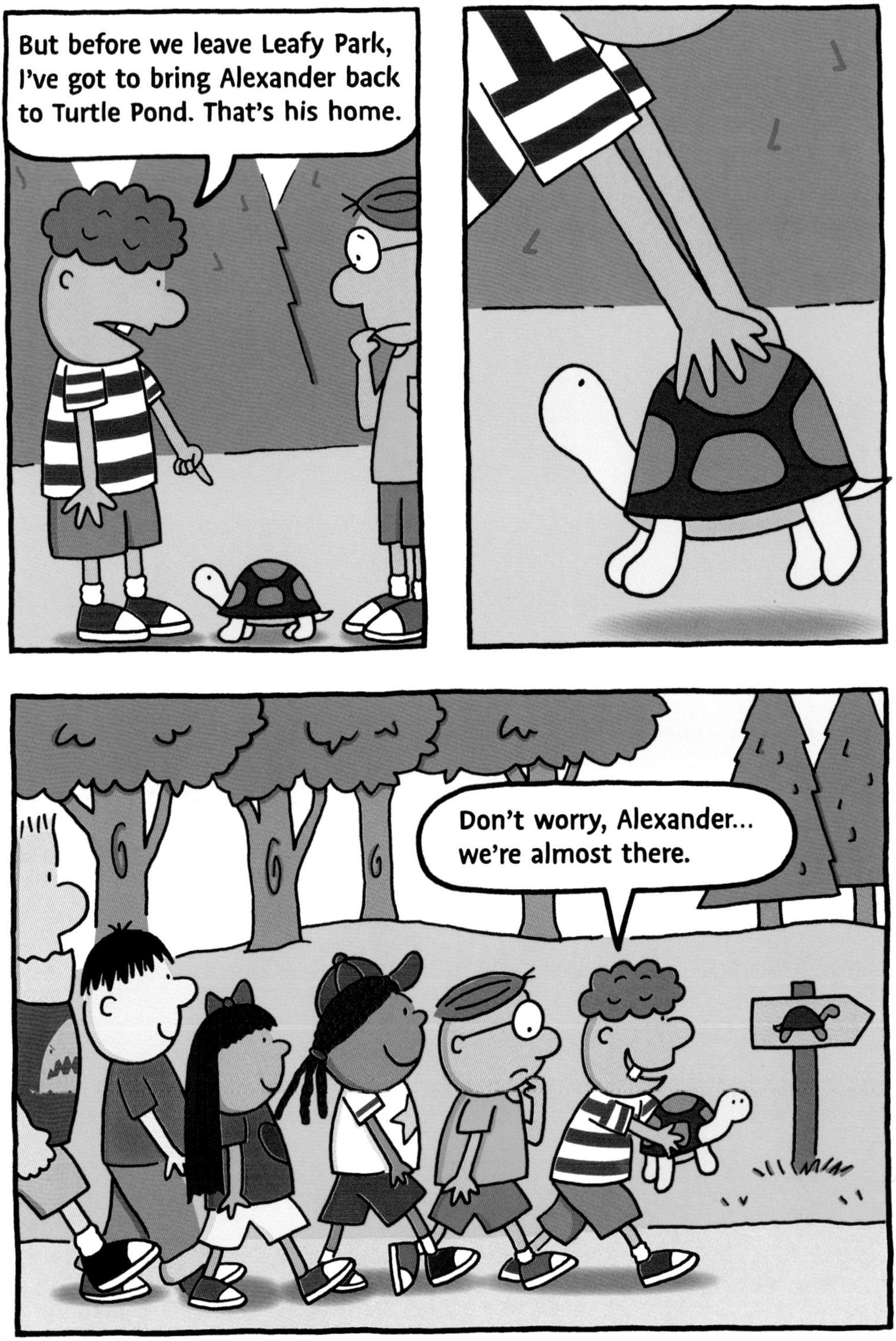
But before we leave Leafy Park, I've got to bring Alexander back to Turtle Pond. That's his home.
Don't worry, Alexander... we're almost there.

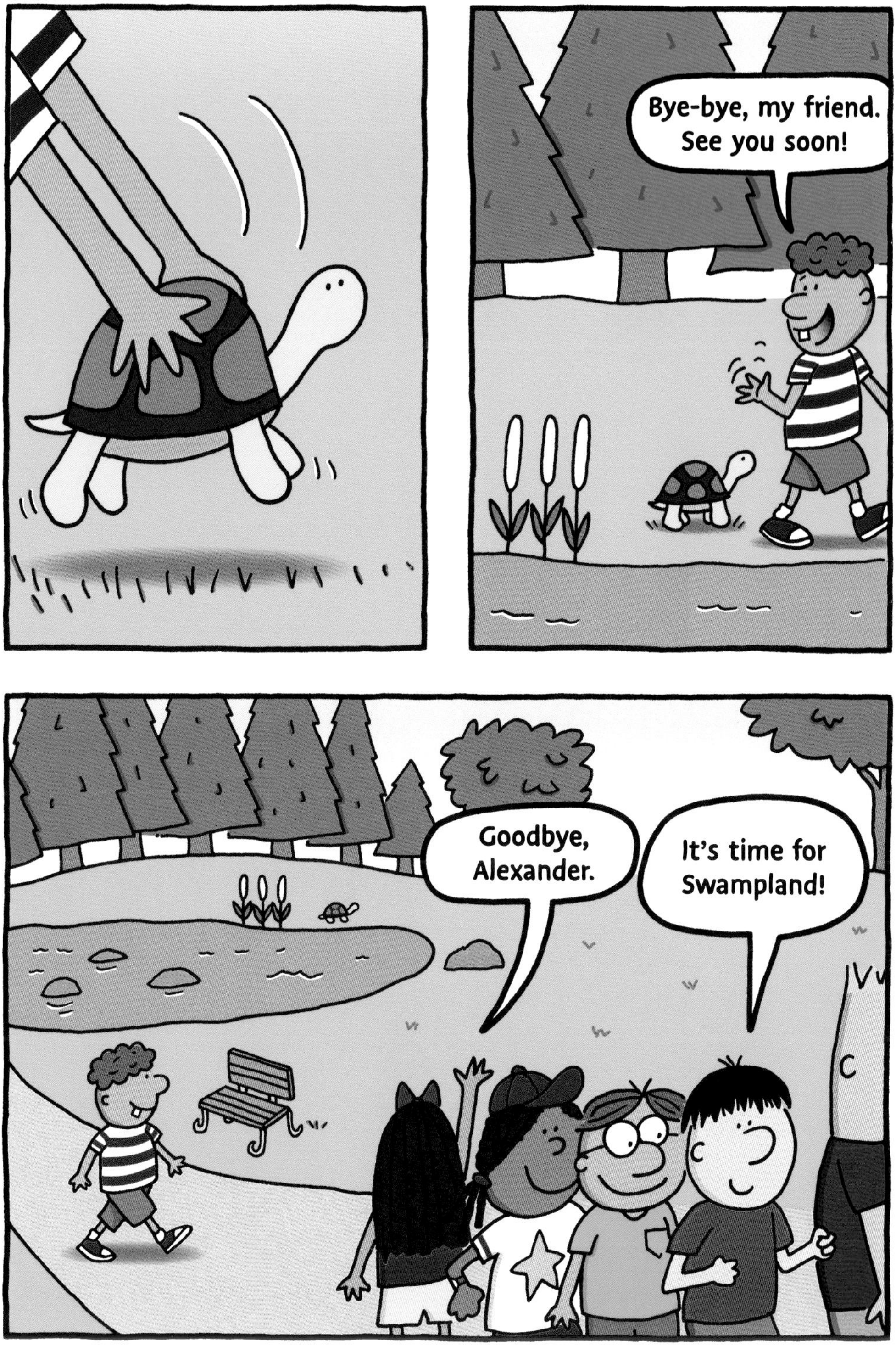
Bye-bye, my friend. See you soon!
Goodbye, Alexander.
It's time for Swampland!

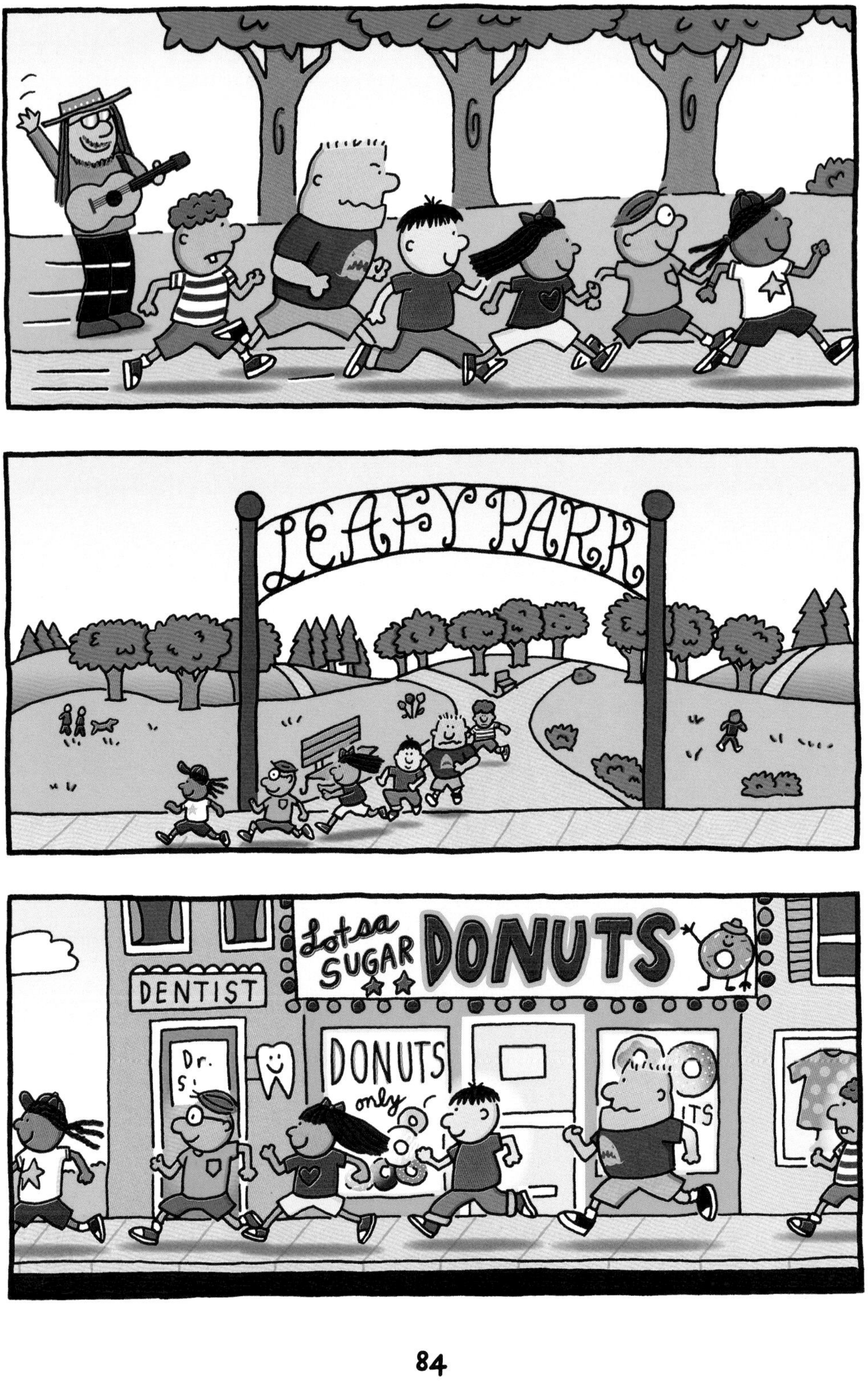
LEAFY PARK
Lotsa SUGAR
DONUTS
DENTIST
Dr. S
DONUTS
only
ITS

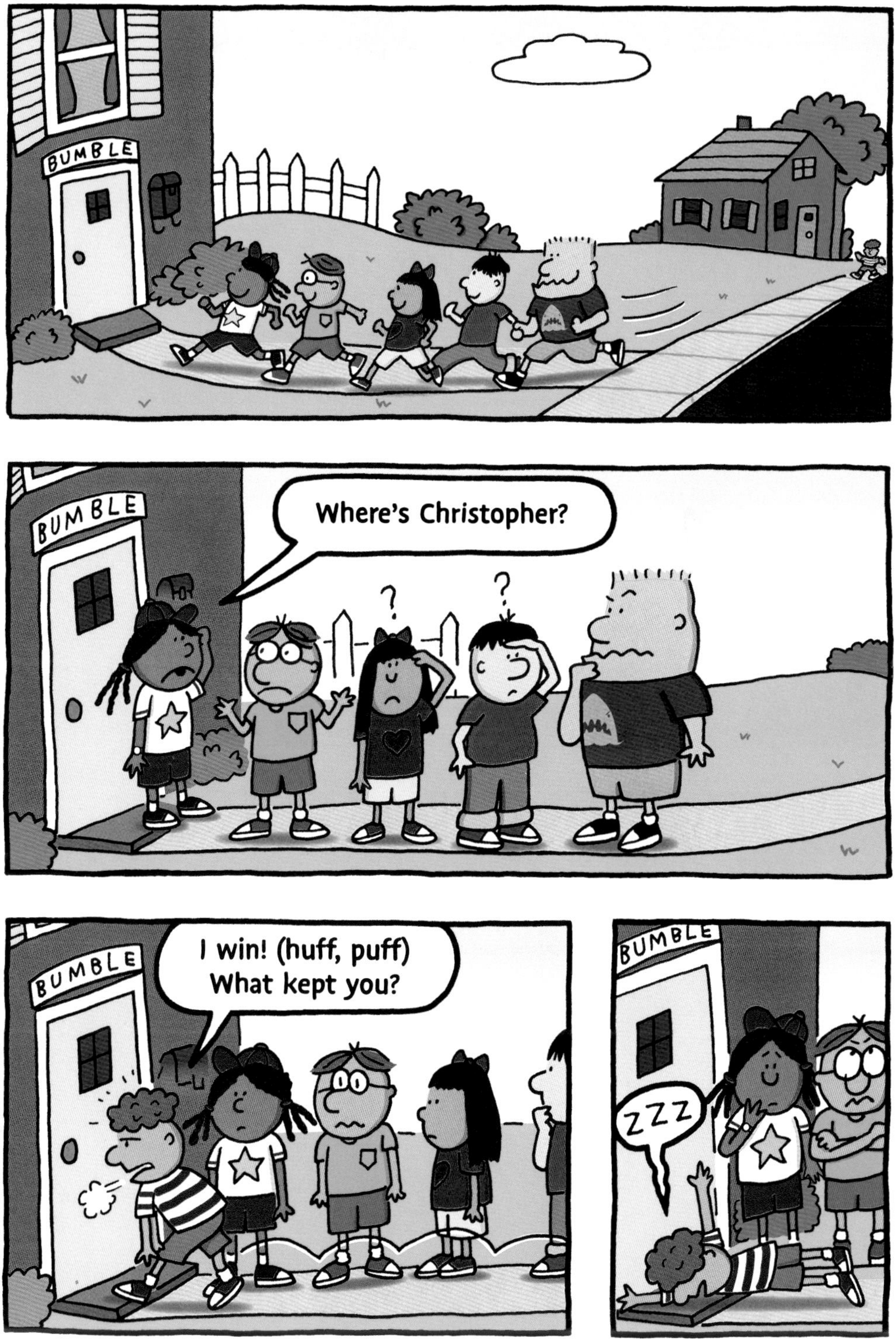
BUMBLE
BUMBLE
Where's Christopher?
BUMBLE
I win! (huff, puff)
What kept you?
BUMBLE
ZZZ

Chapter 10 – Let's Play!

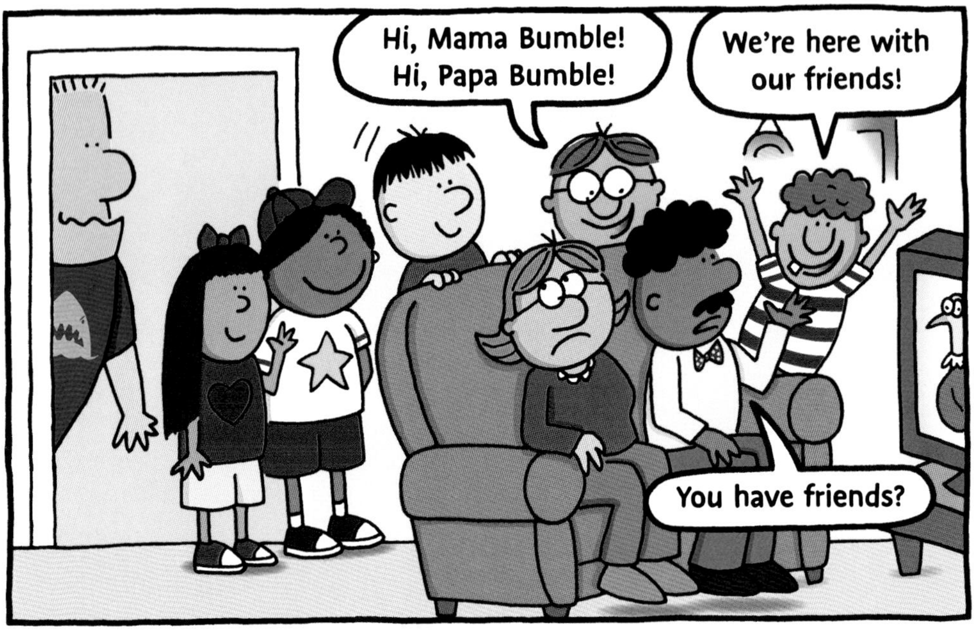
Hi, Mama Bumble! Hi, Papa Bumble!
We're here with our friends!
You have friends?

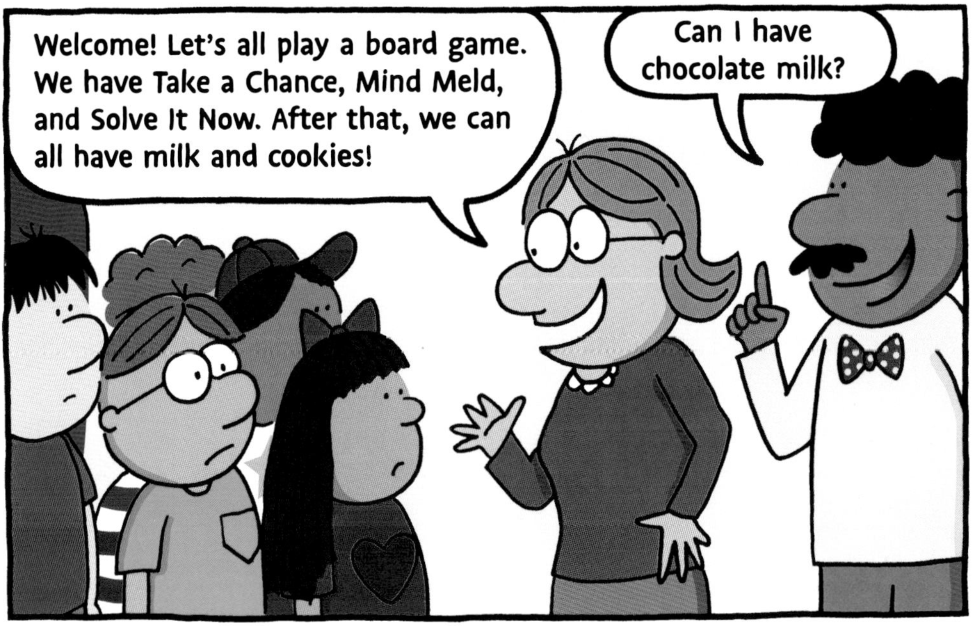
Welcome! Let's all play a board game. We have Take a Chance, Mind Meld, and Solve It Now. After that, we can all have milk and cookies!
Can I have chocolate milk?

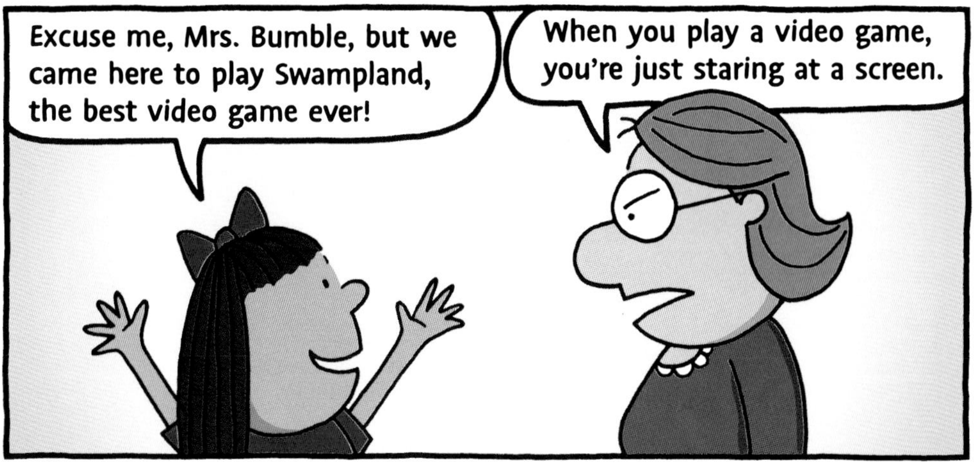
Excuse me, Mrs. Bumble, but we came here to play Swampland, the best video game ever!
When you play a video game, you're just staring at a screen.

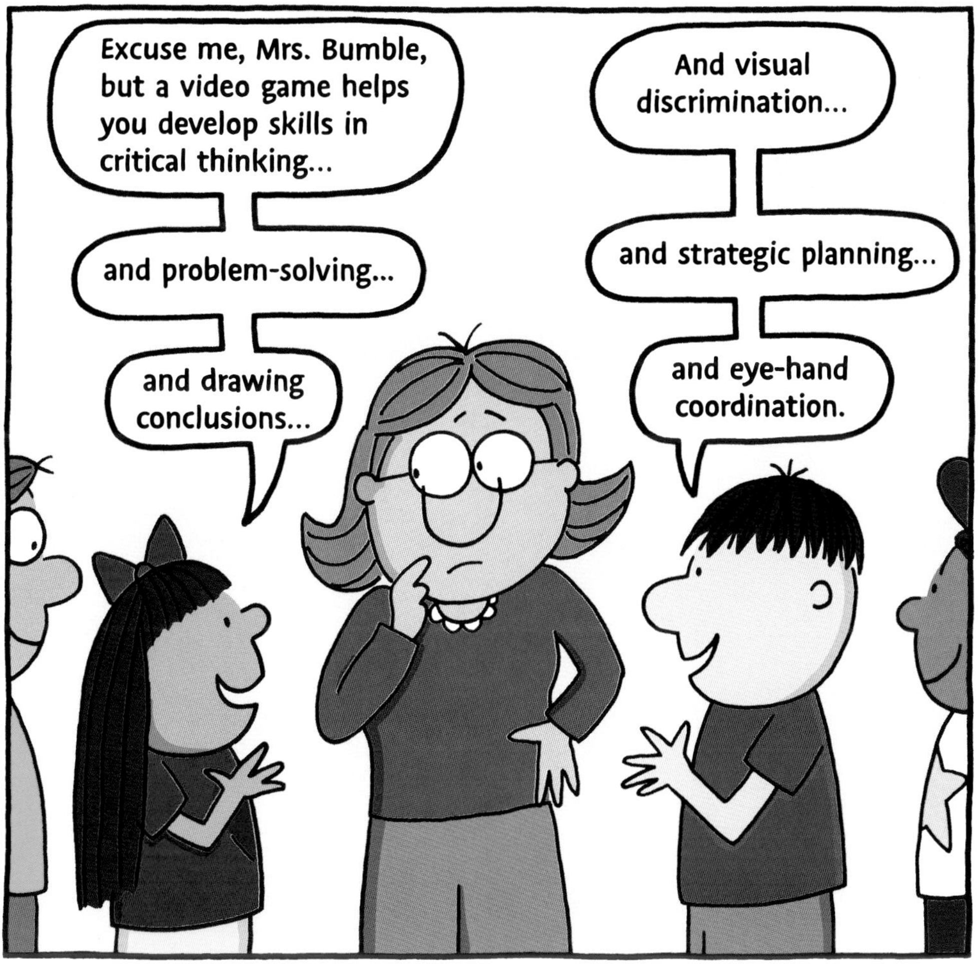
Excuse me, Mrs. Bumble, but a video game helps you develop skills in critical thinking...
and problem-solving...
and drawing conclusions...
And visual discrimination...
and strategic planning...
and eye-hand coordination.

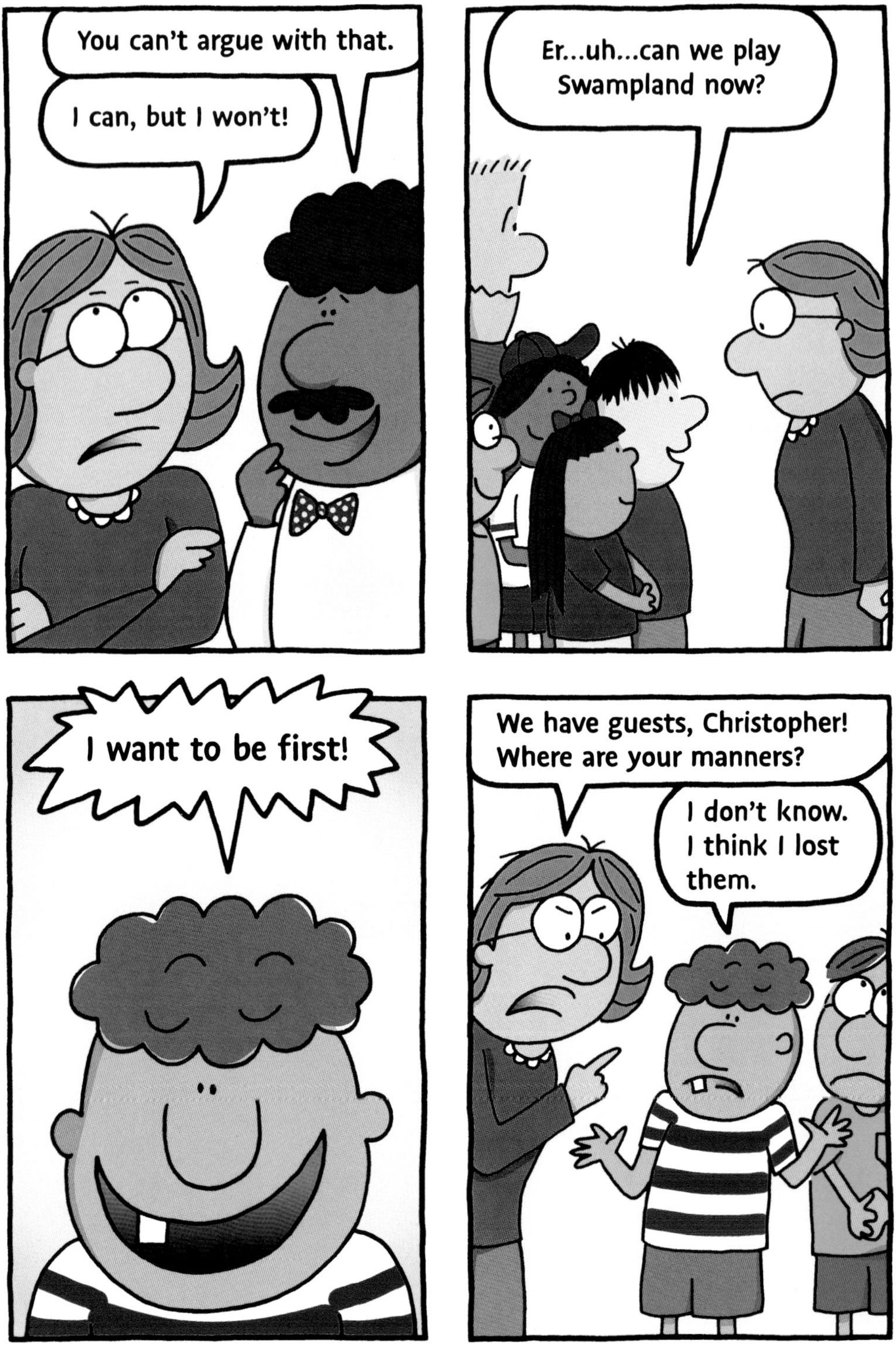
You can't argue with that.
I can, but I won't!
Er...uh...can we play Swampland now?
I want to be first!
We have guests, Christopher! Where are your manners?
I don't know. I think I lost them.

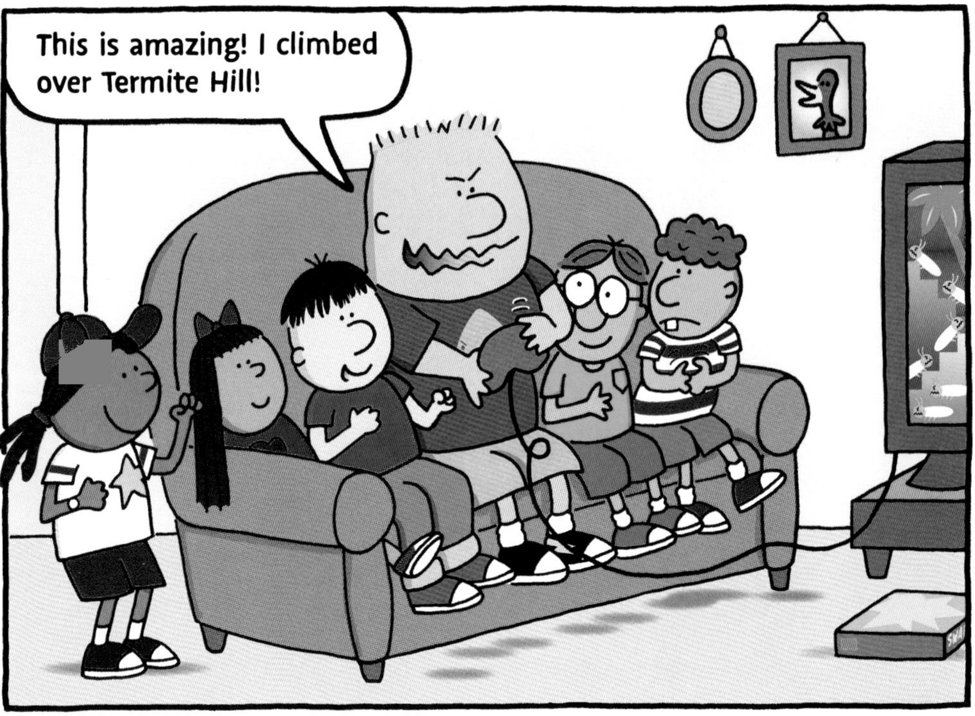
This is amazing! I climbed over Termite Hill!

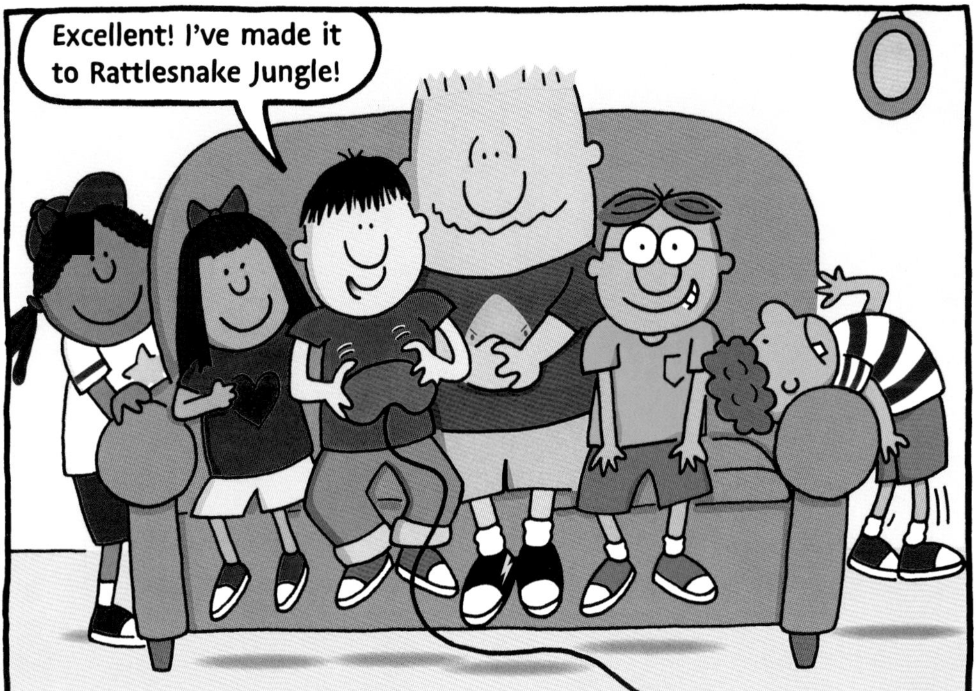
Excellent! I've made it to Rattlesnake Jungle!

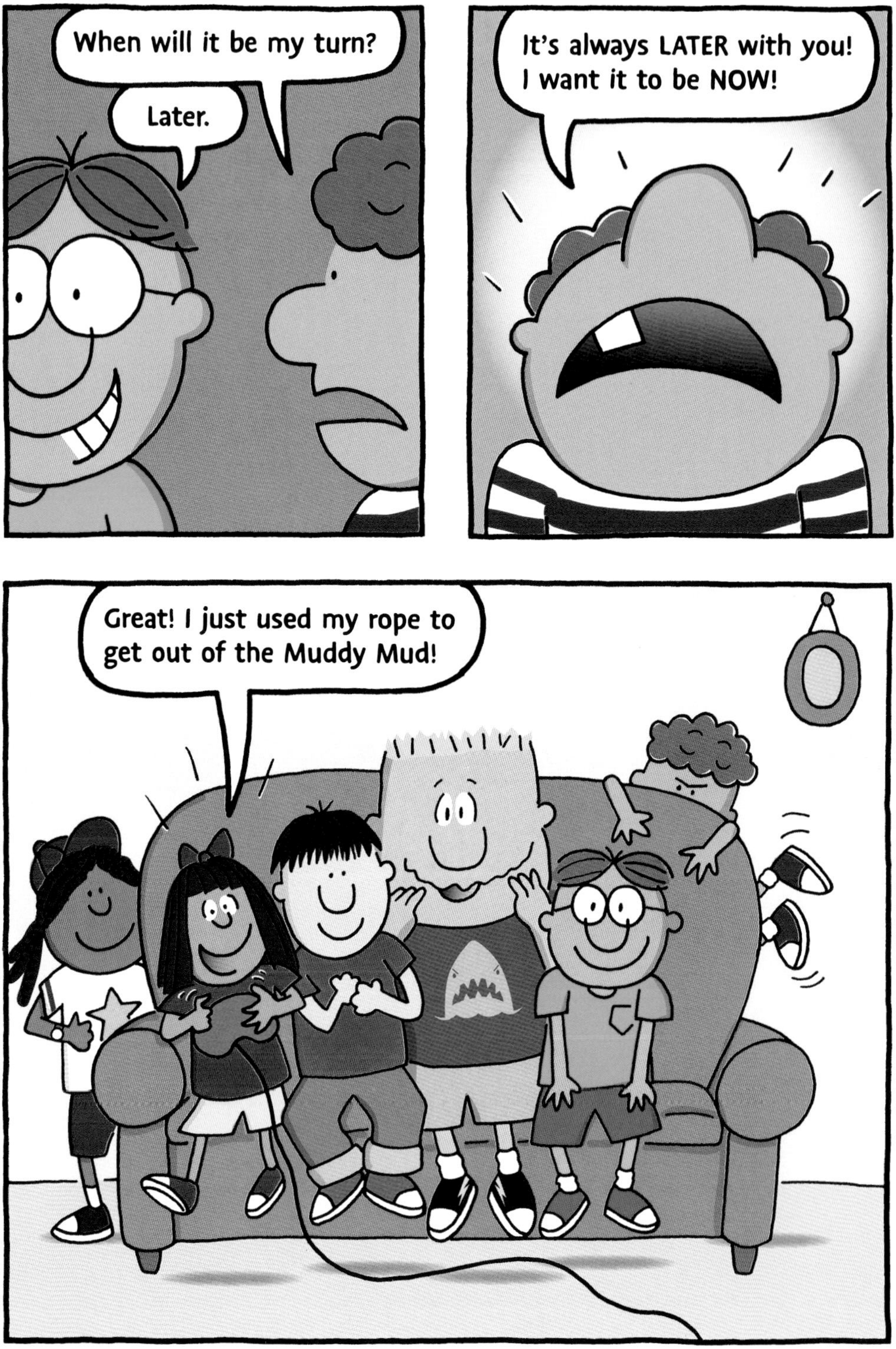
When will it be my turn?
Later.
It's always LATER with you!
I want it to be NOW!
Great! I just used my rope to get out of the Muddy Mud!

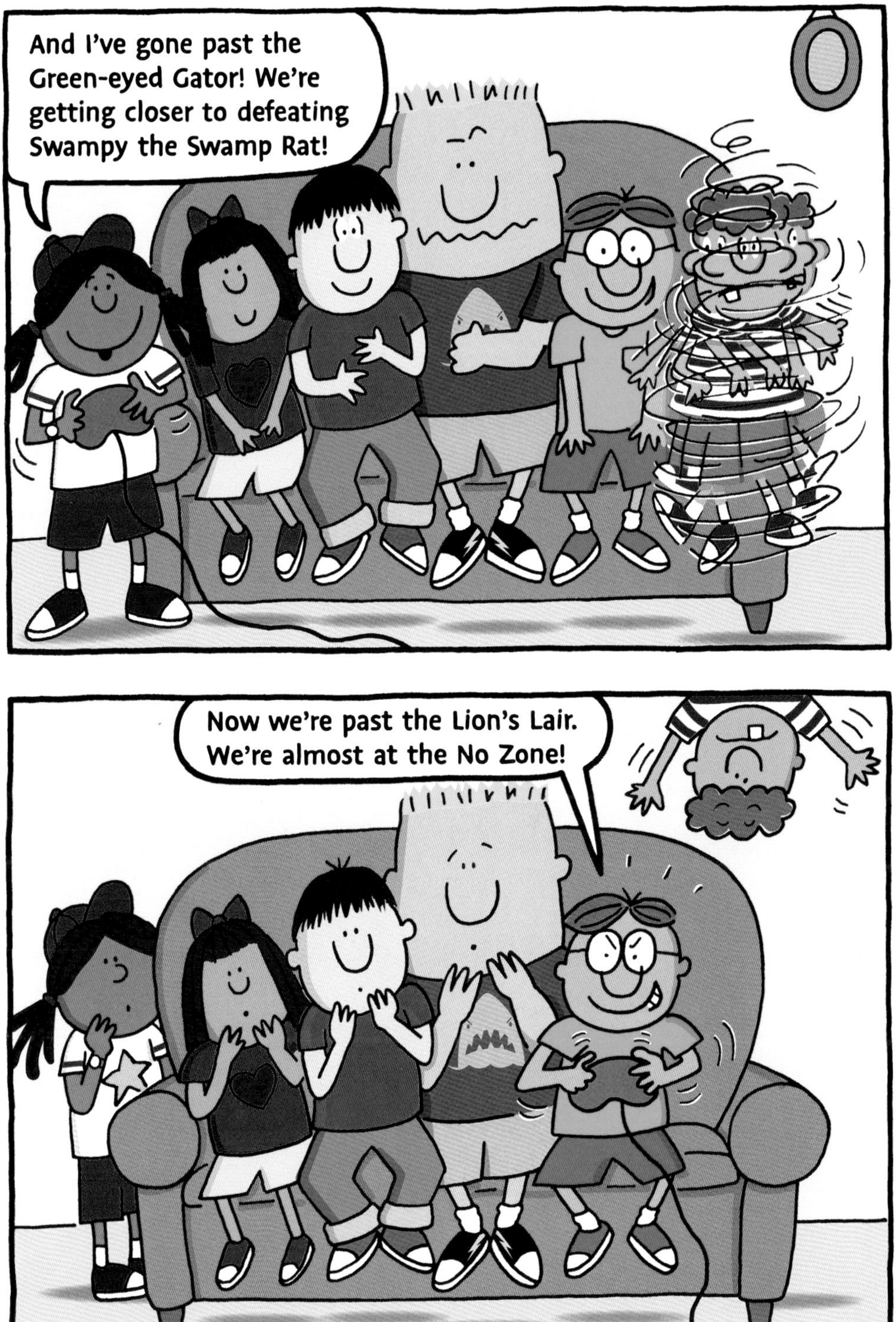
And I've gone past the Green-eyed Gator! We're getting closer to defeating Swampy the Swamp Rat!
Now we're past the Lion's Lair. We're almost at the No Zone!

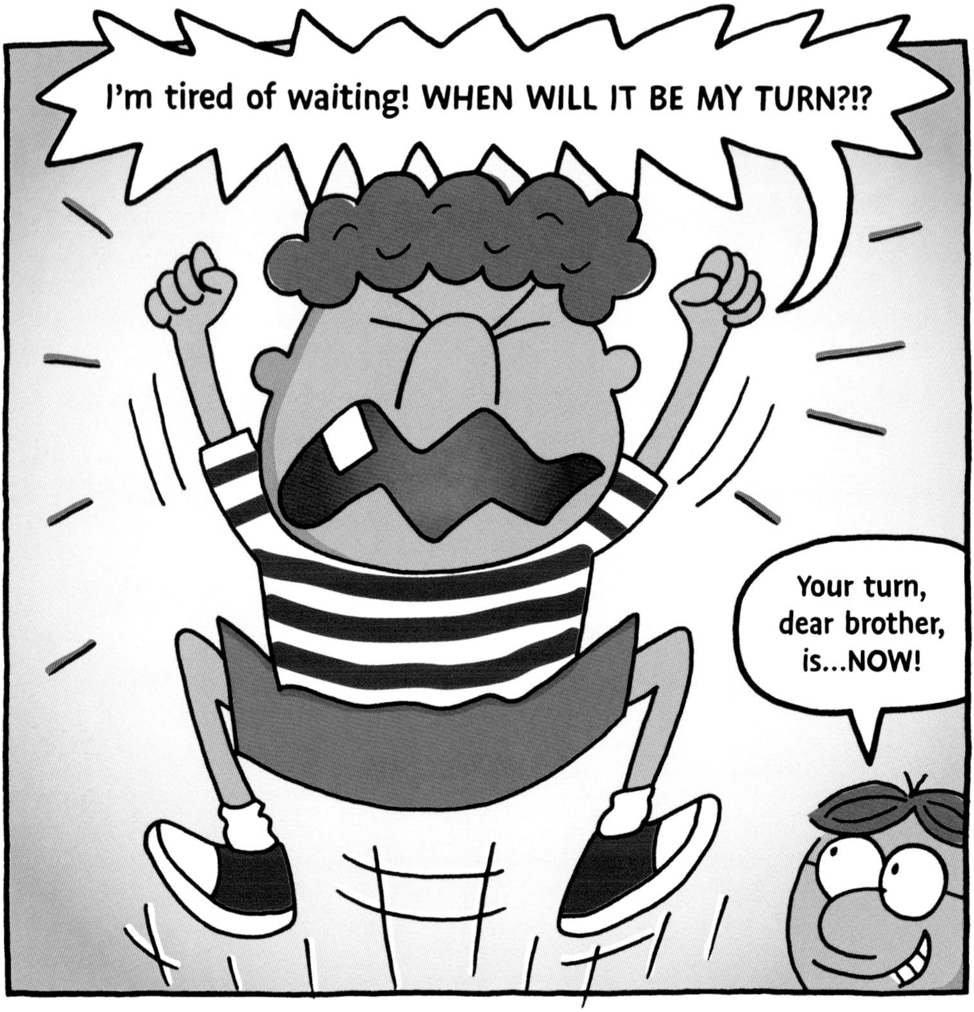
I'm tired of waiting! WHEN WILL IT BE MY TURN?!?
Your turn, dear brother, is...NOW!

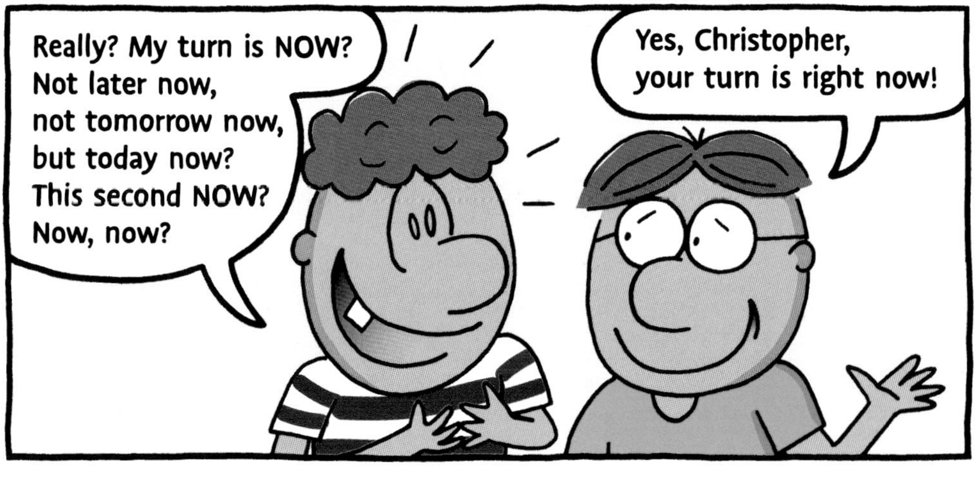
Really? My turn is NOW? Not later now, not tomorrow now, but today now? This second NOW? Now, now?
Yes, Christopher, your turn is right now!

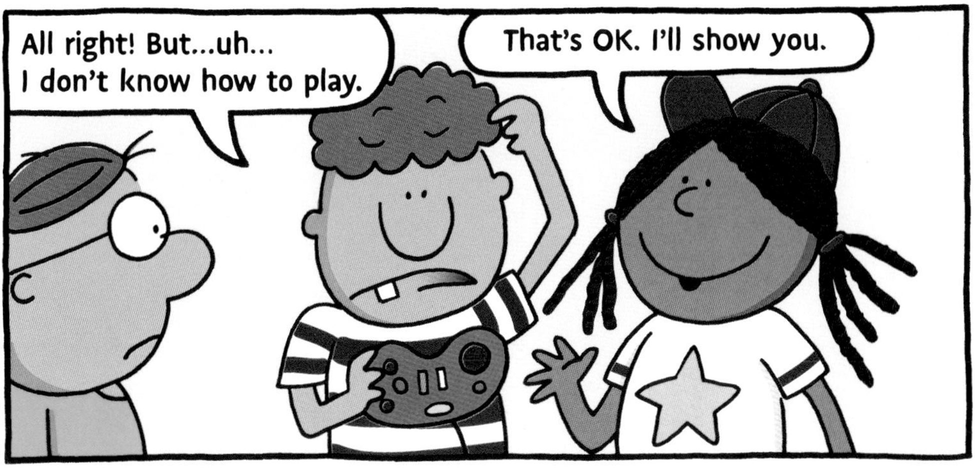
All right! But...uh...
I don't know how to play.
That's OK. I'll show you.

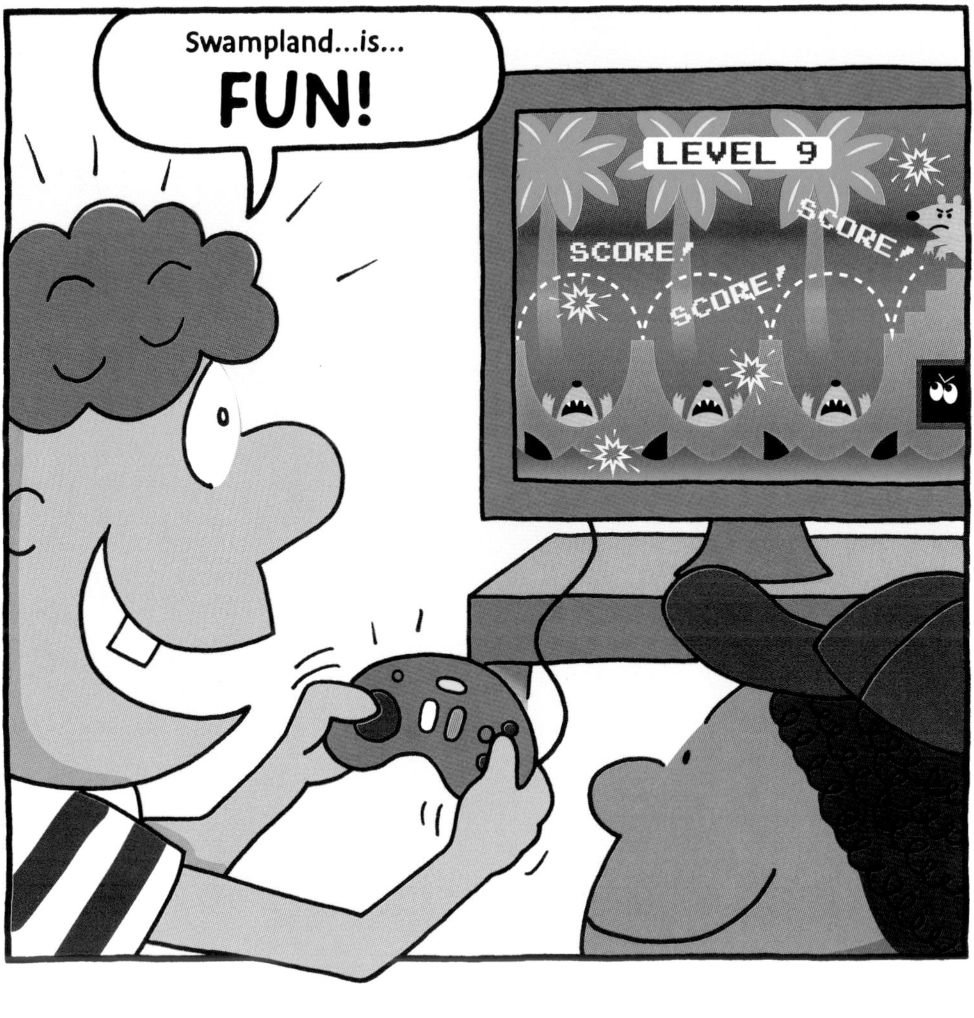
Swampland...is...
FUN!
LEVEL 9
SCORE!
SCORE!
SCORE!

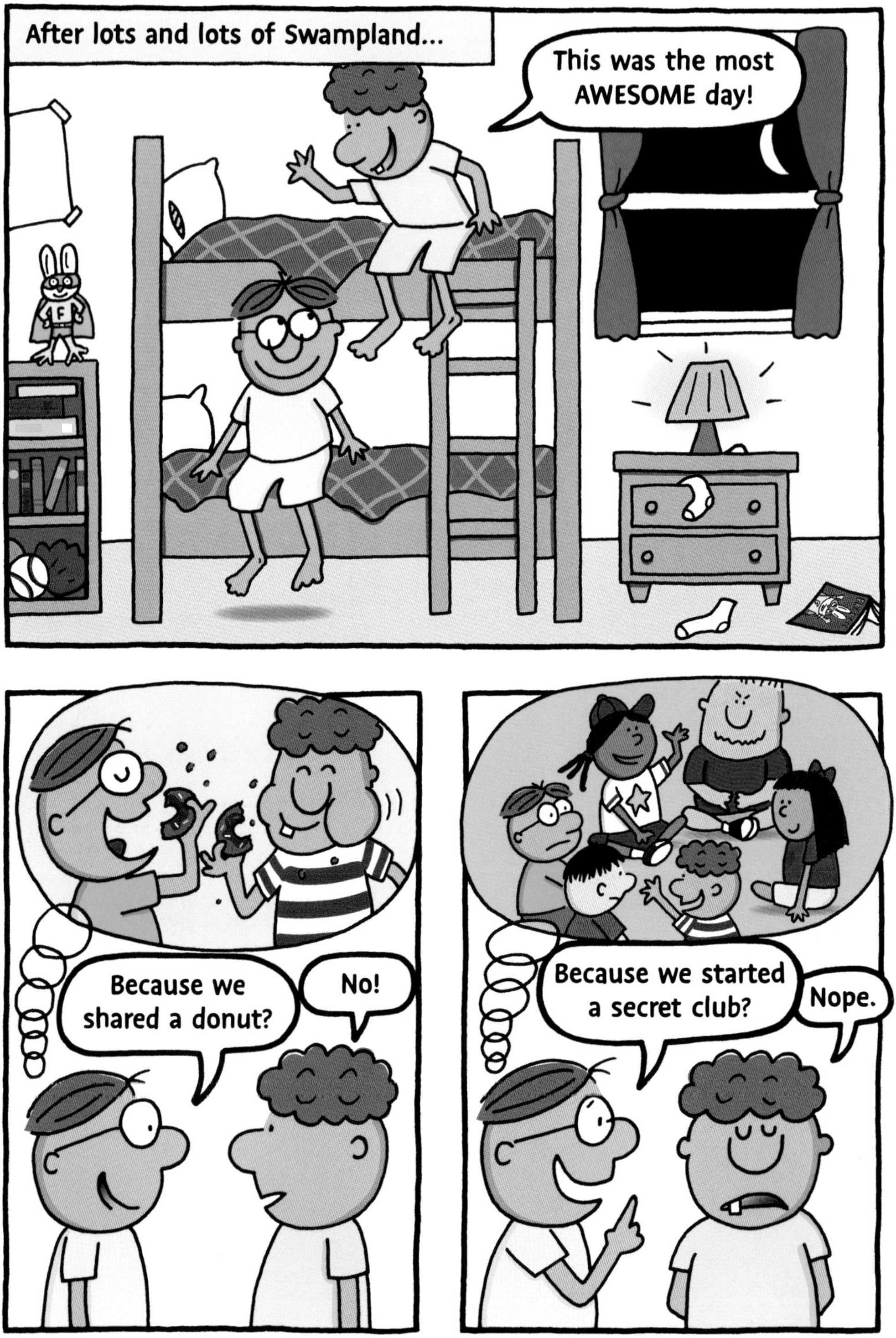
After lots and lots of Swampland...
This was the most AWESOME day!
Because we shared a donut?
No!
Because we started a secret club?
Nope.

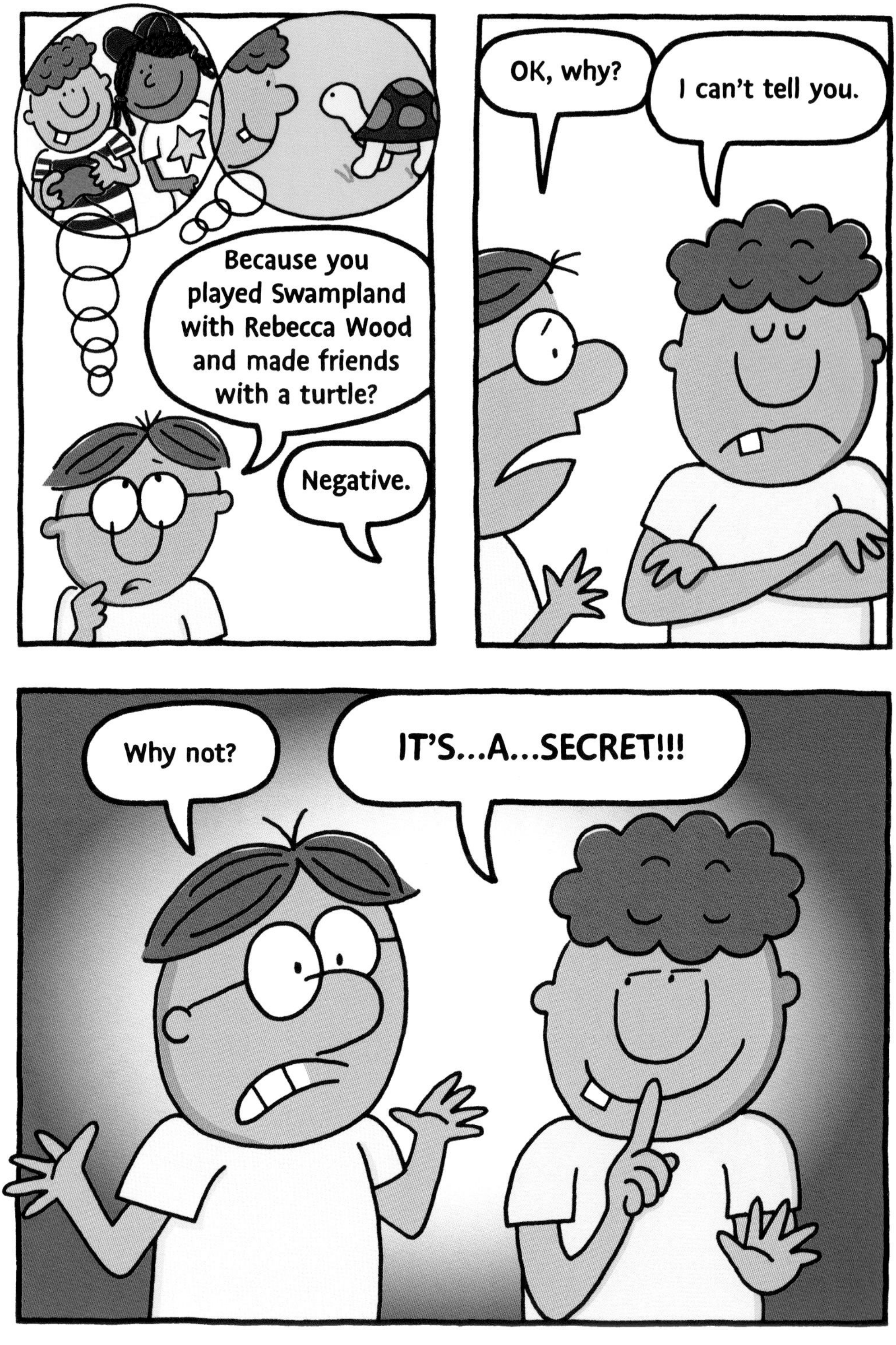
Because you played Swampland with Rebecca Wood and made friends with a turtle?
Negative.
OK, why?
I can't tell you.
Why not?
IT'S...A...SECRET!!!

Steve Metzger is the bestselling author of more than eighty children's books, including *The Way I Act, Detective Blue* (IRA-CBC Children's Choice List. SLJ starred review), and *Pluto Visits Earth!* (ABC Best Books for Children). His latest book, *Yes, I Can Listen!* received a 2019 Eureka! Honor Award from the California Reading Association. Steve lives in New York City with his wife and daughter.

Brian Schatell has illustrated sixteen books for children, some of which he has also written. For many years Brian has chaired the Rutgers University Council on Children's Literature's annual One-on-One Plus Conference. He has also taught children's book illustration and writing at Parsons School of Design. Brian lives in New York City.

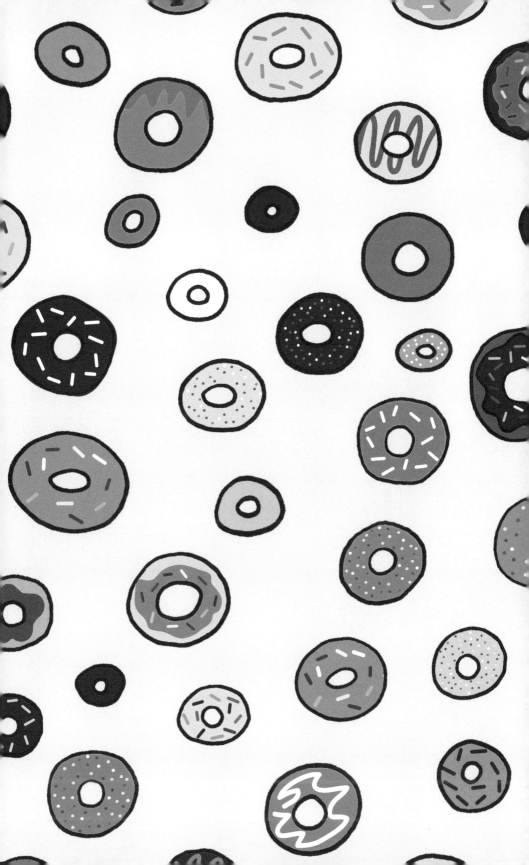

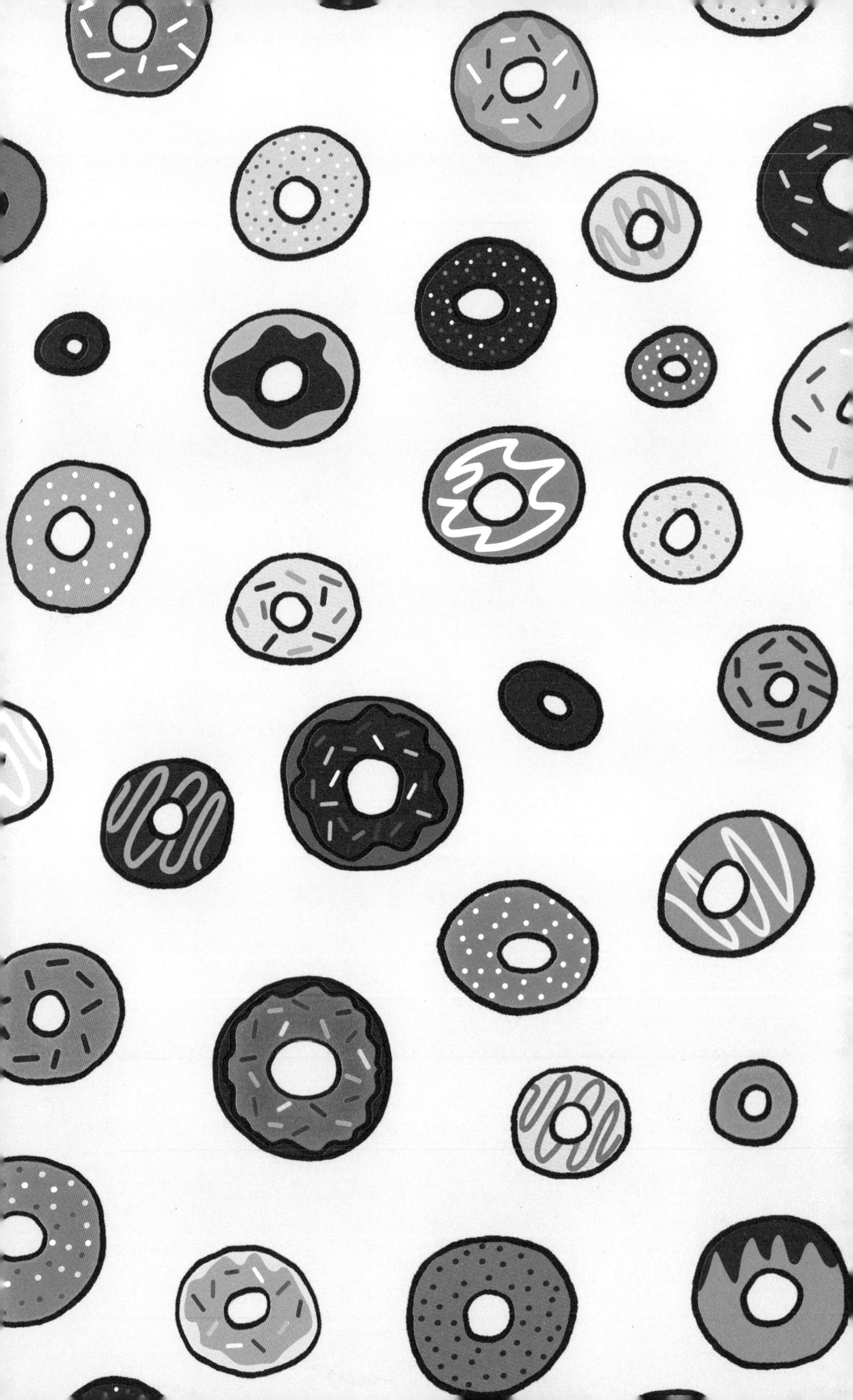